FINAL KILL

S. T. ASHMAN

DEDICATION

To all my amazing readers. I am so grateful. Thank you. ☺

CONTENTS

THANK YOU! 1

PROLOGUE 2

CHAPTER ONE 5

CHAPTER TWO 16

CHAPTER THREE 19

CHAPTER FOUR 31

CHAPTER FIVE 35

CHAPTER SIX 40

CHAPTER SEVEN 50

CHAPTER EIGHT 54

CHAPTER NINE 57

CHAPTER TEN 69

CHAPTER ELEVEN 74

CHAPTER TWELVE 84

CHAPTER THIRTEEN 90

CHAPTER FOURTEEN 95

CHAPTER FIFTEEN 104

CHAPTER SIXTEEN 118

CHAPTER SEVENTEEN 127

CHAPTER EIGHTEEN 135

CHAPTER NINETEEN 147

CHAPTER TWENTY... 155

CHAPTER TWENTY-ONE 158

CHAPTER TWENTY-TWO 169

CHAPTER TWENTY-THREE.. 178

CHAPTER TWENTY-FOUR... 183

CHAPTER TWENTY-FIVE... 188

CHAPTER TWENTY-SIX 192

CHAPTER TWENTY-SEVEN 196

CHAPTER TWENTY-EIGHT 210

CHAPTER TWENTY-NINE.. 221

CHAPTER THIRTY 229

CHAPTER THIRTY-ONE.. 234

CHAPTER THIRTY-TWO 241

CHAPTER THIRTY-THREE.. 244

CHAPTER THIRTY-FOUR... 250

CHAPTER THIRTY-FIVE.. 255

CHAPTER THIRTY-SIX..263

CHAPTER THIRTY-SEVEN..270

CHAPTER THIRTY-EIGHT..272

CHAPTER THIRTY-NINE 281

CHAPTER FORTY...288

CHAPTER FORTY-ONE...291

CHAPTER FORTY-TWO 296

CHAPTER FORTY-THREE 299

CHAPTER FORTY-FOUR 307

CHAPTER FORTY-FIVE 312

CHAPTER FORTY-SIX..315

CHAPTER FORTY-SEVEN 318

CHAPTER FORTY-EIGHT..323

CHAPTER FORTY-NINE 328

CHAPTER FIFTY..333

COMING SOON!..339

THANK YOU!

Dear Reader,

Thank you for reading "Final Kill." If you enjoy the book, please consider leaving a review on your preferred retailer's website (like Amazon, Goodreads, Barnes & Noble, etc.).

https://www.amazon.com/dp/B0D5V4BG8W

As a mom and indie author, every review, share, and kind word makes a huge difference and means the world to me.

Newsletter for bonus chapters:

https://www.ashmanbooks.com

Instagram: https://www.instagram.com/booksbyashman/

TikTok: https://www.tiktok.com/@ashmanbooks

Join Ashman's Dark Thriller Facebook Group to Meet the Author:

https://www.facebook.com/profile.php?id=100094353614873

Contact: hello@ashmanbooks.com

Thank you for your support.

S. T. Ashman

PROLOGUE

"Momma?" The man's low voice churned like gravel into his cell phone. His gold front tooth flashed as he spoke. "I'm … I'm watching her again."

An exasperated sigh resonated from the other end. A pause followed it.

"Pookie," an elderly woman finally responded with authority. "No, no, no, Pookie. No, I says."

The man's brown eyes narrowed at the sight of a prostitute at the far end of the dimly lit alley. Her ample breasts nearly spilled out of her skimpy dress as she leaned into the rolled-down window of a newly arrived car. The dress barely covered her buttocks, leaving little to the imagination about what was underneath.

A surge of desire thundered through the man's cock, a wave of lust threatening his control. The urge was so intense he nearly stepped out from the shadows to claim her in full view of anyone who might see, including the driver of that car. But a deep, shuddering breath steadied him.

"Momma..." A growl rumbled from his throat as he watched the prostitute climb into the car and bend over the driver's lap. Her head began to bob up and down in quick succession. "The devil is back. I can't tame the devil inside me anymore, Momma."

"Yes you can, Pookie." The woman's voice came through clenched teeth, like a desperate prayer. "Listen to the voice of our Lord Jesus, Pookie. The devil is a filthy liar. He plants those sinister thoughts in your mind. You must—"

He hung up and turned off his cell.

The prostitute climbed on the man's lap, riding him energetically, her long blonde hair bouncing in rhythm with her movements under the faint glow of a nearby streetlamp.

This thirst. It was overwhelming. Consuming.

For weeks, he'd watched her. The way she fucked and fucked and then drove back to her trailer, where her mother cared for her children while she indulged in her sins. There was something addicting about this one.

He needed her. The devil wouldn't stop tormenting him until he did as he was commanded. The fight was over. The man knew he'd lost.

Immersed in the shadows, he observed the woman step out and snatch the cash from the man. With practiced ease, she wiped the semen off her thighs with a tissue as the car drove off.

The urge intensified, making him tremble like a puppy in the bitter cold. Oh, all the things he'd do to her. And how it would make him feel.

Power. Control. The thrill of her screams.

His lips twisted into a smile.

A sudden feeling of being watched made him whip around. Was that a shifting shadow? Was it her?

That strange letter flashed vividly in his mind. Mailed to him from an unknown sender. Whoever had sent it knew who he was and what he did ... yet he was still free. No arrests. Not even a call from the cops.

After praying to the devil about it, the man had concluded that his dark lord himself had sent the warning. To protect their work, of course.

"One of your kind has broken the pact of evil and turned on her own," the letter read.

The message included a photo of a renowned pianist—not his type. Most women were weak and useless unless they brought him pleasure. But he'd manage.

He glanced back down the alley where the prostitute was counting her earnings. Tonight belonged to her. But after that ... the pianist would get what she deserved.

CHAPTER ONE

Leah

This wasn't a piano recital. It was a battle.

I pounded Beethoven's Appassionata into the keys in front of me like it was a duel to the death. Jan Novak consumed my thoughts day and night. Sleep eluded me, and though I forced myself to eat, I continued to lose weight. No matter how I approached the situation, I had nothing with which to take on a man with such power, especially not with the little evidence I had.

I knew it was him.

He was the Train Track Killer.

My gut told me so, and the evidence we'd gathered was persuasive enough for me. But Richter and Rose had doubts. They were hesitant because of the missing gunshot wound on Novak's shoulder. I understood their concerns. Their thought process and happiness—unlike mine—were heavily based on emotions. Inadvertently killing someone who wasn't the Train Track Killer would devastate them.

My only hesitation had been the fear that killing an innocent person would turn me into the monster I hunted. Yet that fear was fading. But why? Had the Train Track Killer pushed me to the edge after all these years?

The confrontation with Jan Novak in the forest replayed in my mind. He'd placed Anna directly on the tracks. I'd fired, striking him in the shoulder. He'd clutched his shoulder, crumbled to one knee, and then escaped with Patel's help.

That escape brought a slew of problems.

Patel.

Kirby.

And heaven only knew how many other demons Jan Novak had recruited for his sick games. All-seeing. All-hearing. Almost godlike, Novak knew everyone's moves—who did what, where, and when. He had the power to manipulate people like chess pieces. The sky was the limit.

My fingers slammed onto the keys as the finale began. I played it at almost twice the speed, seeking exhaustion as much as releasing frustration.

When the last note echoed through the mighty Boston Symphony Hall, I sat in silence, surrounded by thousands of empty seats.

My eyes fell to the spot on the stage where my attacker had taken his own life shortly after shooting McCourt. I'd canceled my concerts until further notice. People had come to lay a sea of flowers at the symphony hall and my home. Much to my annoyance, they held hands, singing "Kumbaya." What nonsense.

But my days on the stage were far from over.

Publicity from the attack had caused the demand for my concerts to skyrocket. And although the news coverage seemed to be waning, the attention was still overwhelming. It would fade quickly—the world had too many tragedies to dwell on mine for too long—but for now, it was exhausting.

"Leah."

Crystal's soft voice pulled me from my thoughts. She had endured what could only be described as a hellish few weeks—managing my PR and dealing with Hieber. I'd tripled her salary. It was perhaps the only reason she'd stayed.

I lifted my head to look at her. Crystal, with her bright red glasses and hair, was the only splash of life in the otherwise silent, vast concert hall.

"I've managed to get rid of the journalists in front of your home and the symphony hall. I've also asked your driver to wait for you at the back exit. Do you need anything else from me? Otherwise, I'll go home."

"No. Thank you. Please go home and rest."

She nodded.

"And take the next week off. I'll make Hieber work for a change."

She grinned. "Thank you."

Then she lingered, awkward, like a kid hoping for a second scoop of ice cream.

"What is it?"

Crystal bit her lip.

I sighed. "No, Crystal. Please, not again."

"But, Leah, you need protection. All Hollywood stars have bodyguards."

"I'm not a Hollywood star."

"You're a star in the world of classical music. And somebody just tried to shoot you."

"My answer remains the same. I can take care of myself."

Crystal bit her lip again. It was a habit she fell back on when she was afraid to speak up.

"Talking about security," I said as I rose. "The symphony hall ... did we switch security companies yet?"

She nodded, clearly puzzled as to why I'd instructed her to change our security service provider for a smaller, pricier company. Crystal didn't know that the new firm was one of the only companies in the entire U.S. that didn't use Jan Novak's cloud storage. And I was tired of him watching me. Tired of his very existence.

"That'll be all, then." My tone left no room for argument. "Take two weeks off," I added, grabbing my cashmere coat from the piano bench.

I checked the time. Nine thirty-one.

The cold night air brushed against my face as I stepped out the back door and headed toward my car. Immediately, I sensed a presence in the dark alley behind me. I slowed my pace and reached for the gun in my purse.

For the past week or so, I'd felt like I was being followed. A strange shadow behind a tree at night outside my home on Monday. Dark eyes peering at me from under a hood on a crowded Boston street on Thursday.

Calmly, I turned, gun drawn. But no one was there. At least, not anymore.

"You okay?" Richter's voice came suddenly from behind me.

I kept my gaze on the dark alley a moment longer, then tucked the gun back into my purse. "A bit risky approaching me in public like this, don't you think?" I asked. I looked into his tired brown eyes. Behind them was a man I knew I could trust to always do the right thing.

"Nah," he said playfully, flashing his FBI badge. "Just checking in on a victim and a main witness to McCourt's attack. And to be honest, it's kinda nice to meet in the open like this. Makes it all feel—"

"Less wrong?" I interrupted.

He frowned. "Easier. That old rope factory is far out, and I almost got jumped by a homeless guy last time we met there. Tried to bite me but ran off when I tackled him."

I strode toward my limousine, where Mark was holding the door open. As I climbed in, Richter remained motionless outside. I raised an eyebrow at him just as Agent Rose approached, balancing two coffees in her hands.

"We've been here for a while," she said, handing a coffee to Richter as they got in. Rose sat across from me, next to Richter.

"Thanks, Mark," Richter said as if they were old friends.

I instructed Mark to drive around Boston. He nodded, closed the door, and slipped behind the wheel. With a soft click, he shut the privacy divider before the car smoothly pulled into motion.

"Why did you wait outside?" I asked. "You could have just texted me to meet up."

"I did," Richter said. "You didn't reply."

"The piano is loud," I said quickly.

That was true. But lately, I'd also been lost in thoughts of Jan Novak.

"Did you do a deep dive into Novak?" I asked. Meetings like this were reserved for sharing crucial information. And meetings with Rose specifically targeted the Train Track Killer. She wasn't involved in our other endeavors: hunting serial killers. For now, everyone seemed content with that arrangement.

"He's tougher to get information on than the President," Rose said, adjusting her suit jacket with one hand while holding her coffee in the other.

"We're trying to keep a low profile," Richter added, "so I'm calling in favors from cyber and even a friend at the NSA."

"On paper, his life reads like a fairy tale," Rose continued. "Some poor kid who worked hard and made billions."

"But?" I prompted.

"But his Oscar-worthy story starts from college," Richter said. "Before that, there's nothing. The only thing we know about his childhood comes from a college entrance essay. In it, he mentions arriving in New York as a kid with his Slovak immigrant parents. And that's pretty much all we have."

"What about his birth certificate?" I asked. "School diplomas? Hospital records?"

Richter shook his head. "Nothing. His past is pretty much a mystery."

"There are no mysteries," I said. "Everything has an explanation."

"And some people go the extra mile to find that explanation." Rose handed me a document. "This is a list of Jan Novak's shareholders. Apparently, the U.S. government forced him to split up his cloud storage company before practically handing him control over every aspect of our American lives, making him the closest thing to God since Jesus."

"How tactful of them," I said.

"Don't give them too much credit," Richter countered. "Every single person on this list is a mega-donor to the dirtiest in Congress."

I scanned the names and pictures of ten men. All old. All filthy rich.

"Surprise, surprise," I muttered.

"Do you recognize anyone?" Rose asked.

My gaze narrowed on Ronald Hubble. "I do."

Rose and Richter exchanged hopeful glances.

Richter leaned forward. "Do you think you can get some information? Discreetly?"

"Me? No," I said. "But I might know someone who can."

"Good. We need more proof that Jan Novak is the Train Track Killer." Richter ran his hand through his hair. "Or any proof at this point, actually. A disgruntled high-class prostitute. A pissed-off shareholder. Even the smallest lead would help."

"I assume Jan Novak canceled his gym membership?" I asked. "If he's had skin grafts to remove the bullet scar, there'd be a scar on his chest

11

somewhere. He could have been hiding it under a towel when we first had him followed in the locker room. We focused only on his shoulder."

Rose shook her head. "Too late for a second try. He canceled his membership, and there's no legal way to make him strip down. As powerful as he is, he could be caught red-handed with a bloody knife over a dead body and still have the connections to avoid a court order for a physical like that. Even inviting him for a chit-chat at the office is impossible based on what we have. Trying anything like that would be textbook career suicide for both of us."

Richter opened his mouth as if to speak, but then his phone rang. "Agent Richter." He listened intently, tilted his head, and stared upward. "Good God. Can you ask her to come back tomorrow?" After another pause, he sighed. "No, no police. I'm on my way."

"Please don't tell me the Night Stalker raped another woman," Rose said.

Richter shook his head as he pocketed his phone. "Thank God, no. Some mother of a missing prostitute is causing a scene in front of our headquarters. Security called me before the cops arrested her."

I listened closely, curious about the Night Stalker.

"Good," Rose said. "We really don't need bad publicity right now. The bureau is having a good streak. Do you want me to take care of this?"

Richter shook his head. "No, you've got a big day tomorrow. Go home and rest. I'll handle this."

Rose nodded, then furrowed her brow. "So, what happens now? How does this work? Do we just talk things over, and then you drop us off at home like an Uber until we have more information on Novak and regroup?"

I texted Mark, who instantly pulled over.

"Not quite. You can get out here," I said.

Richter smiled. "Feels like a one-star ride-share. Still, beats a rainy dock and factory any day."

"Mm-hmm." Rose placed her hand on the door handle.

"Wait," I interjected.

Both turned to me.

"I think ... I'm being followed."

"By Novak?" Richter asked, his voice concerned.

"I don't know."

"Why would he follow only you?" Rose asked. "Why not go after all of us? Kill us or at least get us fired—whatever it takes. He knows we're on his trail."

"I wish he'd come after me," Richter said. "If I see him outside my house at night, that's all the reason I need to put a bullet in his head." Suddenly, he tensed. "He wouldn't go after my daughter, would he?"

"No. He won't hurt her," I assured him. "Children are sacred to him. The Train Track Killer isn't an out-of-control sociopath like Grand or the College Snatcher. He's calculated. Everything he does has a purpose, a reflection of what he aspires to be. He has never hurt a child. It would go against who he is. Everything he built."

Richter ran a palm across his cheek in thought. "People can act out of character when they're cornered."

"I doubt he feels cornered by us," I said. Silence followed the heavy truth of that statement.

"I wonder if we should have stayed under the radar," Rose said. "Used secrecy and the element of surprise as our weapons."

I leaned back, gazing out the window as a drunk couple stumbled past on the deserted streets of downtown Boston. "There's no secrecy with a man who sees and hears everything and has the entire government in his pocket. If he knows we're on to him, it might force him to make a mistake to protect himself. I recommend you get the FBI's cloud storage contract with Novak's firm terminated as soon as possible, or he'll know every breath you take."

"That will be ... quite a mountain to climb," Rose said, opening the car door. After a brief silence, she stepped out.

Richter scooted over but then paused, fixing a deep, searching look on me. "Why do I get the feeling you're up to something?"

"I can't say. I'm hardly the right person to ask about interpreting your feelings."

He studied me. "I'm serious, Leah. Is Novak getting to you?"

I met his gaze. "He doesn't have that power over me. No one does. Except myself."

"Do you want me to watch your house for a while, see if someone's following you?"

I managed a faint smile. "Cute," I said. "But that won't be necessary."

Richter nodded, then got out. I closed the door.

As Mark drove off, I mulled over Richter's question. Not his offer to camp outside my house like a scene from an undercover cop movie. Rather, his suspicion. Richter seemed to have acquired the ability to see right through me. It was something nobody had ever managed to do.

And that could be a problem. Especially because he was right. My plans for tonight would only confirm his suspicions.

CHAPTER TWO

Liam

I was sitting next to Mrs. Moore on the cold stone steps in front of FBI headquarters. I'd invited her inside, but she'd declined, saying her grandkids were asleep in the car parked in front of us. It was a chilly fall night, and the air felt crisp. She wore a sweater with an image of a dog drinking wine. Her white hair looked unkempt and neglected, and she had dark rings under her swollen eyes.

"I'm sorry I called your security 'assholes,'" Mrs. Moore said, wiping away tears. "It's just ... I don't know what to do anymore. The police don't care. Nobody seems to care that my daughter is missing." More tears began streaming down her face. "I thought Nathalie worked night shifts at the corner store. That's what she always told me. Then the police said all these things about her. Called her a cheap prostitute."

I stayed silent.

"But in the end, what does it even matter how she earned money for those kids' clothes and food? She was one of the best mothers I've ever known. She had so much love in her heart. No matter what she did, she is still my child. Or was..."

I gently placed my hand on Mrs. Moore's shoulder. "We don't know for sure that she's gone."

"But I can feel it. Like something dark swallowed her. Took her out of the light. It's like a piece of my heart has been ripped out. And the kids." She nodded toward the car, where I could see a glimpse of a blonde scalp in the car seat. "They can feel it too."

Of all the burdens that came with being an FBI agent, dealing with families was the most heart-wrenching.

"I'm a parent too," I told her. "And I can't begin to imagine what you're going through right now." Mrs. Moore's crying intensified as I strengthened my grip on her shoulder. I glanced at the rundown car with the kids inside. "But the kids need their beds. As much of their normal life as they can get."

Mrs. Moore used her sweater sleeve to wipe at her tears.

"How about I get on this first thing in the morning when people are back in the office, and you all go get some rest? I'll give it my all, I promise."

Mrs. Moore's swollen, red eyes lifted to mine. She stared at me as if trying to figure out if I was all talk or really meant it. Finally, she nodded and rose to her feet. So did I. But instead of walking to her car, she tilted her head back and looked up at the night sky.

"We're not supposed to outlive our children," she said softly.

"No, we're not. But until we find a body, there's still a chance she's out there. Alive."

Mrs. Moore kept staring upward.

"I hope so. Because God be my witness, I won't be some forgiving, sweet old lady if we find my little girl dead in some ditch." Her voice quivered. Her eyes met mine again as tears streamed down her face. "I'll carry hatred and rage in my heart until the very last breath I take. And I'll pray to God, Satan, or anybody else who'll listen to bring nothing but pain and misery to whoever did this to my daughter."

I nodded.

Many people measured a parent's abilities by their financial success or educational background. But from what I'd seen on the job, real love wasn't about material wealth or a perfect resume. True affection came from the mom who played Uno with one hand while holding a cigarette in the other or from the mom who lost her temper in the parking lot during her kid's tantrum but covered them with kisses and hugs before bed.

"Thank you," Mrs. Moore finally said, her voice soft and hoarse.

"Of course. I'm sorry you're going through this. Let me know if you need anything. Just call my cell."

As I watched her drive off, a dark feeling settled in my stomach.

Mrs. Moore could be right. A missing prostitute, ten days gone. All signs pointed toward the worst. I'd still give it my all, hoping for the best. But if all was lost and we found a body, at least Mrs. Moore and the kids would have a grave to lay their flowers on. To some, this meant something. And I'd do all I could to give the Moores at least that.

And maybe more.

If her daughter had really been murdered and I found out who did it, her killer might get the brutal end he deserved. I happened to know someone good at that sort of thing. And I had a feeling Mrs. Moore would be okay with it.

CHAPTER THREE

Rose

Disturbingly, I found myself enjoying the thrill of lurking in the shadows. I stood in a narrow alley between two imposing townhomes on Beacon Hill, just across from Leah's mansion. Was this the same thrill that drove serial killers when they stalked their prey?

I'd been here for over three hours, and the deserted streets felt apocalyptic.

A twinge of guilt washed over me for not telling Leah or Liam about my decision to tail her. But when she'd said she was being followed, I'd decided that doing nothing wasn't an option. And my secrecy was meant not to deceive or betray her but, rather, to ensure success. Real-world surveillance was nothing like its fictional portrayal. Parking a mysterious car in front of a house for days on end was a surefire way to attract attention. People were conditioned by what they saw on the movie screen. Tracking someone else's stalker presented an even greater challenge. Stalkers were already on high alert.

So the first rule of my mission to find out who was following Leah was secrecy.

I was mentally prepared for a long night of nothingness when Leah's Audi emerged from her driveway. It was after midnight. Where the hell was she going?

I sprinted to my car, which I'd parked behind a store at the first intersection out of Beacon Hill. Sure enough, Leah's car paused at the intersection's red light. I slid into my seat and waited for the light to turn green. Then, pulling out of the parking lot slowly, I began following her.

She drove west through the city, heading toward the Children's Hospital. Then she pulled over and parked on a dark residential street.

I watched in shock as Leah Nachtnebel, the world-renowned pianist, emerged from her car, utterly transformed. She now sported short blonde hair, a skimpy mini-dress, and a leather jacket. Heavy makeup concealed any trace of the elegant artist I'd sat across from just hours earlier. Even her nose and eyes looked different.

She walked about a mile before arriving at The Thirsty Monkey, a dive bar on a dimly lit corner. Its neon "OPEN" sign flickered wildly, fighting off the dark. The bar's broken windows told of better days gone by.

Without hesitation, she pushed through the bar's door.

I pulled over and turned off my lights and engine. The lateness of the hour meant the area was relatively quiet, but I still blended in perfectly with the occasional car and late-night pedestrian.

As I watched people come out of The Thirsty Monkey for a cigarette, a feeling of worry overcame me. I had no idea what the hell Leah was doing here, but something deep down told me it wasn't a night of karaoke.

Leah

Pushing open the door to the bar, I was hit by a blast of loud music and the stench of cigarette smoke mixed with the greasy aroma of chicken wings. Slurred voices and clumsy laughter echoed from the crowd of drunks scattered around the dimly lit room. Its walls were plastered with broken neon beer signs and sun-bleached band posters. The tables were scuffed, bearing the scars of endless rough nights. In the corner, an old jukebox gathered dust.

I hadn't even reached the bar before the first drunk man leaned into my path and asked if I wanted a drink. I ignored him and ordered a whiskey from the overworked bartender, who acknowledged me with a nod while continuing to fill another order.

"Hey there, pretty," another man—in his forties, reeking of booze—said as he leaned against the bar next to me. "Can I buy you a drink?"

"No." I grabbed the glass of whiskey from the bartender and was about to turn when the man blocked my path.

"Why not?"

I glanced at the barbecue sauce stains on his white shirt. His half-shut eyes indicated he was one step away from being blackout drunk.

"I'd rather not say," I replied, trying to walk around him.

He blocked my way again. "You think you're too good for me?" he slurred.

I drank about half of my whiskey in a smooth swig, then sighed. "Of course I do. It's not even the fact that your fingers are yellow from cigarettes, or that your breath stinks, and you don't know how to eat chicken wings, which literally don't require utensils."

The man's eyes widened as disbelief washed over his flushed face.

"Quite frankly, what disgusts me the most is the wedding band mark on your finger. Your hand is tanned except for the white where you usually wear the ring. You took it off when you came here. So if you sleep with anyone tonight, it should be your wife, who I personally don't think deserves the horror of having someone like you in her bed."

His brows furrowed. "You arrogant cunt."

I smiled as I finally managed to pass him. "Thank you."

It took another rejection before I was able to sit at a high table in the middle of the bar. Every now and then, another adventurer tried to strike gold. I denied all of them. I wasn't here for that, although I'd craved good sex ever since Emanuel died. Not that I'd find it in this bar anyway. I wasn't here for fun. I was here to present myself. I was here as bait.

Rose

It took less than an hour for Leah to stagger back out of The Thirsty Monkey.

"What the hell is going on here?" I mumbled, straightening up from my slumped position behind the wheel of my parked car.

For a moment, I was concerned she might attempt to drive in that state, but then she stumbled away from the direction of her car.

Once she'd turned the corner, I followed her on foot, leaving plenty of space between us.

A few streets later, Leah made her way into Ramler Park, a small public area known for its tranquility and flowers. Its secluded walls of bushes swallowed her instantly. When the street was clear, I walked around the park, then climbed the black metal fence to enter through the bushes. Not far from me, Leah sat in the darkness on a bench near a fountain, smoking a cigarette and looking at her phone. The screen lit up her face, which looked nothing like her. The disconnect added an eerie and bizarre layer to this already strange night.

I was about to reveal myself and ask her what the hell was going on when a dark figure hurried past to my left and hid behind a nearby tree. A rush of adrenaline surged through me, and I hid behind another tree so that whoever was lurking to my left wouldn't see me.

Fuck.

Was that Jan Novak? It was too dark to tell.

I drew my gun and peeked at Leah again. She continued scrolling on her phone, seemingly oblivious. What the fuck? Was she trying to get raped or killed?

Then it dawned on me. No, she wasn't drunk or clueless or suicidal.

She was on the hunt. But who was she after?

My grip tightened around my gun as my heart quickened. I readied myself to bolt toward the tree to my left and tackle whoever was hiding there. However, another shadow emerged from the dimly lit street. This one moved with a confident stride.

A man, perhaps in his late thirties, swiftly walked down the path toward the fountain where Leah was sitting. There was something creepy about him. Maybe it was the way he didn't slow down. Leah was still engrossed in her phone. Didn't she see the man approaching?

The creepy guy adjusted his pace, striding even faster toward Leah. Before she could look up, he grabbed her and wrestled her to the ground, pinning her beneath him.

I glanced to my left to ensure the man attacking Leah and the figure hiding behind the tree weren't one and the same. The dark figure was still there, watching everything unfold. Was that a golden shimmer I just saw from the shadow? It was tiny, almost as if it had come from his mouth. A gold tooth?

If I burst into the open now, the man hiding would see me and escape. But I couldn't just stand by and let Leah get hurt.

Damn the stalker. I had to act.

I was ready to jump into action when, suddenly, the man on top of Leah let out a scream. In seconds, the scene on the ground had completely changed. The man had rolled off, screaming in pain. Leah jumped on top of him as the glint of a knife flashed. She drove the blade down quickly and with force.

I watched, frozen, as the knife struck him two more times.

What the fuck was wrong with me?

I had to get out there and stop her.

Now, goddammit!

I was an FBI agent. And the man on the ground with her most likely wasn't even a serial killer. Everything here pointed toward an attempted rape, which was now turning into a murder by the supposed victim.

My gaze shot to the man behind the tree. He was still there, watching, the golden shimmer from what I thought looked like his teeth now constant.

Then, all of a sudden, he rushed off.

"Shit!"

What now? Stop Leah? Run after this man?

My phone vibrated. I prayed it was Richter, then realized it was the flip phone.

It was her number. A text.

FOLLOW HIM!

Leah

From the corner of my eye, I saw two shadows darting through the park—one after the other. One of them was Rose, likely. Good. She'd gotten my text and followed my instructions.

I snapped my attention back to the Night Stalker. In the brief moment I'd been distracted by my phone, he'd managed to slip out from under me and roll me onto the gravel. My eyes locked onto the whimpering man. Should I just end him now? A few more quick stabs or slit his throat?

This was uncharted territory, dangerously exhilarating. A rapist. No murders in his past—yet.

I got to my feet and drove my knee into his back, pinning him to the ground as he squirmed, desperately trying to crawl away. His pleas for mercy pierced the night, but I was unyielding. I'd already sunk the blade into him five, maybe six times. Still, he'd survive if I walked away now.

"Not so much fun when you're the one pinned down, is it?" I asked. "I heard the youngest of your rape victims was only fourteen, right?"

My gloved left hand clutched his thick hair and yanked his head back to expose his throat. Thanks to a hacker I'd paid on the dark web, I'd tracked down the famous Night Stalker in less than two weeks. The idiot had boasted about his rapes in an exclusive forum, a sanctuary for perverts like him, hiding behind anonymous usernames. These depraved scumbags chatted about rapes like nerds talked about video games. During one of their twisted chats, they'd pushed the Night Stalker into planning his next rape at this park—famous for the migratory birds that paused here to drink. "Rapes n' chirps," they'd called it, laughingly. So I'd decided the last laugh would be mine.

Night after night, I'd waited here. And now, here he was, just as he'd promised. Rapes n' chirps. No mystery on his end—just a sick fuck living out his twisted fantasies.

But the real question was, what the hell was I doing here?

This man wasn't a killer. He'd shattered women's lives in other ways, stealing their confidence, their self-worth, their peace of mind, and, for some, their will to live. Wasn't that a form of murder too? Maybe. But he wasn't my usual prey.

Without realizing it, I'd placed my knife against his throat. The blade pierced his skin slightly.

He begged and whimpered like a coward, which only fueled my desire to kill him. But if I did, what then? The monster lurking within me—would Richter finally see it and sever ties?

I sighed, then rolled the Night Stalker over, yanked down his pants, and, in a few swift cuts, severed his penis.

A screech of agony tore from the Night Stalker's throat before he slumped into a half-conscious state, mumbling incoherently.

"Quite small for a man acting so big," I said calmly as I tossed the severed penis into the fountain. Then I walked away through the bushes, avoiding the main paths.

I ducked into a dark alley to wipe the blood from my neck and arms. My mind spun with questions. I knew Rose had been following me ever since I'd left my house. But why hadn't she intervened tonight? Would she report this to Richter? It didn't matter; he'd probably figure out it was me anyway.

I took off my wig, letting my real hair fall loosely over my shoulders. Then I pulled a pair of leggings from my purse and slipped them on, tucking the dress in like a shirt. I looked like a completely different person—enough to make it back to my car, which I'd parked in a blind spot away from security cameras.

As I moved, my mind wrestled with the night's events. Something inside me was shifting, and I wasn't sure if it was for better or worse. Tonight felt different—off. The target, the method—everything was out of place. Sparing the Night Stalker's life felt like a shallow gesture of justice. For the first time, I found myself wondering whether I was truly driven by a sense of justice when I hunted monsters. Or was it the thrill that kept me going?

Rose

I followed the man down the street. He was clad in a dark sweater and a baseball cap, and he walked calmly to fit in with the occasional dog walker. Unaware of my pursuit, he likely believed he had successfully stalked Leah and was now nonchalantly continuing on his way. He acted as if he were on a Sunday stroll, not a man who'd just witnessed a murder.

Crossing to the other side of the street, I tailed him for another block, then watched as he climbed into a red pickup truck. I paused to memorize his license plate. A chilling thought struck me: Whoever he was, he was good at what he did. The plate was probably fake. Panicking, I scanned my surroundings.

Just then, a police car drove past, heading away from us. I turned and sprinted after it. Before long, the officer noticed me. He stopped the car and rolled down the window, his expression a mix of confusion and irritation.

"Why are you chasing me?"

"FBI," I panted, flashing my badge. "That red truck at the end of the street—follow it, pull him over. Record his face and license with your body cam. Make up some excuse for why you pulled him over, then let him go."

"What?"

"Now, goddammit!" I snapped.

The officer flicked on his lights and took off.

From a safe distance, I watched the officer do as I'd instructed. Good. Even if this wouldn't directly point to Jan Novak, we were one step closer to catching someone. And maybe Leah would be able to get this man to talk.

But what about the rapist in the park? He was probably dead by now. Strangely, I didn't feel a thing for him. I didn't take any joy in his death, but I also couldn't muster any pity. Maybe that's why I hadn't stopped Leah.

I wasn't sure who that guy was or exactly what Leah was doing, but there was a real chance she'd picked up a new hobby—one that wasn't just about killing serial killers. One that involved taking out any kind of bad guy.

I shook my head. None of this was good. As much as I wanted to avoid an uncomfortable conversation, I had to talk to Richter about all this. ASAP.

CHAPTER FOUR

Liam

Cowboy and Rose stood next to me. We were staring through the window of a private patient room on the Intensive Care Unit floor of Mass General Hospital. The strong smell of disinfectant mixed with the rhythmic beeps of hospital machines.

On the other side was a man in his late thirties. His face looked tired but was in pretty good shape otherwise—something one couldn't say about the other half of him.

"Well, who gets a gold star for this masterpiece?" Cowboy asked. "Chopped his dick right off. The doctors couldn't reattach it. Apparently, there were fish in the fountain that nibbled on it for too long."

"Jesus," I grumbled. "How sure are we he's the Night Stalker?"

"Very sure," Rose said. "A DNA sample connected him to eight of the Night Stalker rape victims. His name is Terry Patterson. Thirty-four years old, works as a mechanic for a local garage. Loner. Coworkers described him as strange. Pedophile kinda type, one of them said."

"He said that, literally?" Cowboy asked, grinning.

"Yup. Literally," Rose confirmed.

"If it looks and talks like a duck, eh?" Cowboy's grin widened.

Rose threw him a scolding look, then continued. "Patterson woke up for a few hours yesterday and denies any wrongdoing. Told the cops that he was hooking up at the park with some woman from a bar called Thirsty Monkey. Then, out of nowhere, she stabbed him and chopped his dick off."

"Well, ain't that a plot twist," I said, narrowing my eyes at Patterson.

Cowboy grinned. "More like a happy ending. Grand. Patterson. That guy strapped to the tree in the woods a few months back. It's almost like some higher power is finally doing some spring cleaning on Earth."

Not some higher power.

Leah.

Staring at Patterson, I couldn't help but wonder if this was her work. It had her signature all over it, except for the fact that Patterson was still alive. But Cowboy didn't need to start connecting the dots here.

"Grand killed himself with drugs. Woods guy was a cartel crime," I said.

"This one, though, has an artist behind it," Cowboy joked, nodding at Patterson. "There won't be a single sane person on this planet who'll feel sorry for this guy. Especially not the fourteen women the Night Stalker beat and raped. The youngest was only fourteen."

We continued watching Patterson for a moment.

"So what do you want us to do about all this?" Rose asked.

"What do you mean?" Cowboy interrupted before I could respond. "Don't tell me we're going after the woman who did this to him?" His eyes were wide with disbelief.

I sighed. "We have to conduct a fair and legal investigation, Cowboy. So please go and talk to the police about their reports and possible witness statements they recorded."

Cowboy lingered, defiant.

"But if nothing comes of it, don't waste any other resources or time on this. We'll just wait for the woman to step forward herself. Ok?"

He grinned. "Yes, siiiir!" Then he walked off.

Rose and I lingered as I shifted my gaze from Patterson to her. Did she know anything about this? She seemed a bit on edge. Conflicted. Still, it seemed unlikely that Rose and Leah had teamed up behind my back to hunt down rapists and pedophiles.

"What's wrong?" I asked.

She looked at me for a moment as if she wanted to say something, then shrugged. "Nothing. Well, the meeting later, it's going to be a bit ... fucked up."

I nodded. "Are you sure you want to do this? I can always step in for you."

Rose shook her head. "No. I'm gonna be fine."

"Just let me know if you change your mind. I gotta get Josie now, but I can drop her off at my mom's if you have a change of heart."

"Thanks, but as I said, I'll be fine. I'll call you after the meeting."

I nodded. Rose left.

I watched as she made her way down the Intensive Care Unit hallway, dodging doctors and nurses who were moving around like busy ants.

Something was off about all this. Why hadn't Rose asked if I thought Leah was behind this? My gaze wandered over to Terry Patterson—or what was left of him. I wasn't disturbed by any of it. Like Cowboy, I agreed that he deserved this. Living the rest of his life without the weapon he used against those poor women was only fair. Still, a heavy clump of worry was forming in my stomach. Was Leah prowling outside her usual hunting grounds? Serial killers required months to years of digging to find and dispose of. But rapists and other lowlife criminals were so plentiful in this country, the corpses would pile up sky-high. And so would the trail of evidence. Cowboy was already beginning to form the idea that someone was out there taking care of monsters. If Leah was picking up a side hobby, I had to talk to her. Now. Before our cover got blown and I was sent to jail before the Train Track Killer was caught.

I checked my phone. It was one in the afternoon. I had to pick up Josie, but this ... this couldn't wait.

CHAPTER FIVE

Leah

I made my way through the lush garden of the mansion situated on a private pond just outside Boston. It was a warm and sunny fall day, and the air smelled of grass and roses.

Luca was sitting on a bench overlooking the pond, where a group of ducks swam peacefully.

"I didn't think I'd ever see you again," he said without turning.

I slowed as I made my way around the bench. "How did you know it was me?"

He lifted his eyes from the pond and fixed them on me. "You're the only person who my men would allow to walk around freely on my property. They'd never dare to deny you any wish."

"Unlike you?" I said as I sat next to him. Dressed in a white suit, he appeared immaculate as always, but his face looked tired and deprived of life.

For a moment, we fell silent, listening to the quacks of the ducks and the warm breeze rustling the leaves of the trees surrounding us.

Luca shook his head. "I know I've failed you. I broke my word when McCourt approached me, asking for the impossible—the impossible promise I made to you. To kill you if anyone ever came to ask for it. But for what it's worth, this is the first time I've broken my word in over sixty years. The first time since I broke it all those years ago and cost my older brother his life in a run-down Italian neighborhood in Boston."

"Sixty years. Unfortunate to break such a streak," I said.

"It is indeed. But at least this time, it saved a life I care about."

I remained silent, giving him space to continue.

He took a long breath as if a painful memory was unfolding before his eyes. "Times were hard back then," he went on. "I was just a kid, but we all did whatever we could to survive. My brother too, when he betrayed the Moretti family and made me promise not to tell anyone about his meeting with the Pallini boys. But when the Morettis came to my father's shoe polish shop and questioned me, I told them—for a dime. I ran off to buy ice cream with my friend while my brother was shot for his betrayal. I didn't know they'd kill him, of course, but that was when I learned the importance of keeping one's word."

"You never told me this story," I said.

"That's because I later killed every single one of the Morettis. Expect for the women and children, of course."

I nodded. "I'm sorry for your loss."

"It was a long time ago. Yet it'll haunt me until the day I die. Even more since I broke my word to you." He turned to look at me again. "But I'd break it a thousand times again to save one of the greatest pianists who ever walked the earth."

We fell silent again. I inched closer to him on the bench. "I need your help."

He leaned forward, a spark of the man I'd once known returning to his eyes. "Anything," he said, his voice firm.

"Your friend, Ronald Hubble. He has something of great value that I need."

Luca looked surprised. "Ronald?"

I nodded.

"Name it. I'll get it for you."

"It might not be that easy. I'm not talking about a piano or painting. I'm talking about the entire share of a company he's invested in. I need his seat on the shareholders' table. It's of great importance to me."

Luca took a moment to process my words before a slight smile crossed his lips. "Let me guess. That company would be owned by Jan Novak?"

I couldn't help but smile back. "I did miss our conversations. Your sharp mind."

"No friendship in the world could make Ronald Hubble give up such a powerful investment. Even if he's dying, his legacy means more to him than heaven and earth."

"Then make him," I said, emotionless. "You can keep the shares. I only need power of attorney to attend the meetings. It would be a financially significant move on your end to acquire those shares. You know they hold more than monetary value. They hold a seat at the table of the most powerful men in the world. And those shares also come with the most powerful weapon in the world."

"Knowledge?" Luca asked.

"Knowledge," I repeated.

Yet he hesitated. I leaned back on the bench.

"Why did you ask me to play for the mafia in Italy?" I pressed. "You knew the risks. If the media found out, my career could have ended overnight. You have everything you could want here in America. Riches, power. So why? What could the Italian mafia possibly offer you that made risking my career worth it?"

Luca paused, lost in thought, his gaze drifting away. "I'm sorry I asked that of you. Truly, I am. But it was of great sentimental value to me."

"Sentimental? In what way?"

He sighed, a shadow of old memories crossing his face. "After I killed the Moretti family all those years ago, I found myself at odds with the Italian mafia. I broke our code of honor, but by then, I was too powerful for them to touch me here in the U.S. So they forbade me from ever returning to Italy. If I did, they'd kill me on sight."

"Even now?" I asked, intrigued.

"Italians don't forget. We are of Roman blood," he replied with a hint of pride.

"I see," I murmured.

"Arranging a private concert by 'the Empress'—someone who has turned down kings, queens, and presidents—was a gesture of such respect to the current Don that I hoped it would erase my past sins. I wanted to return home, to smell the olive trees, to visit the family I still have there, before I die."

"Well, you're welcome for the favor," I said bluntly.

After a brief silence, Luca narrowed his eyes at me. "If I was to get these shares ... will this ... make us even?"

I nodded.

"Consider it done then," he said, his intense gaze locking onto mine.

I stood to leave, but he gently caught my wrist. "Will you stay a bit longer?" he asked, his voice soft, almost hopeful, as he released his grip. "I've missed you so much."

"I'm afraid I have another engagement today," I replied. "But let's do dinner soon?"

His face brightened. "How about Luigi's? He keeps tuning that old piano for you. Swears his grandma's soul is in that thing."

I smiled. "People are peculiar." I turned to leave but then stopped and glanced back at him. "McCourt."

"What about him?" Luca asked.

"Please, leave him alive. For now, he might be useful to me."

Luca hesitated, conflict flickering in his eyes, then nodded reluctantly. "If that's what you want. But he'd better stay out of my sight."

"He will," I assured him. Then I made my way through the lush garden and back to my car.

CHAPTER SIX

Liam

I was sitting in my car in front of the metal gated driveway of Leah's townhome mansion. My mind raced as I gripped the steering wheel with both hands. The street was covered in flowers and candles that Leah's fans had left in a statement of support. The story so far was that a criminal had planned an attack on McCourt from the start. Luca had been clever, hiring a man with a criminal record, substance abuse issues, and schizophrenia to carry out the assault. No one questioned the scenario of a mentally ill attacker targeting a high-profile FBI agent at a concert. Yet, most of all, the world mourned Leah—the tragic genius who'd endured so much trauma.

"Dad," Josie called from the driver's seat in a voice tinged with annoyance.

"Hmm?"

"I thought you said you gotta talk to the woman in this house for a minute."

We'd been sitting here for a few minutes as I went back and forth about bringing Josie even close to Leah. But my visit to the Night Stalker that morning had left me very worried about Leah picking up a side gig that could endanger us all. And she wasn't answering her phone—again. Which also worried me. Something had been up with her ever since Jan Novak had entered our lives.

"I do need to talk to her," I finally said.

I spent another moment sitting there.

Josie cocked an eyebrow. "Well, usually people move their legs when they want to get somewhere. If you need to talk to her, you'll have to start by opening the car door. Then, you use your legs to walk to the house."

A proud grin spread across my face. "Sarcasm, first class. Just like me. Love it."

"All jokes aside, the movie starts in thirty minutes, and I don't want to get stuck in the huge candy line again."

I sighed, gave it one last thought, and opened the car door.

"Don't open the car for anybody. I'll lock it and take the keys with me. If some weirdo knocks at the window, you call me. Where's your phone?"

Josie pulled it out of her backpack and held it up for me to see.

"Good. It'll only be a minute."

I quickly walked through the entrance next to the metal gate and knocked on the door. To my surprise, Leah herself answered. A flicker of astonishment crossed her face.

"Another risky check-in on the shooting victim?" she asked, stepping aside to let me in.

"Something like that," I said, leaving the door wide open so I could keep an eye on Josie. Leah followed my gaze to the car, where Josie was watching us.

"Hmm," was all she said before stepping into the office off the hallway. "So how can the poor victim help you today, Agent Richter?"

"Well, first off, by guaranteeing me that you aren't the artist behind the Night Stalker's attack by the fountain."

Leah leaned against her desk. She wore a cream-colored pantsuit, and her long, dark hair was pulled up in a lazy bun. She looked stunning, as always.

Her green eyes found mine. She looked as if she was debating. "I'm afraid ... I can't do that."

I sighed in disbelief. "Leah, what the fuck?" I stepped in front of her, keeping my voice low. "Do you have any idea how dangerous this is? For you? For me and Rose? What's going on with you?"

Much to my surprise, she had no snappy reply. She just looked at me as if she, too, was searching for an answer to my question.

"People are starting to notice that bad guys are having a rough streak," I said. "Not enough for anyone to connect the dots yet, but if this becomes your new side gig—with all the fucked-up people out there—we'll have enough dead bodies to wrap around the earth twice."

"That doesn't sound like a bad thing," she said.

"Leah, I'm serious. I didn't sign up to be Robin to your serial killer Batman."

"Good. Because I'm not planning to involve you in any of this."

"I'm already involved," I countered, frustrated. "Not only is this dangerous, but the margin for error is too close for my comfort."

Her eyes narrowed at me as she studied my face.

I exhaled heavily. "This is also taking energy away from Jan Novak. We need to focus on him. It'll take all we have, and even that might not be enough. Do you really want to risk the chance of bringing him to justice for the sake of your new hobby, or whatever the hell this is?"

There was a brief, intense silence.

"Rose found out who's following me," she finally said.

My head jerked back in surprise. "Rose? What? When?"

"She texted me shortly before you came here. I was about to set up a meeting for tonight."

"How did she get that info?"

"She followed me after our meeting."

This was outrageous. "After our meeting? You mean before you chopped off the Night Stalker's dick? Did you know about this?"

Leah shook her head. "Not until I noticed her following me to the park."

"This is dangerous. Why the hell is everybody starting to do side missions?"

"Because it needs to be done."

I threw her an angry look. "At least people could tell me about these things."

"I'm telling you now. It made sense to follow me. We needed to know who my stalker is."

I thought about it, then nodded. "Fine. Then tell me. Who is it?"

"I haven't gotten much information on him yet, but he seems to be a turkey farmer west of Boston. Carl Carr. He drives a red truck with the license plate MA 3333. The plate is fake, but we have his address from his driver's license."

"Carl Carr?" I repeated. The morning was full of surprises. Then it hit me. "A red pickup truck?"

Leah nodded.

I drew my phone from my suit jacket and called Cowboy. "It's me," I said. "Remember Mrs. Moore and her missing daughter? Can you check surveillance cameras near Fifth and Riley? Where Nathalie Moore disappeared on the twentieth? We're looking for a red pickup, MA 3333."

"Sure thing," Cowboy said.

I hung up.

Leah watched me curiously.

"Just a hunch ... but not a good one," I said.

She had opened her mouth to say something when the sound of piano keys echoed into the office from the library across from us.

Both of us hurried over. My hand was on my gun when we found Josie sitting on the grand piano's bench, looking over her shoulder at us with the stare of a kid who knew she was in trouble.

"Josie!" I yelled.

Her eyes widened. "I ... I'm sorry. I just—"

"I told you to stay in the car!" I shouted again, my voice louder and harsher than I intended.

Josie froze, fear washing over her.

"Richter..." Leah reprimanded me as Josie's eyes welled up with tears.

"I was looking for you," she mumbled. "The movie, it was getting late. Then I saw the cat by the open door—I'm sorry."

"Fuck," I muttered as I walked up to her and placed a hand on her shoulders. "I'm sorry, Muffin, Daddy is just..."

What could I say? *Daddy is just worried about you meeting a serial killer who kills serial killers?*

"How about we get going, and you can get whatever candy you want? No limits."

But the crying didn't let up as Josie buried her face into my stomach.

"I'm sorry," she kept saying. "I followed the cat and saw the piano. I started playing at school, and I'd never seen a piano like this."

I rubbed her back, feeling like the biggest jackass. "I know, Muffin. Daddy is so sorry."

"You must be Josie," Leah said, her eyes still giving me a scolding look as she spoke. "My name is Leah."

Josie immediately stopped crying. She turned her head to Leah. "You're that pianist, aren't you? The one my dad watches on TV all the time," Josie said.

Leah smiled gently. "I'm afraid the cat has left, as you can see," she said, glancing around her elegant piano room. "But I heard you're learning to play the piano?"

Josie nodded, wiping her tears with her sleeve. "For my dad. He watches you all the time."

Jesus. How could I have been such a jerk?

"I see. Would you like me to play something for you?" Leah asked, catching me off guard.

"Really? For me?" Josie asked in disbelief, wiping her eyes one last time.

"Of course. It would be my pleasure."

"You don't have to," I interjected. "We're actually late for the mov—"

"Please, Dad!" Josie cut me off. "Please!"

Leah and I locked eyes. She gave me a look—the one all women have when a man is being a complete idiot.

"All right," I agreed.

Josie jumped up from the bench and grabbed my hand, her face lighting up. We watched as Leah took her seat behind the grand piano.

"I'm afraid I don't know any children's songs," Leah said quietly. "But I did hear a lullaby on the radio once that stuck with me. It's rather sad, though."

"That's okay," Josie replied. "I'm sad a lot when my mom and dad fight, and I was sad when I couldn't see my dad anymore."

Her words pierced me like a knife straight to the heart.

"I can understand how the thought of losing your dad could feel overwhelmingly sad," Leah said softly. "There's a song called 'You Will Be Okay' by Sam Haft. I think you'd appreciate the piano version by Annapantsu."

She settled at the piano and began to play, her fingers gliding over the keys. Then she sang, her voice rich and haunting. It was the most amazing voice I'd ever heard.

The melody filled the room, wrapping us in a tapestry of sorrow and solace. The song was about facing darkness and the inevitability of endings. It spoke of the fading of life and the stark weight of silence. Yet, amid all the despair, it offered a promise—that even when everything went to hell, when she was gone and the world seemed to collapse, those left behind would find a way to be okay.

As she reached the final, heartfelt notes, Leah lifted her gaze from the piano. Her piercing green eyes met mine, leaving me breathless.

Josie and I stood there, frozen after the last echo faded into silence. I was an utter mess inside. Emotions swirled through me: guilt for Josie and all she'd been through. Sadness for Leah and her tragic life, as well as for myself—for the man I'd become or, more likely, the man I'd always been without knowing it.

A murderer.

Even if it was bad people. I was still a killer.

But I felt something else—something I couldn't put a finger on. Or something I was too scared to think about.

Suddenly Josie started clapping. "That was amazing!"

Leah smiled. "I usually don't sing, so I hope you both still enjoyed the piece. It's a simple song to play, so if you keep practicing, you'll be able to play it soon."

"Can I hear another one?" Josie begged.

"Oh no, Muffin, we really need to go," I said. "And Leah is busy."

"Your dad's right. Maybe next time," Leah said.

"Okay," Josie said, disappointed.

On the way out, I stopped and looked back at Leah. "Thank you," I said.

"It was my pleasure. I'll talk to you soon, Agent Richter."

I nodded. Our issues weren't resolved, but now wasn't the time.

As Leah closed the door behind us, Josie and I walked to the car. I was deep in thought about both the song and our conversation before it.

"Dad?" Josie asked as we passed through the gate. Her voice was soft and curious.

"Yeah?"

"I think ... she played that song for you," she said, her brow furrowed in thought.

"What makes you think that?" I asked.

"The way she looked at you," she replied, her eyes searching mine.

I smiled softly and shook my head. "Nah. That song was for you, Muffin. It was all for you."

CHAPTER SEVEN

Luca

Luca opened his arms wide for an embrace as he made his way through Ronald Hubble's grand bedroom. His smile was sincere, creating a bizarre contrast to his mission.

Ronald had been bedridden for a few weeks. Doctors and nurses buzzed around him as he vegetated on death's doorstep, too afraid to let go of the spectacular life he'd been granted.

"I was hoping you'd show up with a bottle of Pappy Van," Ronald huffed, using the electric controls on his bed to adjust his position until he was sitting upright. He looked like a ghost, pale with dark rings around his eyes. Yet his mind still seemed sharp.

"I did." Luca smiled. "But one of the pretty nurses took it from me before I entered."

Ronald's blue lips split into a cheeky grin. "I should have picked them by their brains, not their looks."

Luca watched as one of the pretty young nurses came to check his vitals and then left.

"No, you did well," he joked, sending Ronald into a coughing laugh.

Ronald's eyes flicked to the chair beside the bed, then shifted to Luca, who remained standing.

"Why do I have the feeling you aren't here to visit an old friend?" Ronald asked in his weak voice.

"Because you and I know each other too well."

"What is it then? How can I help you in my last days before I go to hell?"

"Ah, there's no such thing, my friend. But if there is, I'll be joining you soon enough." Luca's expression turned serious. "But you're right. I'm here for more than a visit. I've never asked you for anything, my old friend. Not even when I took care of that whistleblower who would've ruined your family and brought your empire crashing down."

Ronald's eyes narrowed. "But you're asking for something now, aren't you?"

Luca stayed silent.

"I see. Well, it's not a big surprise. I always knew you'd come calling for a favor someday. I just didn't think it'd take this long."

"It took this long because you never had anything I wanted," Luca shot back.

"But now I do," Ronald said.

"Now you do."

"So what is it? What does the mighty Luca Domizio want from his old friend on his deathbed to repay an old favor?"

S. T. ASHMAN

"All of your shares in Obligato Corporation," Luca said, adjusting his white suit jacket. "I'll pay you for them. Market value."

Ronald lay there for a moment, silent, before ripping off his oxygen mask. "Let's skip the whole you-must-be-joking shit. I know you're dead serious. What I don't get is how you can seriously ask me for this. You know I can't do that, Luca. This company ... it's not like the others. And the fact that you're asking for it only proves you know that. This investment isn't just about money—and, by the way, my shares are worth over a billion. It's about the seat at Novak's table, a stronghold of power only a few in this country will ever hold. My son will take my place there and continue our legacy."

Luca let out a sharp, sarcastic breath. "Ben is an idiot. The only tables he'll ever sit at are the poker table and the judge's bench—to settle all the lawsuits against him."

Ronald didn't argue. "Ask for something else," he said, his voice firm.

"I'm afraid, my old friend, I'm asking for this. I'll have to ... insist. And you know what that means."

Ronald started coughing violently, then took a deep breath from his oxygen mask to calm himself.

"So after all these years," he huffed under the mask, "you now threaten me. Our lifelong friendship gone. For power. Greed. My legacy destroyed."

"Those shares will hardly destroy your legacy. If you upset me, on the other hand, that will. Everything you see with your tired old eyes will be gone. Hubble will be a name of tragedy and ruin. I'll pay you a decent sum

52

for the shares. And you'll still be filthy rich after that. Now, do I leave here with those shares? Or do I leave with your family's ruin?"

"Higgins," Ronald wheezed, coughing violently as if this might be his final breath. "Higgins will arrange the paperwork and have it to you by this evening."

"Thank you," Luca replied.

"Get the fuck out," Ronald growled. "I never want to see you again."

Luca let out a short, disbelieving laugh, his brows furrowing. "You really believe that out of the two criminals in this room, I'm the evil one, don't you? Meanwhile, you robbed hardworking families of the roofs over their heads for your own gain. You took the little they had to feed their children because towers of gold weren't enough for you. I stayed in the shadows where I belong. But you, my friend—you feasted on women and children and honest men."

Turning his face away, Ronald pouted like a stubborn kid.

Luca nodded once. "Farewell, old friend."

"I'll see you in hell!" Ronald shouted after him as Luca made his way toward the door.

"You can count on that," Luca muttered, flashing a flirtatious smile at the nurse as he left.

CHAPTER EIGHT

Rose

McCourt's office seemed bigger. It was as if the walls had stopped trying to close in on me.

McCourt was sitting across from me, popping pain pills in silence. I had to give the old bastard that. He was resilient. The gunshot wound was a clear shot through his chest. No arteries, no internal damage. Lady luck was on his side once more. Kind of ironic, considering how many good people she passed every day without making a stop. After the incident, which had been deemed an attack by a mentally ill drug addict, McCourt was hailed as a hero by both the reds and blues in Congress. No FBI director had ever been elected so fast. He'd run the bureau from Boston while the new assistant director represented him in DC for a few months until he was fully healed. Then McCourt would pack up and ship to DC to be right in that swamp.

"Congratulations on making FBI director," I said. "Sorry I missed the ceremony in the hospital. Looked really good on TV, though. Like that of the surviving hero who'll lead us to great victories."

With a swig from a water bottle, he swallowed the pills. "Cut the bullshit, Rose. What do you want?"

I smiled. It felt incredible to be out from under his thumb. The constant pressure. The feeling of being controlled. Gone.

"I think a bigger question would be what you want. I can only assume that staying alive and keeping your seat in the chair are on your list. Probably at the top."

McCourt narrowed his eyes. "So you're part of all this now? Them?"

"It's complicated," I said.

"There's nothing complicated about how you betrayed me. The bureau. The badge."

"You must know," I countered calmly.

A heavy silence settled over the room as I stood.

"No need to drag this out," I said. "Operations continue as usual. We catch bad guys. The only difference is, there'll be no sniffing around in the BAU or the Boston Concert Hall. That's it."

"Oh, that's it, huh?" he shot back.

"Pretty much. You can still play the big boss. But if I were you, I'd tread carefully. Your little arrangement with Luca Domizio didn't exactly go as planned. You'd better steer clear of pissing him off for a while."

His eyes flared with a mix of disbelief and fury.

"And maybe just check under your car for a bit," I added. "You know, for bombs. I think Luca Domizio agreed to leave you alone, but with the mob, you never really know. From what I've gathered, he seems quite fond of the pianist you tried to have killed. Oops. My bad." I turned toward the door.

"Fucking bitch," I heard McCourt mutter as I left his office. But to me, it wasn't an insult. Not the way he said it, laced with defeat and rage. He was like a child throwing a tantrum, with no other way to vent. In this context, it was almost a compliment. Maybe the only time in my life when being called a bitch felt like one.

With a grin, I walked past the secretary. "Have a good day," I said, "and make sure he remembers to take his pills. The FBI needs him in top shape."

My smile faded as I took the stairs down to the BAU. I had texted Carl Carr's info to Leah before I'd even talked to Richter about it. And then there was the hospital, where I'd had the chance but hadn't told him about Leah and the Night Stalker. What really troubled me, though, wasn't Richter. It was why I hadn't said anything. Did I feel like I owed Leah for the McCourt incident? Or for saving my life? Or, maybe worse: Did I, deep down, support her missions, no matter what?

I was dancing with the devil now, fully caught in the tango. And the thing about dancing with the devil was that once you started, you didn't get to decide when the music stopped.

CHAPTER NINE

Leah

Carl Carr.

I'd been waiting for hours for the sun to descend beyond the edge of a small patch of woods bordering Carl Carr's turkey farm. It had started to rain. I was wearing a black coverall, and I'd brought my bag of goodies in case my hunch about my stalker turned out to be true. Richter was still waiting for the results of viewing hundreds of hours of surveillance footage. But I had all I needed to visit Carl Carr and scout out the farm under the cover of night. This man had stalked me for weeks. It was time to return the favor.

As twilight faded, I followed a narrow deer path through the woods. It led straight to a field of turkey barns surrounding a small, old farmhouse.

Emerging from the woods, I was enveloped by the night sounds and smells of the farm. Soft gobbles and clucks of turkeys mixed with the faint hum of distant machinery. The air smelled like grain and turkey manure. Large holding houses loomed in the dark, their structures casting long shadows across the open fields. In the back, a meat processing facility stood out with a single bright light outside, creating a stark contrast against the darkness.

I made my way to the small, rundown farmhouse off to the side, not far from the holding houses. Its white paint was peeling, and weeds grew tall around it.

I approached it, stepping carefully to avoid making noise. The dim light from inside flickered through the gaps in a flowery curtain. I peered through the window. An old woman sat in a worn armchair and smoked a cigarette. Her face was deeply sun-tanned and lined—a testament to a life spent farming. She wore a faded pink nightgown that looked like it was from the sixties. Her eyes were fixed on the television, some old movie in black and white.

Next to her was a man in his thirties, lounging on a battered sofa. He looked unkempt, with a scruffy beard and long, oily hair. His overalls and denim shirt needed a wash. He stared at the screen, occasionally glancing at the old woman as if seeking some form of approval.

Leaving the farmhouse behind, I made my way toward the large processing facility and stepped inside. The metallic stench of meat—thick and repulsive—hit me. Despite the overhead lights buzzing faintly, the place was deserted. No workers. No cameras. Not anywhere on the property. Curious. Very curious.

I kept close to the wall, moving carefully, until I spotted a red door at the far end of the machinery room, where turkeys were being ground into meat. The door was reinforced, solid steel, and locked tight. Far too secure for a place like this.

Quickly, I used my tools to unlock it. Then I slipped inside. The small room was dusty and filled with cleaning supplies. To most, it would look like a janitor's closet. But that heavy steel door had me on edge. Why go to such lengths to guard a few rags and buckets?

I swept the room with my flashlight, whose beam cut through the dust. That was when I saw them—footprints, faint but distinct, leading to a rug in the center of the room. The prints looked like they belonged to a man about the size of the one I'd glimpsed at the farmhouse. And they stopped right at the rug.

I shut the door quietly behind me and walked over, then lifted the rug. Beneath it, I found a wooden hatch—the kind used to access hidden basements. It took some effort, but I managed to pry it open, revealing a set of wooden stairs leading down into darkness. A chill ran through me as the stench of feces and death hit, along with the cold certainty that something dark was waiting below.

I'd been right to come tonight.

And I'd be right to end whatever this was.

My flashlight illuminated the wooden stairs as I descended. Noise dampers lined the reinforced walls. When I reached the dark room at the bottom of the stairs, the reek of rotten meat hit me, forcing me to gag. But what I saw next in my flashlight's beam hit me even harder than the smell.

Bright, fresh blood mingled with dark, dried stains splattered across every surface, creating a gruesome tapestry on the walls and floor. Metal hooks dangled from the ceiling. One of them pierced a decomposing human leg, crawling with maggots that wiggled and squirmed. I swept my flashlight to the left, revealing a long wooden table covered in tools—a blood-soaked chainsaw, a rusted axe, and a set of butcher knives, their blades stained and dulled from repeated use.

A metallic clinking of chains echoed to my right, and I spun my flashlight in that direction. The beam landed on a chained, naked woman huddled in the corner of the room, her body trembling. She blinked rapidly against the sudden brightness. Filled with fear and desperation, she murmured pitifully beneath the duct tape covering her mouth. Next to her was a large shelf containing several jars, each with a preserved human head inside it. All women, swollen and soaked from having sat in the solution for a long time. Their eyes, open wide in horror, matched those of the woman chained to the wall. The agony of sitting here in this hell, all alone, in the dark, was unthinkable. She was still alive, but her blonde hair was sticky with blood, and it looked like someone had cut chunks of flesh from her arms and legs. The exposed areas were swollen and oozed pus.

I was about to rush over to the woman and remove the tape from her mouth when a groaning sound from the red door at the top of the stairs echoed down into the room.

Quickly, I turned my flashlight off and squeezed between old boxes under the stairs.

The light snapped on, casting a harsh glare down the staircase. A tense silence followed, as if the person above was straining to hear any sound. The wooden stairs creaked ominously above me as someone descended slowly, step by step. Each heavy footstep thudded, echoing through the quiet.

I grabbed the gun from my bag, ready to shoot. Carl Carr had probably noticed the door was unlocked. His slow, cautious steps confirmed my worries.

He was looking for me. And if he looked long enough, he'd find me.

I had only one option.

When he was almost right above me, I aimed the gun upward, took a deep breath, and unloaded the entire magazine through the wooden steps. He screamed as his body tumbled down the stairs. With practiced ease, I reloaded my gun and carefully emerged from my hiding spot.

I found Carl at the bottom of the stairs. He was clutching his chest and grunting in pain. But he wasn't entirely out, maybe still able to fight. I changed plans and ran over to the table with the tools. There, I grabbed the axe.

"You cunt," Carl Carr spat, his moment of brave defiance fueled by the flicker of evil in his dark eyes. "I'm not afra—"

Before he could finish, I swung the axe high above my head and brought it down on his right ankle, severing his foot. Blood sprayed across my face as his scream ripped through the air.

"I don't need you to be afraid," I said coldly, wiping the blood from my cheek. "I just need you to be in pain."

His screams filled the room, unrelenting.

"In just one strike. Would you look at that," I mumbled to myself. He was immobile but not dead. Just what I wanted.

Calmly, I checked the door at the top of the stairs. He'd locked it behind himself.

Perfect. Nobody would hear his screams.

"Please stop!" he cried.

"Shut up. We're just getting started," I said, scanning the table of tools. I spotted a roll of tape and grabbed it to cover his mouth. He was too busy sobbing over his severed foot to put up much of a fight. When he started crawling toward the stairs, I took advantage of his desperation and taped his legs together just above the stump.

He managed to worm his way to the base of the stairs, so I decided to take his arm too. My first swing missed. It took a few chops to sever his arm at the elbow. His cries turned into desperate sobs. Then he went still.

"I hope the bastard didn't die on us," I said to the woman in the corner. Her eyes were wide with a mix of horror and something like satisfaction.

I checked his neck for a pulse.

"No, just passed out," I said, grabbing a rope from the table. I tied it around the stumps as a tourniquet to slow the bleeding. He'd been shot a couple of times, but from what I could see, there were only two bullet wounds—one in the shoulder and one in the leg. Neither was bleeding too badly. Technically, he could survive all this.

"Where does he keep the keys to your chains?" I asked.

She nodded toward the table.

It didn't take long to find them nestled between a bloody knife and a rotting finger.

For a moment, I stood there, staring at her. This was a problem. A witness. But it was too late to worry about that now. This was the first time I'd ever saved a life before taking one, and I found a strange satisfaction in it. So much so that a warmth spread through my chest—a warmth that might have been happiness. Or maybe joy?

"I'm going to remove the tape from your mouth, okay?"

She nodded, her blue eyes wide, a mix of fear and hope.

"Thank you," she choked out, sobbing the instant the tape was gone. "Thank you, my guardian angel. Thank you."

Guardian angel...

The irony hit me, considering I'd just hacked off a man's arm and foot. Then I noticed the small silver cross around her neck. She must be religious.

"I'm going to unchain you now, but you need to promise me you won't run. He can't hurt you anymore, understand?"

"Yes, I promise," she wept, her tears flowing freely.

I used the keys to release the chains from her wrists and ankles. The moment she was free, she sprang up—not to run, as I'd expected, but to throw her arms around me in a desperate embrace. The foul odor of urine and feces filled my nostrils as she clung to me, squeezing so tightly that she forced the air from my lungs. Yet that strange, warm glow inside me remained.

I stood there, my arms dangling motionless by my hips, frozen, as the naked woman sobbed into my neck, thanking me over and over again. Nobody had ever hugged me like this before.

Finally, I gently pushed her off and grabbed her by the shoulders. "I need you to focus now. We don't have much time, you understand?"

The woman nodded.

"I have two options for you," I said calmly. "We can call the police, and the man might survive and will be arrested. The horror of all of this will publicly haunt you and your family for the rest of your life. You'll never be able to leave the house without people taking pictures of you. And the police might come looking for me."

The woman's blue eyes stared straight into mine. "Or?" she said, her tears dying down.

"Or I'll take care of this monster. Nobody will ever find him. As of now, the police don't know who he is or what he's doing. It'll look like he just left his old life behind. People disappear all the time. And you ... you run back home and tell your family whatever lie suits you best. To explain your temporary disappearance."

Surprisingly, she didn't need time to think about it. "Kill him," she spat as her gaze wandered to Carl on the floor. "Make it painful."

I nodded. "Go now. Use the woods to get to the road. Make sure nobody sees you."

But instead of fleeing, the woman slipped her silver cross necklace over her head and placed it into my bloody, gloved hand.

"I have no use for—"

"Thank you from the bottom of my heart," she said, closing my hand around the cross. "I have two kids, and thanks to you, they still have a mom. Even if it's now a broken one, they still have her."

Then she turned and bolted toward the stairs. I watched as she snatched a dirty dress from the floor and pulled it over her head. In a flash, she was up the stairs and gone.

I stood there, clutching the silver cross necklace in my bloody fist. She'd called me an angel and hugged me. And, for a moment, it had felt ... good. But as my gaze shifted back to Carl Carr, I remembered what I truly was.

A monster.

If I had more time, I'd make Carl Carr feel every ounce of my rotten core. But time was a luxury when one was committing murder.

I walked over to my bag by the stairs, deliberately stepping on Carl Carr as if he were nothing more than a rug. He let out a pained groan and twitched slightly. In a rare moment of sentiment, I slipped the silver necklace into my bag. Not that it would suddenly make me religious or give me a warm feeling every time I saw it, but leaving it here didn't feel right.

Frowning, I pulled out my phone and dialed Richter.

He answered immediately. "Are you alright?"

"I found a woman with long blonde hair and blue eyes in Carl Carr's hidden basement. She might be your missing prostitute. She'll be home soon."

"You what?" his voice echoed back.

"I still have to deal with Carl Carr. No help needed. Resume business as usual."

"Resume business as usual? Leah, this—"

"Oh, one more thing. I got the shares to Jan Novak's company. Tomorrow, they hold a shareholders meeting, which I'll attend. I'll meet with you after that."

"Are you kidding? What the hell—"

"I don't mean to be rude, but I have to go."

"Leah, wait!"

"Don't eat turkey for a while."

"What? Goddamn—"

I hung up and turned off my phone.

Richter was upset. Of course he was. But, lately, I'd found myself caring less about consequences. It was as if Jan Novak was taking hold of my mind, clouding it.

Carl Carr groaned, tearing me away from my thoughts.

I walked over to him and pulled the tape off his mouth.

"Mama ... help me," he huffed weakly.

"Stop that, you piece of shit. Your mama won't help you. But I'll make it quick if you tell me why you were following me."

After a moment of defiant silence, Carl Carr coughed up blood. He looked like he was about to pass out again, so I stepped on the stump of his arm.

"Aaaaaa—!"

"You know I can keep you alive for weeks down here. Stop by every night, just to torture you and take a piece off you inch by inch, starting with your dick."

Carl Carr whimpered like a child.

"We could even bring your mama down here. Show her your work. Make her watch. I mean, she kinda already knows what you were doing down here, doesn't she?"

He kept whimpering, so I grabbed the axe and dragged it over to him.

"Fine, let's just get to work."

"W-w-wait!" he stuttered hysterically. "The devil. The devil told me a-about you."

I sighed. "What utter nonsense." I lifted the axe high above his leg.

"Wait! No! It's true!" he screamed, finding a new will to live.

I paused.

"He sent me a letter and picture of you and warned me about you. I know it was the devil. He watches over me. Warned me. Said you turned on your own. That you're a traitor." He spat the last two words in disgust.

I almost laughed as I lowered the axe. "Turned on my own? Ridiculous. You're not my kind. You're a monster from pure darkness. I'm a monster walking in the light."

"I ... I need help." Carl started crying. "My arms. I'm bleeding. Please call an ambulance. I'm really hurt."

I lifted the axe again. "Well, aren't you slow, Carl boy. That's the whole point of it."

"Wait!" he begged beneath his tears. "I told you about the letter. What are you doing?"

"Chopping you up, of course, so I can carry you over to the meat grinder. You're too big for me to carry all at once. I'm petite."

"You're crazy! Somebody, help! Heeeeeeeeeeelp!"

I dropped the axe with speed onto his upper thigh. After a few strikes, I'd chopped it off.

It would take a few trips, but I ignored him as I taped his mouth shut again and began hauling his severed leg up the stairs to the meat grinder. Disposing of Carl Carr in a meat factory seemed like the most fitting end. Sure, I could leave him down here, but I didn't want the heads of the women in those jars to spend another minute in this bastard's presence.

Grinding him up would be quick and clean. No trace of him left behind. And in a sick, twisted irony, Carl Carr would finally serve life rather than take it.

Tonight, there wasn't enough time, but in a few weeks, once the dust settled, I'd try to return and bury those poor women's heads somewhere peaceful in the woods, far from this hellhole. It wouldn't be a happy ending, but in a fucked-up world like this, it would have to be enough. For now.

CHAPTER TEN

Richter

Rose and I were waiting in an SUV not far from the Moores' trailer. It was already three a.m., but after Leah's call, I had to see for myself if Nathalie was safe. And Rose had insisted on tagging along the moment I'd texted her.

"So what else did she say?" Rose asked, her eyes locked on mine, concern creasing her brow.

"That's all she said. Carl Carr was taken care of. And if the woman in the basement was Nathalie, she'd be home safe soon."

Rose sighed. "So how does this work, exactly? I mean, this whole taking-out-serial-killers thing. This isn't exactly covered in the FBI training manual. So far, it seems a bit ... well, risky."

I ran my hand through my hair. It had been months since this business with Leah had started, and I still had no idea how it was supposed to work. How the hell did Larsen operate like this? Or had Leah changed? Had she gotten more out of control? Leah should have run this mission by me first. There was no pattern, no order to anything anymore, and I had a feeling Jan Novak was the reason why Leah was becoming more aggressive. But Rose didn't need to know any of that. We needed her on board without doubts— or at least with more commitment to us than against us.

"There isn't really much to it," I said. "We find bad guys. She disposes of them."

"Mm-hmm. Disposes of them," Rose said. "Just curious. What evidence do we have that Carl Carr was really a serial killer? Did she say anything about that? Because the guy in the park—"

I cut her off, facing her. "Yeah, let's talk about the guy in the park."

Rose's gaze dropped to her hands.

"Because I'm still a bit confused about all of that, to be honest. How exactly did you come by the information about Carl Carr again?"

"I ... I followed Leah after our meeting. So I could catch her stalker and get his ID. Worked out quite well, if you ask—" Her voice broke off the moment she saw the look on my face.

"Worked out great, didn't it? Especially the part where you knew Leah stabbed the Night Stalker and decided not to mention it. I assume that was to protect her?"

Rose's lips moved as if to respond, but no words came out. Finally, she spoke. "It wasn't like that. And it's not like she needs protection. I followed her to catch her stalker. Everything else that happened ... it just happened. And I knew you two would sort it out eventually. Aren't you supposed to be a team or something? You're acting like I should know exactly how to handle situations like these. But guess what, Richter? There's no manual on how to operate in an office with serial killer coworkers, okay? But I'm here, aren't I?"

I nodded. "Yes. You are."

"Then please tell me Carl Carr was the bad guy we were after because if I'm responsible for the brutal murder of some random—"

Rose stopped mid-sentence when a shadow emerged from the dark road.

Nathalie!

She was hurrying along the narrow flower path to her trailer's porch. There were only a few streetlights, which made it hard to see her face, but the limp and the way she clutched herself told a story of horror. She stopped under the porchlight, which illuminated her blood-soaked blonde hair. She was wearing a large jacket, probably given to her by someone on her way here, but her legs, exposed beneath the blood-stained mini-dress, bore what looked like deep, ragged wounds as if something had gnawed at her.

"Fucking Christ," Rose muttered, gripping the car door handle, ready to leap out.

I grabbed her arm. "Wait!"

We watched as the door opened. Mrs. Moore and Nathalie fell into each other in a tearful embrace.

"It's her!" Rose said. "I can't believe it. It's really Nathalie! Fucking Carl Carr. We gotta talk to her."

"No." I shook my head. "Nathalie didn't call the cops. It would be suspicious for us to be out here in front of her home at this time. We have to wait and see what the Moores tell us about what happened. Nathalie might never mention Carl Carr to protect Leah and her family from the media."

Rose leaned back in her seat as a loud breath escaped her lips. "This ... is nuts, Richter."

We watched as Nathalie and Mrs. Moore closed the door to the trailer.

"Pretty much," I agreed. "But it also feels pretty damn good, doesn't it? Seeing Nathalie back home. Carl Carr gone. I know it's wrong. And yet..."

Rose's gaze met mine. "It does feel pretty damn good."

For a moment, we just sat there and let the beautiful feeling of Nathalie returning home alive sink in. She had been through hell and would carry scars for the rest of her life, but she was alive. If she was half the fighter I made her out to be, they'd be alright someday.

"So what exactly happened to Carl Carr?" Rose asked. "It would be nice to retrieve the missing bodies of the other women from his farm. I have a feeling this was a thing for that sick fuck."

"I've thought about that," I said. "But we need to give this some time, let things cool down. I'll pull Cowboy off the search for the truck. In a few months, we'll come up with a plan. Maybe something like a hiker's dog finding evidence on Carr's property."

Rose nodded. "You said Leah got the shares to Jan Novak's cloud firm?"

"Yes. She'll meet us after she attends that shareholders meeting with Jan Novak."

Rose crossed her arms. "I don't want to jinx it, but things might be looking up for us."

"Amen to that," I said.

"Might even get some sleep tonight," she added, smiling faintly.

"Wouldn't that be a plot twist for these two burnt-out, emotionally drained, walking-on-the-sword's-edge FBI agents?"

She smiled. "It would, indeed."

The car engine kicked on with a roar as I turned the key. "Just don't eat any turkey meat for a while," I said.

Rose's smile vanished. "Jesus fucking Christ, you serious?"

"'You don't look a gift horse in the mouth,' my German grandmother always used to say," I said.

"I guess not," Rose responded as I pulled the car onto the road.

CHAPTER ELEVEN

Leah

Dressed in a hand-tailored white pantsuit and carrying a Hermès Birkin, I walked into the heavily guarded underground hallway of Obledalo Corporation. The setting felt more like a secret military base than a corporate office. My hair was styled in a sleek chignon, adding a sharpness to my look. Walking beside me was Ronald Hubble's lawyer, Jeff Higgins. He was a short, elderly man well past his prime and seemed almost out of place. We approached a massive metal door guarded by two men in black suits standing sternly in front. To the side, a young woman sat behind a desk, typing on a computer.

As soon as she spotted us, the woman jumped to her feet. "You can't be here!" she exclaimed, her voice laced with shock as the men beside her tensed, hands hovering near their weapons.

Higgins, cool and composed, retrieved a document from his suitcase and handed it to her. "This is Ms. Nachtnebel," he stated firmly, "the representative for the new owner of the Hubble family's shares in Obligato Corporation. Mr. Hubble sold them very recently. Now, tell those men to open the door or risk a lawsuit for denying a shareholder the ability to attend a corporate meeting."

The woman's eyes widened as she scanned the document. Then her gaze lifted to meet mine. "Ms. Nachtnebel, I apologize for this incident. We take security very seriously around here. I hope you understand."

"Of course," I replied smoothly.

She nodded to the guards, who reluctantly stepped aside and opened the wide metal doors.

Higgins stood still until I glanced at him. He shook his head in response.

"Only you can enter, Ms. Nachtnebel," the woman said in an apologetic tone.

When I stepped through the doors and into the grand meeting room, its sheer scale instantly struck me. Warm light from crystal chandeliers bathed the space in a soft glow, reflecting off polished mahogany walls adorned with intricate carvings. Illuminated cases lined the walls, showcasing ancient Egyptian artifacts. To the side, a sophisticated bar, stocked with top-shelf spirits, stood next to a cluster of plush leather armchairs and a velvet sofa. This cozy lounge area sharply contrasted with the imposing dark wood table gleaming under the lights in the center of the room. High-backed chairs with rich red upholstery flanked the table on either side, giving it a regal feel. To the left, four elderly men sat in impeccably tailored suits, exuding an air of arrogant authority. I recognized them immediately—America's wealthiest and most influential figures, mega-donors to politics, representing both old and new money.

On the right side of the table, three men sat beside an empty chair, presumably reserved for Hubble. At one end of the table, a larger chair was occupied by a man whose back was to me. On the opposite end sat Jan Novak. Dressed in an elegant suit, he radiated power and confidence. His sharp blue eyes surveyed the men around the table. Clearly, he was the one in charge.

As I stepped inside, the room buzzed with a heated discussion. None of them noticed my entrance.

"China slashing its cloud storage prices in half is a direct attack on Obligato," said Edward Wallace, whose tall frame and silver hair boosted his commanding presence. He owned one of the largest airplane companies in the world. His voice brimmed with urgency as he continued: "They're aiming to secure contracts with our allies. Sensitive information in China's hands would be catastrophic!"

"Absolutely," agreed Thomas Whitmore, his gruff voice matching his stout frame. He came from old money, as his family had made their fortune in the late 1800s through oil and railroads. His eyes flashed with anger behind gold-rimmed glasses. "But some of our allies are willing to risk it for a cheap price. Just like when Europe ran to Putin for his cheap oil, not even realizing the power he'd gain over them. Truly idiotic."

"We all know what happened next," said Harold Lytton, his voice low. He was a thin man, always calm, with a neatly trimmed beard. He ran a massive beef business, feeding half the world. "Putin invaded Ukraine, and Europe had to beg the Saudis for oil while we drained America's emergency reserves to stabilize global markets and help them get through the winter. We can't let them make the same mistake again."

"Fucking idiots," snapped Richard Caldwell, whose booming voice cut through the room. His white hair and dominant presence made him hard to ignore. As heir to the world's largest pharmaceutical empire, he had the confidence of someone used to getting his way. "This isn't just about national security. It's about global security," he added, taking a sip of whiskey and scanning the table.

The argument intensified as I approached. It wasn't until Jan Novak rose from his chair that the room fell silent. His piercing eyes locked onto mine, betraying a mix of shock and cold calculation. The men stopped talking, and all eyes turned to me.

"Well, if it isn't the world-famous Ms. Nachtnebel," Jan Novak announced, his voice slicing through the stillness with surgical precision. "I must admit, I'm quite surprised to see you ... *here.*"

"I'm here to attend the shareholders' meeting," I replied calmly.

"Ms. Nachtnebel," Thomas Whitmore said, rising to greet me with genuine warmth. He shook my hand as three other men followed suit. "That attack was awful. My wife and I were so relieved to hear you came out unharmed. She thinks you're the closest thing to Jesus. We were at Mr. Hubble's birthday concert, and being so close to the piano was an experience like none other—"

"I'm afraid this is a closed meeting," Richard Caldwell cut in, his tone sharp as he stood to face me. "For shareholders only. There must be a mistake. Please excuse us."

The men who had greeted me quickly returned to their seats, visibly uneasy after Caldwell's authoritative interruption.

"There is no mistake, Mr. Caldwell," I replied. "I'm here on behalf of Domizio Investment Corp, which now holds Mr. Hubble's entire share of Obligato Corporation. And with that, the empty seat at this table."

"Luca Domizio bought Ronald's shares?" muttered Thomas Whitmore, disbelief clear in his voice. "How is that possible?"

"It's quite simple," I said. "Luca Domizio wanted the shares. Now he has them."

I walked to the vacant seat amid the murmurs of the group. Jan Novak's gaze followed my movements. A smile played on his lips the entire time.

I pulled back the empty chair and was about to sit when Novak nodded subtly at Caldwell. "Why don't we welcome our new member to the table by offering your seat at the head, Caldwell?" Novak suggested. "Right across from me."

The room fell silent. Richard Caldwell, likely the wealthiest in this room after Jan Novak, was a man who had influenced and sponsored the last few presidents. He wasn't accustomed to this sort of treatment.

"My seat?" Caldwell echoed, his voice laced with confusion and disbelief. "But I own the most shares after you—nearly double what Ronald Hubble had."

"You do indeed," Jan Novak replied smoothly. "But ... I'm afraid I have to insist. As the only woman at this table, Ms. Nachtnebel should be made to feel welcome, sitting right across from me."

Caldwell scanned the room, searching for support, but found none. With a slow, reluctant motion, he began gathering his papers as if preparing to leave.

"That won't be necessary," I said, sliding into Hubble's old chair. "It's just a chair. You can sit back down, Caldwell. Let's get back to discussing China's advancement in the cloud storage industry."

Jan's grin widened as he leaned back in his seat, his attention fixed on me.

Caldwell cleared his throat, clearly irritated. "Ms. Nachtnebel, now that you're here ... maybe you'd like to enlighten us on how to solve this problem?" His voice oozed with condescension. He was trying to catch me off guard. To him, I was just a woman, out of my depth.

All eyes turned to me, brows furrowed and curious.

"Well, I might not represent enough shares to decide the matter alone," I began, "but I'd suggest raising our cloud storage prices domestically while lowering them internationally for our allies who are seriously considering China's offer."

Caldwell laughed. "We can't raise domestic prices high enough to offset the discount needed to stay competitive internationally. And cutting prices without making up for it would hurt shareholder profits unless we cut workers' benefits or salaries—something Mr. Novak strongly opposes. Any seasoned businessman knows you have to balance what you take with what you give to maintain profit margins. It's basic math. Unlike music, which is more like child's play with sound—no real structure, no logic, just whatever feels good at the time."

A few men chuckled. I waited for them to finish.

"Quite simple math indeed, Mr. Caldwell," I replied smoothly. "Which is why we could offset the international price cuts further with a targeted tax break for the tech industry, specifically cloud storage. I estimate a point-five percent tax decrease should cover it, though it could be closer to point-forty-four percent if I'm not mistaken?"

Caldwell hesitated as the room's curiosity shifted toward him. "Are you a comedian too now, Ms. Nachtnebel? Who's supposed to fund this tax break?"

"I'm not naive enough to think it would come out of your pocket," I said. "Otherwise, you'd just accept a lower profit margin after reducing prices for our allies internationally without raising them domestically. From what I've gathered, those margins are still more than substantial. But given your company's history—such as those recent government contracts that inflated medication prices to boost profits after two record-breaking years—I'd bet you'll find a way to pull funds from a social security program to cover the proposed tax break. Food stamps. School lunches. Medicaid. Your choice. Make the poor poorer but safer, right? That's what you'll tell yourself while you sail the world on your nine-hundred-million-dollar yacht. By the way, I completely agree with the public—the large ivory dolphin sculptures placed along the railings on the first deck are a tasteless monstrosity."

The room fell into dead silence. Caldwell's face was as red as a lobster. Not that I took any pleasure in his defeat. The idea that another social program would be cut just to make the rich even richer was repulsive. But this wasn't my company, and someone else would have made the same suggestion anyway. The world worked that way, and my battle was with a different kind of monster. For now.

Caldwell opened his mouth to speak, but Jan Novak cut him off. "I see now why Luca Domizio trusted you with his seat," Jan said, a faint smile playing on his lips. "Shall we vote on Ms. Nachtnebel's proposal? All in favor, raise your hand."

Everyone in the room, except Caldwell, raised their hands.

"It's decided then," Jan said, rising from his chair. "Well done, Ms. Nachtnebel. Be sure to send Luca Domizio my regards and congratulate him on his wise choice of representation. We'll meet again next quarter."

The men stood and chatted among themselves as they scattered. I was heading toward the door when Jan Novak stopped me.

"Quite impressive, Ms. Nachtnebel."

"There's nothing impressive about greed," I replied.

"Yet here you are."

Standing close, he towered over me by nearly a head. He was slim but muscular. Not classically handsome, but his power, influence, and confidence radiated off him in waves. Even I could feel the pull. Had I not known the monster he truly was, I might have found myself drawn to him.

"I'm here for many reasons," I said. "Some of them you might not like."

"Try me. I might surprise you."

"Not many things surprise me anymore, Mr. Novak."

"Challenge accepted. Will you join us for a drink?"

"Another time," I said. "I have another engagement today. I'll see you at the next meeting."

I turned and walked away, but his footsteps followed close behind. He wasn't the type of man used to hearing the word "no."

"Let me walk you out," he said, holding the heavy metal door open for me. "It was good to see you again. It's been a while since our last and very interesting conversation at the Smithsonian Museum."

"It has indeed," I said. "Yet I have a feeling you saw me more often than I saw you." I locked eyes with him. He held my gaze without flinching. Unfazed and playful. Nobody ever did that except for Richter.

"May I invite you to dinner at my house this Friday then?"

I could almost hear Richter screaming *no*. That it was too dangerous. That he would come along. But I was who I was.

"I would be delighted," I said as I looked into his icy blue eyes.

Strange.

I'd thought seeing him again would spark a fire of hatred within me. He'd killed Emanuel. Shouldn't I slit his throat right now, right here, no matter the consequence? Yet as we stood there, just as we'd done back at the museum, I failed to see the monster in his eyes as I did with all the other killers.

Jan Novak was truly one of a kind. A master. Of everything.

"It's settled then," he said.

"Jan!" Caldwell shouted from the metal doors. "Could we have a word, please?"

"Of course," Jan responded.

"Why do I have the feeling that I'm the root of this 'word,'" I said.

Jan chuckled. "Because you are. Ruffled quite some feathers. But you're a shareholder's representative and free to speak your genius mind. I'll handle the children. Don't worry."

I nodded.

"Friday then," he said. "I'll have my driver pick you up at your house."

"I assume you know where I live."

"Of course I do," he said, his grin vanishing.

Then he turned and disappeared through the metal doors.

For a moment, I looked down the hallway of the most modern tech facility I'd ever seen.

This dinner with Jan Novak could be the step forward we needed to gather the proof to get him. Or it could be my end. He could kill me, and nobody would be able to prove anything.

I wondered if I should mention the dinner to Richter. I already knew he'd be against it. Yet open disagreement with him wouldn't break trust. Hiding things from him would. Especially after the Night Stalker incident. And Carl Carr.

I didn't have my phone, which I'd been forced to leave at the entrance of the building—no electronics were allowed. But as soon as I had access to it, I'd text Richter for a meeting tonight. I had a feeling it would be among our most tense ones yet.

CHAPTER TWELVE

Liam

"No. Absolutely not, no way," I said in a tone that should have left no room for debate. However, I was talking to Leah. "You can't meet him for a private dinner at his house. It's out of the question."

We were in her study. It was late afternoon, and Rose was late.

Leah sat behind her desk, leaning back in her chair, her eyes drilling into me with a cold, merciless stare. For a long moment, she said nothing, just watched me in silence.

"It's too dangerous," I continued when she didn't respond. "What would stop him from killing you and dropping you in some river like he did with Anna? I wouldn't know for weeks what happened to you. Maybe months. There has to be another way."

Another moment of silence stretched between us. It was broken only by the crackling of the fire in the fireplace.

"Are you done?" she finally said.

"No." And I wasn't. "After everything we've been through together. Everything we survived together. You think I'll just let you get killed over caviar and a bottle of fancy whiskey? Just keep attending those meetings. Something might come up."

Leah rose. "Something did come up, and I intend to take the chance."

I stood from my seat across from her desk. "Leah. Be honest with yourself. Don't you see how dangerous this is? This is madness."

"Of course I do. But we need to know if Jan Novak is the Train Track Killer. You said you want real evidence. I plan on delivering it to you."

"But not like this. No," I countered. I could barely control myself. How could she do this to our mission? To us as a team? Without her, our work to rid the streets of monsters was over.

"Larsen and I hunted the Train Track Killer for years before you came on board," she said. "With no leads. Nothing. He's not like you or me. Don't you understand what we're dealing with here? Do you want him to continue murdering innocent people? Like Anna. Hundreds and hundreds more of them. Gone."

This stuck me. Of course I didn't. Of course I wanted him dead as much as Leah did. But not like this.

"Besides," she continued. "If Jan Novak wanted us dead, we'd all be dead. Or at least fired. Have you ever asked yourself why he doesn't just call in a favor and have both you and Rose removed from the FBI altogether? Publish some scandal about me in every news outlet owned by his rich friends?"

"Of course I have," I shot back. "Many times. And none of it adds up."

"Then you know we're running out of time. This might be our only chance to get the evidence we need to prove he's the Train Track Killer—before he decides we're no longer fun and wipes us out. We need to move now. If I can confirm he's the killer, I can finally rid this world of one of the worst monsters ever to walk it."

The room fell into silence once more. She was right, as always. And I hated that I'd known it all along. But why was it so damn hard to let her go, knowing she might be sacrificing herself?

"Besides, if he kills me, you'll be able to connect him to the murder. I know you will. You know where I am. If I disappear, you'll go after him publicly. I'm not Anna. The world will care if I disappear. Jan Novak is powerful, but not even he can make a world-famous pianist disappear without a trace if a hungry FBI agent is on his heels. You'll get him. If anybody can, it's you, Richter. I have faith in you."

A wave of ice-cold dread washed over me, settling deep in my gut. Was this her strategy? Getting herself killed for the greater good of taking down Jan Novak? Sure. In this fucked-up world, it would be an honorable sacrifice. A killer for a killer. One life for saving hundreds. But something deep inside me couldn't accept this.

"No," I said, shaking my head. "No, Leah, please don't do this."

Her forehead furrowed as she slowly circled the desk, finally stopping in front of me. "Why defy logic, Richter? Is there another angle I fail to see that prevents you from accepting this mission?"

She stared into my eyes. Inches away from me. I could smell her perfume. I wanted to say something but just stood there like an idiot. Lost. The way she laid it out made sense. So why fight it? Had I grown attached to a killer?

Was I creating some fucked-up version of Starsky and Hutch after all? But after all we'd been through together, could anyone blame me?

"No, Leah … I can't sanction this suicide mission."

Her green eyes narrowed as the air between us became suffocating. For a split second, her hand lifted, reaching for my arm. Instinctively, I stepped back as if her touch might turn me into something else—something from which I could never return. She noticed, of course. Which only made it worse.

A sudden knock on the door shattered the tension, startling us both.

Without a word, Leah crossed the room and opened the door for Rose.

"Sorry I'm late, but I had to write a shit ton of fake interview reports about the shooting at your concert to explain why Richter and I have these meetings at your house." As they walked into the study, Rose handed a few papers to Leah. "Here are the copies for you to read so our stories about the interviews match."

Leah accepted the papers and placed them on her desk. The room fell into an awkward silence.

Rose looked between Leah and me, her brows raised. "Did the old married couple fight again?" she joked, though the heavy air quickly smothered her words.

"I'll drive you so Novak knows I'm not far," I announced as I walked toward the door. "And that's what I'll do no matter what you say."

"Drive her where?" Rose asked as I walked past her.

"Leah will bring you up to speed. I'm late to pick up Josie for bowling."

Without glancing back, I left, pulling the heavy door of Leah's Beacon Hill mansion shut behind me. I made my way to my SUV, which was parked just beyond the gate. The air was still heavy with everything unspoken.

I hated how much this mission messed with me—how it angered me, worried me, made me sick to my stomach. Thoughts of Leah being raped, or drowned in some river, spun through my head. And then there was her stare. Those intense green eyes, just inches from my face.

If he laid even a finger on her—if he so much as pulled a single strand of her hair—I'd shoot him. Literally, I would.

I couldn't let my mind wander down the path of how she'd get the evidence we needed. It wouldn't come from small talk. There was only one way to confirm that he had a skin graft, and it involved him taking off his shirt. Which probably meant she'd have to take hers off too. For a monster. Forced to sell herself out like an enslaved prostitute.

My fist pounded against the steering wheel. Once. Twice. Again and again.

"Fuck," I muttered, tipping my head back against the seat and staring at the roof of my car as helplessness coiled tightly in my chest. I felt sick.

I had to do more. No, I had to do everything. This would be the first and last time Leah would risk her life for this murdering psychopath.

I had to be ready to act the moment she walked out of there alive.

Doubt weighed on me like an anvil. I was nobody compared to Jan Novak. What was I even trying to pull off? Arrest the most powerful man in the nation? It would cost me my job. But if Leah was willing to risk her life to stop this killer, to save more victims like Anna, what kind of coward was I to worry about my career?

No, the moment she had the evidence to tie him to the Train Track Killer, I'd act. No matter the cost.

And there was only one way.

With an army of loyal people. People who weren't slaves to money like Congress was. People who still gave a damn about the world. Convincing them wouldn't be easy. It would take a hell of a lot of effort. But if Jan Novak was taken down in broad daylight, that alone would send a message to his allies: cut him loose, make him too dangerous to be associated with.

It was a crazy mission, no doubt. But inside that house was a woman ready to sacrifice her life and her body to make the world a better place.

And I'd do the goddamn same.

First, I needed an ally. Someone who'd proven his loyalty to Leah more than anyone else.

Luckily, the answer was simple.

Luca Domizio.

CHAPTER THIRTEEN

Rose

Leah quietly took a seat behind her desk and started reading the papers I'd handed her. I studied her fancy study for a moment. The large fireplace. The antique books on the mahogany bookshelves along the walls. I walked over to one that caught my attention.

The Bible.

I pulled the large book off the shelf and opened it. It was heavy as hell. A handwritten manuscript with ornate illustrations, bound in leather with metal clasps, showcasing exquisite calligraphy and craftsmanship.

"You don't strike me as religious," I said, wondering why I was even still here. I should have left with Richter. Instead, I was wandering around as if I were more loyal to her than to him. Which concerned me to the core.

"I'm not religious," she said. "In fact, I don't put my faith in anything beyond the immense strength we all possess—the strength to achieve extraordinary things. But as you know all too well, some of those things can descend into pitch-black darkness. That's the nature of human potential. It's capable of both brilliance and horror."

I absorbed the weight of her words, my brow furrowing slightly. "Why have a copy, then?"

"This is a rare version of the Bible that includes the Lost Gospel—possibly one of the oldest fully transcribed copies in existence. There are only two like it. It reads like the most brilliant fiction novel—if you can read Aramaic."

"What's the Lost Gospel?" I asked.

"The Lost Gospel is a 1,500-year-old manuscript that was excluded from the conventional Bible. Some interpretations suggest it contains hidden references to Jesus and Mary Magdalene having a child. However, mainstream scholars and the Catholic Church largely regard it as a fictional narrative involving biblical figures rather than a historical account of Jesus's life."

"Hmm. Interesting. Well, it would make sense for Jesus to have a child..." I mumbled.

Leah looked up from the papers. "Why is that?" she asked.

"I mean ... who'd be a better dad than Jesus?"

To my surprise, Leah smiled. "I never thought about it that way."

I quietly set the book back in its place and nodded toward the door through which Richter had just walked. "So ... what was that all about?"

"I'm going to meet with Jan Novak for dinner this weekend. Richter objects, of course, but at this point, it's the only way. We might be running out of time. I don't know how much longer Jan Novak will let us interfere with his life. To be honest, it's a mystery to me why he's put up with us for so long."

I nodded.

Leah lifted an eyebrow. "No objections?"

I shrugged. "It's the most logical strategy on our end. You can always kill him if he tries anything stupid."

"Interesting," Leah said, leaning back in her chair, her eyes still on me.

I was ready for her to ask why I hadn't told Richter about her and the Night Stalker, but instead, Leah pointed at an empty glass of wine.

"Would you like some?"

I shook my head. "No, thank you. I only drink on Thanksgiving and Christmas."

"I see."

Warm memories of better times washed over me. "My mom used to drink wine only on Thanksgiving and Christmas. Every year. It drove my dad crazy when she went to the store and bought the really expensive wine. She told me that alcohol killed more good people than bullets and that this was her rare treat."

Leah filled herself a glass. "If alcohol kills good people, I have nothing to worry about," she joked.

I couldn't help but smile.

"Sounds like your mother was a wise woman, though," she added.

"She was. She was the kindest and strongest person I knew."

Had I just opened up to Leah Nachtnebel? The woman who brutally murdered bad guys? I never opened up to anybody. My memories were mine.

"Sorry. I didn't mean to sob on you," I said.

"Not at all," she responded. "I personally don't attach myself to memories, those of others or my own, but I enjoy good stories about good people."

I held her gaze for a moment before looking away. I was beginning to understand why Richter was so drawn to her. There was something about her—something that made you realize, almost instinctively, that she was different. Special.

"So you're meeting Jan Novak for dinner. Did you consider that men act irrationally when they feel cornered?"

"Yes. But I don't think Jan Novak feels corn—"

"I wasn't talking about Jan Novak," I said. "I was talking about Richter. I think he's starting to take this whole thing with you personally. Richter's the kind of man who gets attached—to memories, to people. He'd do anything for those he cares about."

She fell silent, taking a long sip from her glass. "I doubt Richter would be foolish enough to get attached to me. He doesn't see me as anything more than what I am."

I wasn't so sure about that.

"Why did you choose him in the first place, if I may ask? From what I've gathered, Larsen seemed to get the job done," I said.

She hesitated. "Larsen ... yes, his performance was satisfactory. But there were other issues with him."

"What kind of issues?"

"He was a killer. Like the ones we hunt. I gave him a chance to prove he'd truly changed, just as he'd tried to convince me. But he failed that test. Miserably. Richter, on the other hand, has qualities that Larsen lacked. Qualities..." She exhaled slowly. "Qualities I lack. And there's no better judge than someone who truly believes in a better world. Even if that sounds like something from the back of a cereal box."

I nodded. "Fair enough. Just make sure you take into account that Richter's judgment might be clouded with sentiment." I turned toward the door. "Thank you for the drink offer."

She remained silent as I made my way out.

And with that, our plan to take down the Train Track Killer was set in motion.

A genius mind would meet another. A killer would meet another killer.

As I walked back to my car, the sun faded into strong orange hues across the sky. I had no idea how any of this would end. But I'd ride it out. As my brother always said, we only got to see what happens if we didn't quit.

CHAPTER FOURTEEN

Liam

I pushed open the heavy wooden door of the Italian restaurant. The warm scent of garlic and herbs welcomed me as I stepped inside. Dim lighting gave the bustling dining area a cozy atmosphere.

The carpet muffled my footsteps as I made my way to the back room.

Looking sharp in a tailored suit, Luca Domizio sat at a round table covered with a white tablecloth. He was eating pasta and sipping red wine across from an older man who was enjoying the same meal.

As I approached, Luca looked up and dabbed at the corner of his mouth with a white napkin.

"The FBI seems to be rekindling its old flame for me," Luca said, his voice smooth but cold. "I didn't like it then, and I don't like it now. I suggest you leave before I call my lawyer and have you fired."

"Don't flatter yourself. It's hardly a spark," I said. "But you might want to hear what I have to say."

He looked me over, unimpressed. "I doubt it."

"We have a mutual acquaintance ... who needs help."

Luca leaned back in his chair, studying me for a moment. "Antonio, give us a minute," he finally said.

"Of course. I'll get more wine from Luigi." Antonio stood and cast an arrogant glance my way as he walked past, then closed the door behind him.

"If you think your relationship with our mutual friend will impress me or make us allies, you're wrong," Luca said. "I'm aware of her odd fondness for you, but frankly, I neither understand nor share it."

I sat down across from him. "Good. Because, frankly, I don't understand or share her fondness for you. But I'm not here for myself. I'm here for her. She's in serious danger, and the fact that you took out McCourt and secured the shares for her tells me you might be willing to help. So can we cut the bullshit? I don't have much time."

Luca sipped his wine. "I deny everything you just said. I had nothing to do with McCourt's shooting."

I sighed, fearing this trip would be for nothing.

"But," he added, "I'll admit, we do share a very special friend. She asks for favors when it suits her. I don't worry too much about it. Her judgment has always been exceptional. A true genius. I prefer to stay out of things unless she asks me directly. And when she does, I'll do whatever is needed."

"Fair enough. But things have changed a lot in the past few months. A threat has emerged—someone with both the power and the will to harm her. And, as crazy as it sounds, this person might be her equal in every way."

"You're speaking of Jan Novak, aren't you?" Luca said, his voice serious.

"Jan fucking Novak," I confirmed.

He pressed his lips together, then sighed. "A very powerful and dangerous man indeed. People look at me and think I'm the bad guy. The truth is, there are plenty of men like me out there. But Novak ... men like him are rare, maybe one in a generation. It would be wise to stay far away from him. Even people like you and me."

"Well, as you know by now, she didn't."

A flicker of despair flashed in his eyes. "No, she didn't. And if that woman ever made a mistake, this might very well be it. But as I said, Leah writes the rules for her life. Unless she asks me, there's nothing I can do about that, or I would have already."

"Fine," I said, standing. "Just remember that I tried. When we find her face down in a river a few months from now, stiff, cold, and blue. Remember that I was here, trying to save one of the greatest musical virtuosos of our time, taken from this world—and from you—by a man who could have been stopped. Because whatever you think you know about Novak doesn't even scratch the surface of what he's truly capable of."

Luca's eyes sparkled dangerously at me.

"Funny," I continued, my voice dripping with sarcasm as a chuckle escaped. "Here I was, thinking Leah Nachtnebel's music might be the last thing that gets you excited when you open your tired old eyes in the morning, still searching for reasons to drag yourself out of bed. Years of murder can dull the senses, make you feel dead inside. So I figured you'd go to great lengths to protect that last real spark in your lonely life. Your kids have cut you off, haven't they? No wife stuck around. But what do I know? Maybe there's still enough in your fancy, empty life to keep you jolly. Plenty of pumpkin patches in full swing, eh? Hardly a match for the melodies of a prodigy like Leah. But then again, what would a peasant like me know about the finer points of life?" I turned, ready to leave.

"Wait," Luca called after me.

I paused, then slowly sat back down, a smirk of victory tugging at my lips.

"What do you want?" he demanded.

"Thought you'd never ask." I took a deep breath. "I'm ... planning to arrest him."

A sudden, deep laugh erupted from Luca. "Jan Novak? Absurd. You might as well try to arrest the president."

"If the president turns out to be a serial killer as well, I just might do that," I said.

Luca's laughter faded. His eyes narrowed as he studied me with newfound curiosity. "If you think Novak is the first sick fuck among them, you're too naive for that badge you flash around," he said. "Most powerful and rich men have some sort of disgusting hobby, and most of them never pay the price for their actions." He shrugged. "The law doesn't apply to the ultra-rich, just like in the days of kings and their subjects."

"Maybe so, but you see, in this case, Novak is messing with the wrong peasant. With enough public involvement, even a commoner like me can make quite a fuss. And as fate would have it, something more powerful than kings and queens has formed in this world. Social media. A direct voice to the people. If you gather enough of us, even kings have to care about the laws again."

Luca frowned. "You want to start a public war with Novak?"

I grinned. "Picture a huge crowd of cell phones pointing straight at him. An army of police officers and FBI agents at my back. Not even Jan Novak or the president could keep that spectacle secret."

"You're really serious about this," Luca concluded, almost in admiration.

"I am."

He shook his head. "Seems like a huge fucking headache if you ask me. Why not just get rid of Novak in, well, simpler ways?"

"That would be the easier method, yes. But it could also complicate things. Nothing is as it seems with Jan Novak. So far, he has held all the cards in his hands. I need to talk to him, force him to make a mistake. I'm an FBI agent, not Al Capone. I can't just start shooting suspects without proof— proof that I need now. All of our lives could be in great danger—hers, other agents', mine, and ... my daughter's. There's no time left for games."

Our eyes met.

"A public arrest of Jan Novak," Luca said. "A spectacle like that would raise a lot of questions and draw attention. Surely, it would also be a quick way to make a lot of enemies for very little return. All this might go nowhere."

"The media brought Epstein down. And he had some powerful sickos on his little island too."

"Indeed he did. And I wish you luck with your plans. But I don't see how a simple construction company owner like myself could be of help in any of this."

"Simple construction company owner, huh? Didn't we say no more games?"

Luca grinned. "We did."

"Good. Then let me tell you how you can help. I need you to have a large group of people ready at the scene of the arrest. Filming every second of it. Saving it online to any data storage company that doesn't use Obligato. As a weapon for the media and social media apps."

"You could pay any homeless fifty bucks to record the arrest. You don't need me for that."

"I need people who are willing to treat the arrest and evidence with the utmost ... well, respect. People who can be trusted to post the evidence on every social platform in this world or delete it. People who do what they're told no matter what."

Luca pondered this for a moment, then narrowed his eyes as he fixed his gaze on me. "But that's not all you need, is it? You need something else from me." He took a sip of his wine. "No more games, remember?" he added.

"You're right." I took a shallow breath, my words catching in my throat. "I ... I also need to know how far your arms reach into the Secret Service."

"The Secret Service?" Luca raised an eyebrow. "Are you planning your crazy mission at the White House or something?"

"No, of course not," I replied.

"Then why mention the Secret Service?"

"The location of the arrest might be tricky. We'll need to strike during a private fundraiser. Jan Novak keeps a low profile, mingling only with the ultra-rich and influential. The next fundraiser that could draw him in might have some very big names on the guest list—potentially as big as the vice president."

Luca shook his head. "Well, in that case, I don't think I can help you. It's only logical that some of my acquaintances will be there. Bullets could fly, and I'm not eager to turn allies into enemies. Dead business partners aren't exactly profitable."

"Nobody will get hurt. That's why I'm here. In case the vice president will be there, I need the CIA to stand down. Focus on getting him out of there. Prevent him from helping Novak so the arrest can take place."

"This is madness. Even if the CIA stands down, what about the police and your own men? Won't they listen to the vice president if he tells them to stop this nonsense?"

"I'll handle the police and the FBI."

Luca sighed. "Let's say, against all odds, you manage to pull this off. David hits Goliath one more time with his little slingshot. Have you thought about the consequences for yourself? A mission this reckless would be career suicide. You'd kiss your badge goodbye. You might end up in prison. Or worse, dead. And if by some miracle you survive, I couldn't risk having you around talking. Do you understand what I'm saying?"

I met his gaze. "I do. But Novak ... if he is who I think he is, someone has to stop him. Not just for Leah but for many others. Including my daughter. Nobody touches my daughter. Nobody. Do you understand?"

Luca folded his hands in his lap as he studied me.

"Nobody will ever know you were involved if that's what you're worried about," I said.

"Don't be ridiculous," he scoffed. "Very few things worry me, and upsetting a bunch of rich old men isn't one of them."

"Then help me save her."

Silence fell between us.

"Leah..." he finally said. "She knows nothing about this, does she? You see how this could feel like a betrayal. That's a risk I can't take. Not again." He looked away. The weight of past mistakes hung between us.

"I'll tell her everything before the mission. I promise."

He nodded slowly. "Still, for now, I won't be part of your Rambo fantasy."

I frowned.

"But," he added, "if you somehow manage the impossible and rally enough fools at the FBI and police to turn fiction into reality, come see me again. I've been known to change my mind about things that interest me. And I have to admit, your crazy mission is ... very interesting."

I grinned. He was right. This was crazy. I knew it. He knew it. But crazy might be the only weapon I had against Jan Novak, and Luca was sharp enough to see that my plan might be the only option.

I was by the door when I turned one last time. "Thank you."

"Don't thank me yet," Luca replied. "But do grab some pasta on the way out. It's the best in town."

CHAPTER FIFTEEN

Leah

I wore a red cocktail dress that hugged every curve, with matching heels and a daring slit up my leg. My hair was pulled into an elegant bun. My makeup was flawless, and diamond jewelry caught the light as I moved.

The crisp autumn breeze brushed against my skin as I pulled my cashmere coat tighter around me. As I stepped out of my townhome, the limousine that Jan Novak had sent pulled up to the curb. Before I could reach it, I spotted Agent Richter leaning against the hood of his black SUV, parked just behind the limo. He was in his usual FBI suit, his badge on full display.

The limo driver got out and glanced between me and Richter, looking confused.

"Thank you, but I already have a ride. We'll follow you," I said.

The driver nodded and got back into the car.

Richter's eyes moved over me, concern flickering across his face. Without a word, he opened the passenger side door for me, then walked around to get behind the wheel. I slid into the passenger seat, and we followed the limousine.

The tension in the SUV was thick, and the silence between us stretched on.

"You got a gun in there, right?" Richter finally said, nodding toward my red purse.

"That and a few more things," I replied.

He nodded. Silence fell again.

"Are you upset with me?" I asked, glancing at him as he focused on the road.

"I'm not upset, Leah. I'm worried. What if he hurts you? Kills you? You said it yourself. Jan Novak is unlike anyone else. Nobody knows what's going on in the head of a psychopath like him."

"I might have some insight into that," I replied.

"So enlighten me. What exactly are you after tonight?"

The scar from a skin graft, I almost said but stopped before I had to explain how I planned to get that information from him.

"I'm … not sure yet. But I have a feeling he invited me for a reason. Novak doesn't strike me as a man who wastes time. This might be our only chance, Richter. We've gotten almost nowhere. The shareholders meeting was supposed to get us a lead. Here it is."

He exhaled, the sound long and frustrated. "I was hoping for something … different."

"Me too."

"Just promise me you'll kill him the moment things feel off."

"That's a promise I can easily make," I said, smiling faintly.

The tension lifted slightly as he smiled back. "Good. I won't be far. If Jan Novak tries anything stupid, it'll be the easiest shot I've ever taken."

"I'll keep that in mind," I said.

We followed the limousine out of Boston, then turned onto a narrow, private road lined with dark trees. After a few more minutes of driving, we'd passed all the other houses in the area.

"Looks like private property. God, this is huge. Right out of Boston, it must be millions," Richter said as we pulled up in front of a large brick mansion that looked straight out of Downton Abbey.

"My estimate would be around a hundred million dollars."

Richter shook his head as we stopped in front of large marble stairs leading to wide-open double doors. Burning torches lined the pathway as if this were an episode of The Bachelor. At the top of the stairs stood Jan Novak, dressed in an elegant tuxedo. I noticed Richter's hand clutch the steering wheel tightly.

"Richter ... don't. It'll be for nothing, and he'll get away."

Richter exhaled, nodded, and got out of the car. He opened the door for me before Jan Novak, who was already descending the stairs, had the chance. I stepped out, watching as their eyes met.

"Agent Richter," Novak said with a smile. "I didn't realize you'd be joining us tonight. I'll have another plate set at the table."

"That won't be necessary," Richter said before I could respond. "I'm just the driver." He turned to me, his tone shifting. "I'll be close by. Call if you need anything." Without warning, he pulled out his phone and snapped a photo of us. The flash momentarily blinded Novak. "For the album," Richter added with a smirk. "Uh-oh. Caught you mid-blink."

Novak smiled faintly, then extended his arm toward me. "Shall we?"

I threw Richter a glance before I locked arms with Novak, who led me up the stairs.

Inside, the grand entrance hall was even more imposing than I'd imagined it would be. Vaulted ceilings soared overhead, and frescoes of mythic scenes stretched across the walls. The polished marble floors reflected the flickering light from candles mounted along the walls. Instead of the knight's armor that one would expect in such a grand space, ancient Egyptian artifacts dominated the room. Their golden hues cast a warm glow over everything.

Novak noticed my curious gaze as I took in the unusual decor. "You know how fond I am of Egyptian history," he explained, his voice echoing slightly in the expansive hall. "My collection is the biggest in the world."

I stopped in front of a large golden mirror shaped like an ankh. It had a smooth oval top and cross-like arms. Its gold frame gave off an ancient feel. "You seem to be especially taken with the ankh symbol," I said. "It represents a mirror, doesn't it?"

"It does indeed," Jan Novak replied. "A window to our souls, exposing who we truly are behind all the smiles and frowns, the shouting and laughing, the words spoken in truth and the ones in lies."

I nodded slightly. "What do you see, Mr. Novak, when you look in the mirror?"

"A man who's getting older," he joked. "But please, call me Jan."

He led me farther into the mansion. Eventually, we stopped at a large dining hall set for an intimate dinner: candles flickering, silver cutlery shining, and wine glasses catching the light.

"And beyond that?" I pressed. "What does it show about your soul?"

Jan pulled out a chair for me and leaned in close to my ear. "That's a secret for another time. We don't want to cut dinner short before it's even begun, do we?"

I watched as he walked to a smaller side table where various dishes were laid out—an assortment of simple yet elegant foods. He picked up two plates, already prepared, and set one in front of me before taking his seat. Then he poured red wine into our glasses.

"Everything here is grown in my own gardens," he explained. "I prefer simple, well-prepared food over the fancy trash they serve at a Michelin star restaurant."

I was surprised to find the starter was a basic garden salad.

"I sent the staff away so we could talk freely," he continued. "But that also means I'm your waiter tonight. I hope you'll enjoy the vegetarian menu. I know you like mushrooms and watermelon, so the chef prepared a cold watermelon soup and mushroom risotto for the main course."

A chill ran down my spine. Mushroom risotto was the first meal I'd ever shared with Emanuel. Was this just a coincidence?

"Thank you. I do like mushrooms. It's almost as if you know me so well," I said.

He gave me a small nod and sat across from me. "So how did the famous Ms. Leah Nachtnebel end up on the board of a tech company?" He sipped his wine before starting on the salad.

I took a bite myself. It was easily the freshest, most flavorful salad I'd ever had. The herbs were likely picked only hours ago, and even the lavender vinaigrette tasted homemade.

"My interest is more in the company's owner," I said, wiping my mouth with a napkin before taking a sip of wine. I placed the glass back on the table. "Eagle Cabernet Sauvignon 1992," I noted. "You shouldn't have."

Jan raised his glass. "Only the best for my daring pianist, who's going to such great lengths to uncover mysteries no one else would dare to dream about."

Our eyes met. "And what secrets would that be … Jan?"

Jan rose to his feet and cleared the starter to place the mushroom risotto in front of me. For a moment, I stared at it, memories of Emanuel flooding me. Where was the rage? The hatred I'd felt every second before I looked into Jan's eyes for the first time at that museum? In some ways, it felt like a betrayal.

"Agent Richter," he said, taking his seat across from me again. "That's quite interesting company to keep. Is it business-related? Personal?"

My eyes met his. "It's nothing of the romantic sort. But my relationship with him is a secret I'll keep tonight, as you seem to guard so many."

"Touché," he said with a charming smile.

We started the course. It was outstanding—the food, at least. Not so much my attempts at getting anything useful out of him.

"Carl Carr," I said, deciding to go straight at it. "Does that name ring a bell?"

Jan briefly furrowed his brows, then continued eating. He held his fork elegantly as if he were some sort of duke. "Why do you ask?"

"I was wondering if we have some acquaintances in common."

Jan's gaze flickered. He appeared to be considering whether to cut through the bullshit. Then he leaned back in his chair and took a slow sip of wine. "I know many people. I'm certain you do as well. Carl Carr ... hmmm. It's almost like it rings a bell, but then it slips me."

This was going nowhere. I placed my napkin onto my plate to signal that I was done with dinner. His eyes followed the gesture, and he quickly rose.

"Do you know how to dance?" he asked.

"I don't dance."

"I'll teach you." He walked over and offered me his arm. I accepted and followed him into a gigantic library where a fire crackled in a large stone fireplace. Slow jazz music played from speakers in the walls.

Jan guided me to the center of the room, then placed one hand gently on my bare back. The other one wrapped around me. Pulling me close, he began swaying us side to side, leading me into a slow, careful dance. I caught the scent of his expensive aftershave—rich with notes of cedar and leather.

"I hope you don't mind the music choice, but I'm personally not a big fan of classical music."

"Not at all," I said, resting my hand on his chest. I could feel the lean muscle even through his tuxedo. This—between the fireplace and the dancing—was headed in only one direction, and I wasn't going to stop it. Talking had gotten us nowhere.

"I apologize if I'm a bit rusty," he said, his hand gently moving up and down my back. "I haven't danced since my divorce."

"You're quite good at it," I replied. "Just another hidden talent of yours."

"I'm trying very hard to impress you. Something extraordinary brought you back into my life, and I'm not going to sit by like I did after we met at the museum." He pulled me closer, his chest pressing against mine. "I know you won't believe me, and I almost can't believe it myself, but our meeting back then—it really was by chance on my end."

I tilted my head back, searching his eyes. I couldn't tell if he was lying.

"Do you believe in fate?" he asked, leaning in, his lips almost brushing mine.

"I don't," I replied just before he kissed me. His kiss was full of desire: confident and sure.

I should have felt repulsed. Angry. Or at the very least guilty. Something uncomfortable. But all I felt was the usual emptiness.

And lust.

That unmistakable heat rising between my legs. It had been too long since I'd allowed myself to feel anything close to pleasure. Months, to be exact. And for someone like me, a psychopath, repressing primal urges for too long could be dangerous.

I caught sight of the couch near the fireplace.

Without a word, I pushed him backward onto it. He landed in a sitting position as I climbed on top of him, spreading my legs over his hard cock.

He grabbed my hips eagerly, guiding me as I started moving against his erection. Quickly, I began unbuttoning his shirt, my breath shallow with anticipation.

The scar ... the reason I was here.

Unbuttoning Jan's shirt was taking too long, so I tore it open, sending buttons flying. As he sat beneath me, bare-chested, everything stopped. My eyes searched his chest, where I expected to see the bullet wound.

No scar.

I checked higher, near his upper chest. Still nothing.

I searched his skin again and again, but all I found were faint patches of discoloration, barely noticeable, stretching across his chest, over his shoulder, and up toward his neck. It could have been anything—a healing sunburn or natural discoloration from birth.

If this was a skin graft, it was a true masterpiece.

"Impossible," I muttered. I knew I'd shot him in the shoulder. I was sure of it. There was no doubt in my mind, not even now.

My gaze dropped to a small scar on his lower abdomen, no more than four inches long. But that couldn't be it.

"Did you find what you were looking for?" Jan asked, confidence dripping from every word. He didn't move an inch.

In silence, I stared at the small scar, frozen. Defeated.

"A parting gift from my father," he continued calmly. "When I tried to stop him from stabbing my mother. One of many times, unfortunately."

I looked into his eyes. For the first time, I saw something. There were feelings there, flickering in the depths. Jan wasn't dead inside like I was. He was a monster but one who could still feel.

"Maybe ... I'm not the man you think I am," he said, his voice softer now.

I should've left. Right then. Instead I stayed, my thoughts drifting to the hardness pressing between my legs. For a shameful moment, the urge to fuck him crept in. The need for release, for something, anything, was almost unbearable. I craved the sensation, the quick thrill of getting off. It had been too damn long since I'd let myself feel pleasure.

Jan groaned, gripping my hips and pulling me closer. I was about to give in, ready to let it happen, when thoughts of Richter flashed through my mind. Guilt hit me like a truck, mixing with the shame that finally, finally washed over me.

I felt something.

At least for Richter, if not for myself or Emanuel.

Jan's hand moved to his zipper.

I rose abruptly, stepping away from him. Emotionless, I adjusted my dress, making myself presentable again. "You might fool the world, but I know who you really are," I said, grabbing my purse from beside him.

He calmly zipped up his pants. With a faint grin, he sat there, watching me with those same eyes—like I was exactly where he wanted me.

For a moment, I considered grabbing the gun from my purse and putting a bullet in his head. It wouldn't mean a damn thing to me. But with the little I had on Novak, that might end my relationship with Richter—and with it, our partnership, which I wasn't ready to lose.

"Thank you. That was quite an interesting evening," I said, turning to make my way to the double doors.

Of course, he didn't chase me. "Oh, we've only just begun," he called out as I strode through the grand entrance hall and out the door.

As I descended the wide steps, I was surprised to find Richter leaning against the SUV, waiting. He looked at me with a frown.

"Let's go," I said, climbing into the car with him.

We drove in silence for a few minutes until we hit the main road. Finally, Richter cleared his throat, careful, hesitant. "Please tell me it's him so this wasn't all for nothing."

"It is," I replied, not a single doubt in my mind.

"Did he admit it? Or did you ... see the scar?"

I shook my head.

"Fuck," Richter muttered, gripping the steering wheel tighter. "Fuck!" He said it louder this time, his hand raking through his hair—something I'd seen him do a hundred times by now.

"It gets worse," I said, my voice steady. "The way he spoke to me. He knows who we are. He knows everything. I'm sure of it."

"Then it's time for us to act," Richter said, urgency creeping into his voice.

I turned to him. "What do you mean?"

"I mean the time for games is over. I mean it's time to make things uncomfortable for him. Create a rift in his perfect world. A rift so big it'll hit his closest allies. Distance them from him. Push him to make a mistake."

"And how are you planning to do that?" I asked.

He was hesitant, then nodded. "An open arrest. In front of the whole world."

I stated the obvious. "That's impossible. We don't hold that power over Jan Novak. Not even the FBI holds that power over him. At this point, nobody does."

"You're right. The FBI doesn't hold that power. At least not by itself. But with allies, it can be done. It will be done. The whole country will watch as Jan Novak is dragged away in handcuffs. We'll put it all over the news and social media. If we shout loud enough, people will notice."

"You'd lose your job overnight."

"I'm not worried about my damn career. I'm worried about my daughter. And ... other people I care about."

This was madness.

Our eyes met. "Richter, please listen to me. Arresting him in broad daylight—"

"We did it your way, Leah. Now we do it mine."

This plan was impulsive. Almost impossible to pull off. I opened my mouth, but Richter was faster.

"How much longer do you think we have before we start finding more corpses in the river? A nice little ankh carved next to them."

I stayed quiet, letting his words sink in.

"Exactly. After tonight, can you really say he won't hurt us? That it won't be Josie we find floating facedown in a river next? He's playing us, Leah. He probably even knew you'd be looking for that scar. Hell, I wouldn't be surprised if he sent Carl Carr to kill you."

He wasn't wrong. Novak was in control of this game—setting the rules, toying with us for as long as it amused him. I'd thought coming here would get me answers. Instead I'd left with more questions than I could count. Questions like why I still couldn't see the monster in him. Why his touch hadn't repulsed me. Though it hadn't made me feel warm and safe, either. But I'd almost fucked him like some wild animal.

"Do you trust me?" Richter's voice broke through my thoughts, his tone serious.

Our eyes locked.

"Do you?" he asked.

Trust? I'd never trusted anyone. Not even myself. But Richter...

"I do," I said, realizing in that moment that it was true. "But if we go through with this arrest, he'll come after all of us. And he won't hold back."

Richter nodded, his grip on the wheel tightening again. "Let him come. I'd rather face him head-on in a fist fight, knowing he's coming, than be caught guessing. I'll have a bullet with his name carved into it, ready for him. Hell, I'll carve an ankh right next to where this asshole drops dead." He exhaled sharply, shaking his head. "Let's take him the fuck down. All we need is one slip-up when we question him. Turn him into the Epstein of murder in the public's eyes. Make him nervous. Corner him for once." He glanced over at me, his eyes hard. "Because you were right about one thing. We're not the predators in this hunt. And if you're not the predator on a killer's playground, there's only one outcome."

"Death," I said, my voice flat.

"Death," he echoed before silence swallowed the car once again.

CHAPTER SIXTEEN

Liam

The dimly lit meeting room buzzed with tension. Chief Murray, stocky and weathered, sat at the long table, his eyes sharp with the same no-nonsense attitude I'd seen during the College Snatcher case. Beside him, Lieutenant Colonel Jason Lewis sat rigid, military discipline carved into his posture. He'd been the one to recover Harvey Grand's charred remains from Ocean City. McCourt, sitting farther down, was silent, his simmering frustration clear in every glance.

Agent Rose sat alongside them. All eyes were locked on me.

As I stood at the head of the table, their stares felt as heavy as lead. Behind me, the evidence board displayed Jan Novak—elegant, composed— as well as the gruesome photos of the train track murders, each marked by his twisted ankh symbol.

The air felt stifling, and the untouched water bottles on the table only heightened the tension.

Murray's voice cut through the room. "So you're telling me this Great Gatsby wannabe is a serial killer dumping people on train tracks? Why the hell haven't I heard about this?"

I kept my voice steady. "The investigation's been kept quiet because Novak is extremely well connected. He's as powerful as the president. His company manages data from Granny's doorbell camera all the way to secret military bases."

"And he has access to all this information?" Chief Murray asked.

I nodded. "He does."

"Is it safe to talk here then?" Lieutenant Colonel Lewis asked, concern lining his features.

Rose shot a glance at McCourt. "The FBI recently ended its contract with Obligato and switched cloud storage providers," she informed us. "It was quite a fight with some members in Congress, but we managed to pull it off."

"And your evidence links him to the crimes?" Murray leaned back in his chair. "In over fifty years on the job, I've never seen anything this insane."

"It does," I replied. "Unfortunately, we live in a world that's produced monsters like Hitler and Dahmer. As crazy as it sounds, it's real."

Lieutenant Colonel Lewis frowned, disbelief etched across his face. "I've been to war more times than I can count. To think a monster like this could hide behind greedy U.S. government officials ... what the fuck was it all for?"

"For the people," Rose cut in. "The same people we're trying to protect by taking down Jan Novak."

"That's all well and good," Chief Murray said, his voice heavy with skepticism. "But if what you're saying is true, how the hell are we supposed to stop him? Any arrest would be blocked by his powerful friends. The evidence we've got might be enough to haul Bobby from down the street in for questioning, but not a man like Novak."

"We're not entirely powerless," I said, locking eyes with McCourt as he pressed his lips together in frustration. "We're part of the system that protects him, and right now, Novak's not getting any sanctuary from the FBI. With this meeting, I'm hoping he won't find refuge with the Massachusetts police or at Hanscom Air Force Base either. It's the closest base to Boston, and it would be responsible for any airborne aid requested during an arrest."

The room fell silent again.

"This mission is a death sentence for my career," McCourt spat, anger flashing in his eyes.

"And 'no mission' is a death sentence to our integrity," I snapped back.

Our brief clash caught discreet glances from Lewis and Murray.

"Look at this man," I said, pointing at Novak's picture. "He's likely one of the deadliest serial killers in history. He's killed indiscriminately—men, women, the young, the old. Who knows when he'll start targeting children? We all have families. Imagine someone you love being laid out on train tracks, knowing the killer walks free. Have you seen what a train does to a body? I spared you those pictures today, but one family found parts of their son's body a mile down the tracks from where the crime happened."

I took a breath, steadying myself, then continued. "I called this meeting because the FBI won't sit back while this monster kills like it's a stroll through Boston Common. We swore to protect the people of this country from enemies, foreign and domestic. Jan Novak is one of the worst domestic threats we've ever seen."

I gestured to the door. "If you want to walk out and save your career, I won't hold it against you. Do it now before we get into the details. I get it. I have a kid who needs a roof over her head too. But remember, I called you because you can make a difference and more so because I trust you. And I trust that when Novak's pile of bodies keeps growing, you'll regret not doing everything you could to stop him. Right now, to achieve that, we need to arrest him for questioning."

The silence in the room felt weighty. For a moment, I thought Murray would get up and leave, but he just leaned back, deep in thought.

Rightfully so.

Here I was, asking these men to risk their careers. Their public images. Their legacies. But stopping Jan Novak was more than just a mission or duty. It was the only way.

"So what do you propose?" Lieutenant Colonel Lewis asked.

Rose got up and handed a printout to the three men. "Our greatest weapon in this arrest will be the public eye. Jan Novak is attending a private fundraiser near Provincetown. Senator Wheezer will be there, along with the ... vice president."

"The vice president?" Chief Murray repeated, his wrinkled forehead creased with shock.

"Yes," I said. "But that'll work to our advantage. We need to let Jan Novak's allies know that associating with him can cost them their elections. We need to make him nervous. Corner him. And to do that, we need to get as high up in the swamp as we can. A few senators won't send a very strong message."

"How do we make sure this won't end up in a shootout between us and the Secret Service?" Murray asked. "Because I'm not willing to stop a murderer by becoming one."

For a second, I let his words sink in. My eyes briefly met Rose's.

"We have a source in the Secret Service," Rose said, "who will make sure the agents on the ground pull the vice president out the moment we arrive. He won't be around to possibly interfere with Novak's arrest."

Chief Murray nodded slowly. "Senators depend on police protection. And since Provincetown's in Massachusetts, that protection falls to me."

I met his gaze in agreement.

"We're hoping Hanscom Air Force Base will stay unresponsive to any requests from Novak's allies," Rose said. "No troop movements, no air support. You're the closest base, and it would buy us some time."

"We'd also need a police helicopter to retrieve the target and drop us off at a location that we'll communicate to the pilot on the scene," I said. "The police use helicopters daily. If we were to request one through the FBI, it could raise some eyebrows."

"What about witnesses?" Lieutenant Colonel Lewis asked. "If your goal is to make this a talked-about arrest, it won't work. Staff at these high-level events sign non-disclosure agreements, and no phones are allowed."

"Our mentioned ally will arrange for a catering service we can ... well ... trust," Rose said. "The source will take over the contract from the current catering service with an offer they can't refuse."

I almost laughed at the irony of Rose using those words on a mission involving a mob boss.

"We have only one shot at this," I said. "If we don't get anything from Novak out of the interrogation or the media doesn't pick up on this, then he walks." I put my hands on my hips, a silent gesture of frustration. "And we'll all be fired. Ruined. Our careers destroyed beyond redemption."

McCourt sighed loudly and shook his head, but he held strong. His eyes met those of Chief Murray and Colonel Lewis, who leaned forward on the table, deep in thought.

"So..." McCourt drawled, his voice dripping with doubt, "how sure are you, really, that Jan Novak is the Train Track Killer?"

I thought about the murky waters of the gunshot wound, the ankh symbol and Novak's strong connection to it, the name of his company. But above all, I thought about Leah, the smartest person I knew. I'd asked if she trusted me, and she'd said yes. And this street went both ways. I trusted not only her judgment but my own gut feeling. I'd seen something in his eyes the night I'd dropped off Leah at his fancy mansion. Something that told me, as clear as the blue sky, that Jan Novak was the Train Track Killer.

"I..." I paused. "I'd stake my career on it. If he's the killer—and I know he is—I'll get the truth out of him during that interrogation, and we'll save countless lives.

"And if you're wrong?" McCourt shot back.

"If he's not, he can cry about his arrest to his thousand-dollar-an-hour therapist and sail off on his billion-dollar yacht to find closure. No real harm done. At least my career would have been gambled on something worth losing it over. Simple as that. *Que sera, sera.* But I'll sleep at night knowing I did the right thing."

Lieutenant Colonel Lewis started nodding as if he'd just come to a conclusion. "I can only speak for myself," he said, "but when I joined the Air Force, I did it to serve the people of this country. Not to protect a bunch of rich sick fucks hurting the people I swore to protect." Something shifted behind his eyes, a darkness settling there. "When they made my airmen carry that bastard Harvey Grand's remains like he was some kind of fallen hero, they took something from us. Our honor. Our pride. At least in the public's eyes. My men and their families received hate messages—hell, even death threats. All because of some dirty politicians. So if I go down for taking out another sick fuck that these dirtbags are trying to protect, at least I'll go out with a big fucking smile on my face."

I gave him a firm nod.

Chief Murray let out a heavy sigh and shook his head. "Fuck it. As crazy as this is ... I'm in."

Relief washed over me. Rose and I exchanged a glance. For the first time, I noticed the beads of sweat glistening on her forehead.

"Under one condition," Murray added. "I'm coming along on the mission, so the blame falls on me, not my men."

"Of course," I said. "The same goes for our agents. They'll simply follow my orders with no more details other than the target. No shot will be fired, no matter what."

Chief Murray and Lieutenant Colonel Lewis exchanged a look, then turned toward McCourt. He rose slowly, leaving the papers untouched on the table. "It's settled, then," he said. "Gentlemen, good luck. We're gonna fucking need it." He didn't wait for a response before striding out of the room.

Lewis and Murray shifted their gaze to me.

"He was just named FBI director. This hit him hard," I explained. "But we're moving forward as planned. Rose will fill you in on the mission details. Will you excuse me?" I hurried out after McCourt, catching up to him just as he stepped into the elevator. I slipped in beside him before the doors could close.

"You're fucking crazy," McCourt barked, jabbing the button for his floor.

"Keep your voice down," I snapped.

"This is career suicide, and you know it," he growled. "I'd rather have Luca Domizio shoot me than get dragged through the media as a lunatic. If this blows up, Congress will make us look like idiots too stupid to hold their own dicks when they piss."

I slammed the emergency stop button, halting the elevator, and stepped in front of him. "Cut the shit. We all know you're just like those scumbags in DC who jerk off people like Jan Novak to keep their power."

McCourt pressed himself against the elevator wall, his eyes widening.

I leaned in closer. "But here's the deal. You're going to stay quiet and play along like a good boy. And if this mission goes south, you're taking the fall right beside me. Got it?"

Shock flickered across his face, his sass crumbling.

"Because if you don't," I continued, "I'll make it look like you were the grandmaster behind everything with Leah. Hell, I'll make you the mastermind behind all the shit that went down with Larsen too. I'll testify that I was just following your orders. I'll have Rose testify about you blackmailing her."

"But ... but none of that's true," he mumbled, panic creeping into his voice.

"You trying to kill Leah is true. You blackmailing Rose? Also true. But above all, the fact that you'd let a murderer like Jan Novak walk to save your own ass? That's why I'll destroy you. And if you think quietly losing your job and rotting in your fancy Nantucket beach house is bad, let me remind you that your other option is prison—where you'll be taking it up the ass from the guys you put there until the day they finally kill you."

I stepped back and hit the emergency button to get the elevator moving again.

"If I were you, I'd shut the fuck up and, for once, do something selfless," I added.

Moments later, the doors opened to reveal two agents, who stepped inside.

"Thank you, Director McCourt," I said, all smiles and respect as I stepped out. "Hey, guys. Hope to see you for drinks later tonight." I flashed a smile at the agents, who nodded and promised to be there.

And just like that, Mission Career Wreckage was officially in motion.

CHAPTER SEVENTEEN

Liam

I stood in front of the men's bathroom mirror at the FBI office, staring at my reflection. My hands were clenched tightly around the edges of the sink, my knuckles white from the grip.

Dressed in a suit and bulletproof FBI vest, I looked every bit the agent ready to take down Jan Novak. Yet doubts crept in. Was this crazy? A mistake?

My gun was secure in its holster on my hip. If all went well, it'd remain there all day—unless Jan Novak tried to hurt anybody.

The bathroom door swung open, and Cowboy stepped in. "It's time," he said.

I took a deep breath as a mix of adrenaline and anxiety coursed through my chest.

"Can't you give me more details than the target's name and picture?" Cowboy begged again like a child. "I thought we're a team."

"We are. But it's for your own good. You're just following my orders. Got it?"

Cowboy muttered something under his breath as I stepped out to meet Rose by the elevator. She looked as anxious as I felt. We exchanged a glance, with no words needed, then stepped into the elevator.

It carried us down to the garage, where a line of ten FBI SUVs sat idling, their engines rumbling. Inside each, agents were prepped and ready to roll.

"Let's fucking do this," I said as I slid into the passenger seat of the lead SUV. Rose was behind the wheel. Cowboy took his usual spot in the back.

Tension hung in the air as our convoy cut through Boston's streets. Every turn and acceleration was charged with purpose. The hum of powerful engines echoed through the city, creating a relentless symphony of urgency.

Pedestrians turned their heads, their eyes widening as we sped past. Some reached for their phones and snapped photos of the black line of SUVs blowing through red lights and weaving through traffic like an unstoppable force. Cars parted for us, their drivers staring as we surged ahead.

When we hit Route 1, the scene shifted. About fifteen police vehicles were lined up along the roadside, forming a wall of authority just outside Nahant. The peninsula was known for its sprawling mansions and old money.

As we neared the line, Rose maneuvered the SUV to the front of the convoy. Chief Murray rolled down his window when we pulled up beside him.

"You're not messing around," I said, glancing at the row of cop cars.

"Figured we'd skip the formalities," he replied, a grim tugging at his lips. He was suited up in a bulletproof vest, just like I was.

I adjusted mine, feeling the weight pressing against my chest. "Might as well make 'em sweat for a change."

"Let's do this. Let's take this bastard down," Murray said, his voice low and full of grit. He turned to his radio and barked orders with sharp authority. On his command, the line of police cruisers surged to life, sirens blaring, red and blue lights slicing through the morning fog.

Our SUVs joined his fleet like a black wave crashing forward.

Together, we tore down the road toward Nahant, ready for whatever awaited us.

As our fleet drove through the outskirts of the city, Senator Wheezer's waterfront mansion loomed ahead on its cliffside perch. When we had neared the massive iron gate, a line of Secret Service agents in sleek black suits stepped forward and halted our advance—just like Luca had warned they would.

I swung the car door open and stepped out, authority in every movement. "FBI! Open the fucking gate!" I barked, leaving no room for hesitation.

The agents exchanged confused glances but quickly obeyed, swinging the gates wide open.

We rolled up the long white gravel driveway and pulled to a stop in the middle of a lavish garden party. The rich mingled over champagne and caviar while the delicate notes of violins serenaded them. That serene bubble shattered the second our caravan arrived. Panic rippled through the crowd as shocked murmurs rose. The partygoers' faces twisted in fear and confusion.

I jumped out. Rose and Cowboy were close behind, with Chief Murray at my side, leading a small army of police and FBI agents. We marched through the stunned elites, who parted like a sea of diamonds and silk until we reached him.

Jan fucking Novak. Flesh and blood.

He stood there, cool as ice, sipping champagne as chaos swirled around him. Beside him, the vice president looked stricken, his thin, wrinkled face tight with alarm. Senator Wheezer, red-faced and trembling, looked ready to explode.

"Get the vice president out of here!" Chief Murray shouted.

Secret Service agents rushed to surround the vice president and quickly guided him toward the black limousine.

"What the hell is this? How dare you!" he yelled, but his protests faded as the car sped off.

"What is going on here?" Senator Wheezer demanded, charging toward me, his face flushed.

I shoved him aside and faced Jan Novak. "Jan Novak, you're under arrest for suspicion of murder."

"Are you insane? Stop this madness!" Wheezer yelled at me, his voice desperate. "Jan, I'm so, so sorry. Don't worry, I'll fix this!"

Chief Murray grabbed the senator before he could interfere more. "Get out of the way, or I'll arrest you for obstruction," Murray snapped.

My hands shook as I pulled out the handcuffs. Novak's eyes met mine. The arrogant grin was still plastered on his face. "You have the right to remain silent," I said, locking his wrists behind his back. "Anything you say can and will be used against you in a court of law. You have the right to an attorney. If you cannot afford an attorney, which I fucking doubt, one will be appointed to you."

He didn't resist, that fucker, just stayed as calm as ever.

Out of the corner of my eye, I spotted the catering staff recording everything—just like Luca Domizio had promised. The vice president's limo was long gone. God bless that old son of a bitch. Domizio had kept his word.

"Let's go, you piece of shit," I muttered, dragging Jan Novak by the arm toward the open field where our helicopter was supposed to land any second. But just as I moved, Murray's phone rang.

He answered, and his face tightened with dread. "Fucking shit!" Murray cursed, slamming his phone shut. "The police helicopters are all tied up, responding to a shooting at a gas station."

"We're not going to make it to the factory by car," Rose said. "The vice president has probably already called for reinforcements from the nearest military bases. Colonel Lewis might hold off on his orders and buy us some time, but the others will respond. We'll never get out by land."

Fuck. Fuck. Fuck.

I scanned Murray's face for a plan, but he had nothing.

"Lady luck turning on you already?" Novak sneered, enjoying every second of the chaos.

"Shut up!" I snapped, feeling the crowd of guests press in tighter around us. Mumbling, demanding that we let Jan Novak go.

Sweat dripped down my face, and my pulse hammered in my ears. We wouldn't make it far without air support. If we didn't get Novak out now, the whole mission would collapse—our asses hauled off in cuffs while Novak waved goodbye with that disgusting grin on his face.

"Let him go right now!" Wheezer demanded, yanking free from Chief Murray's grip. His face was twisted with rage. "Your careers are over! Don't you idiots know who I am?"

I barely heard him. Everything blurred.

My career? Over. Rose, Chief Murray, Lieutenant Colonel Lewis? Done. And Leah? Probably dead—killed by Novak in some twisted act of revenge.

I'd never imagined my downfall would come on a manicured lawn at some pretentious garden party.

My grip on Novak's arm started to slip as defeat settled in. Rose hissed a string of curses under her breath. We were so damn close. So fucking close. Life had screwed me over before, but this—this was the worst. Everything I'd fought for, everything I'd sacrificed, would be erased. All for nothing. And this bastard would walk free. Exhaustion hit me like a freight train. How easy it would be to just let go. To stop fighting. Let fate have its way.

But just as my fingers began to slip from Novak's arm, a deafening roar shattered the chaos—the unmistakable thunder of helicopters.

Rose, Murray, and I shot each other shocked looks. My head snapped up as five Air Force helicopters ripped across the sky, their blades slicing the air. Party guests screamed and ducked for cover as tables flipped, champagne flutes shattered, and chaos exploded around us. The helicopters hovered low, whipping up a storm of debris, and then descended onto the open lawn, kicking the panic into overdrive.

"Is that the fucking U.S. military?" Wheezer shouted, his voice cracking with disbelief. "Our military?"

I couldn't help but grin as I caught Chief Murray's eye. Satisfaction lit up his wrinkled face.

"For the record, I know exactly who you are," I yelled over to Senator Wheezer, who was now crouched like a scared child, hands over his head. "But you forgot who we are. We're the people who put you in power to serve us—not the other way around. So don't ever insult the U.S. military again, you greedy piece of shit."

I shot him a wicked grin as I stared at his wide, shocked eyes. If I was going down, I might as well go out with a bang.

I yanked Novak toward one of the helicopters, then spotted Colonel Lewis in the front seat next to the pilot. I shoved Novak inside as Rose followed. Cowboy was about to hop in, but Rose pushed him back as the helicopter lifted off.

"Figured I'd make sure my last mission counts," Lieutenant Colonel Lewis yelled over the deafening roar of the blades. "Let these bastards know where the U.S. military stands when this shit hits the fan."

"Oh, they'll know," I shouted back, handing him a piece of paper with coordinates. "Please drop us off at the first location, then send the other choppers to the second. That'll buy us more time."

He nodded sharply.

With that, we lifted off, the chaos below swept into the whipping winds of the helicopter's blades. This was probably my last day as an FBI agent. Especially given that Rose, Leah, and I had agreed to interrogate Novak at Leah's factory—far from government eyes. That decision alone would bury my career. Taking a suspect to private property instead of a federal facility or FBI headquarters? There was no coming back from that. My career was over.

But the chances of Novak talking? Slim to none. The smug grin on his face told me that he was thinking the same thing. What that arrogant bastard didn't know was that it wasn't me he'd be up against.

It would be someone far more persuasive.

The only person on this planet who could break him.

So I grinned right back.

CHAPTER EIGHTEEN

Leah

I stood in the shadow of the dark hallway of the old rope factory that I owned outside of town. The stench of urine lingered—a testament to the homeless who sought refuge here. Their makeshift mattresses and trash bags were scattered beneath graffiti-covered walls.

When I heard the distant thud of helicopter blades, I was impressed. Richter had actually pulled it off. He'd managed to bring Jan Novak here on a mission that was close to suicide.

My grip on the gun tightened as I watched Richter and Rose drag a handcuffed Jan Novak into the expansive factory hall. Richter believed I could make Novak talk, but I saw only one inevitable outcome.

One of us had to die, and it wasn't going to be me.

My time as a famous pianist would surely end, likely in a high-profile prison. But I held no attachment to the life I'd led—not the crowds chanting my name, not the luxurious life that came with it, and especially not my personal life. I'd never been foolish enough to hold myself in high regard. Even if I told myself that I was different from Carl Carr or Jan Novak, I was still a killer. And today, I realized just how tired I was—tired of the hunt, tired of the games. Tired of waking up each morning fighting the same fight.

The only regret I harbored was for Richter, the trouble this brought him, and the possibility that he might not see his daughter for a long time.

Glass crunched under my shoes as I strode down the corridor and headed into the hall of abandoned machinery where Richter, Rose, and Novak were waiting.

Richter was the first to notice me. His eyes darted to the gun I now aimed directly at Novak.

"Leah!" he yelled, pushing Novak toward Rose. "No! Don't!"

Jan Novak's eyes—an icy blue—met mine. His demeanor was calm and composed. "I have to say, this is quite impress—"

I squeezed the trigger.

The gunshot rang out. The bullet bounced off the factory walls before the sound faded into silence. Richter spun around, expecting Novak to drop—but he was still standing. Rose, panic written all over her face, glanced at Richter, then turned to me, her eyes wide with shock.

I kept my gun steady, smoke curling from the barrel. "The next bullet goes right between your eyes unless you answer me—truthfully," I said, my gaze fixed on Novak.

He frowned briefly, then found his cool, old self. "Is this the moment in movies when they make deals? Well, I guess here's mine. Uncuff me, and I'll answer your questions. Otherwise, do as you wish."

Rose and Richter exchanged glances.

136

"Uncuff him," I said.

"I don't think that's a good idea," Rose muttered, looking at Richter. But after a tense moment, he nodded. With a sigh of protest, Rose uncuffed Novak. He rubbed his wrists, then straightened his tuxedo jacket like he wasn't standing in the middle of his doom.

"Your turn," I said, my gun still pointing at Novak. "Why did you send Carl Carr after me?" I bypassed the question of whether he was the Train Track Killer. That would be confirmed by his answer to this one.

"I didn't send him after you," he said.

My finger tightened slightly on the trigger as I stepped closer, now only a few feet away. I'd shoot him—no doubt about that.

"Wait!" Jan said quickly, his eyes watching my every movement. "Let me finish, please."

I narrowed my eyes but eased up on the trigger slightly.

"Here's the problem with your perception about all this," Novak said, his tone calm, almost patronizing, like we were students who'd fumbled an easy equation. "Carl Carr—I didn't send him after you. I sent him *to* you."

Richter and I exchanged confused glances. "We don't have time for this bullshit," Richter snapped. "You're the sick fuck putting people on train tracks, aren't you?"

Novak didn't flinch. "My dear Agent Richter, life *is* a game. And today, you've played yours in ways I couldn't have imagined. Quite frankly, I'm impressed. Utterly stunned." He began clapping slowly, the sound echoing through the hall. "Bravo. Really. You've made today quite the headache for me. A career suicide mission for you, of course, but your passion, Agent Richter—it's remarkable. I'm starting to see what *she* sees in you."

"Answer the fucking question!" Rose barked, her voice cutting through the tension.

"But I just did," he countered. "Carl Carr—I didn't send him after you but *to* you."

Richter's hands trembled as he drew his gun, the weight of the moment etched in his face, tension tightening every muscle. "This is all the proof I need," he muttered, aiming at Novak. "If you don't do it, Leah, I will. I can't let him hire some top-notch lawyer and walk. Not after what he did to Anna and all the countless other lives he's ripped apart. He won't stop. He's sick. He'll do it again and again. We all know that."

"Richter, wait!" I snapped. Something wasn't adding up.

He shot me a troubled look. His gun was still trained on Novak, but he lowered it slightly.

"What do you mean you sent Carl Carr to me?" I asked, turning toward Novak. "You knew what I'd do to him, didn't you?"

"Of course I did," Novak said like it was the most obvious thing in the world.

That lingering question, the one that had gnawed at me from the start— why I'd never seen the monster in Novak's eyes—fought its way to the surface. And when a possible answer formed, a sickening knot of horror twisted in my gut.

"Let's move this along, shall we?" Novak said, his hand sliding toward his pocket.

Instantly, three guns were on him.

"Oh, please. You really think I'm stupid enough to pull a gun like this is some Patterson novel?" His hand moved slowly and pulled out a phone. "Like I told you, I'm not who you think I am. And here's the proof."

He walked over to a rusty metal table, set the phone down, and propped it up against an old typewriter.

"You might want to come closer," Novak said, his voice smooth and unsettling. "It's about Anna—sweet Anna. A little memoir about her life."

"You sick fuck!" Richter shouted, his voice trembling with rage.

I moved toward the metal table, my gun hanging loosely by my side. Deep down, something told me the real enemy in this room wasn't Jan Novak—it was whatever waited for me on that phone.

"Access personal storage file labeled 'Complete.' Play video one hundred fifty-three," Novak instructed calmly.

"Password?" the phone's robotic female voice responded.

"Mojca," Novak answered.

The phone turned on and played a video of what looked like a college party. At first, it showed the floor and the feet of people dancing to rap music. Then the camera shifted up to show a teenage girl held down on a couch by several young men and ... a younger version of Anna.

"Fuck the slut!" Anna shouted with an excited grin as a young man walked up and tore down the girl's panties. He rammed himself inside, moving his hips wildly to the girl's screams.

Richter and Rose approached the table, watching in horror as one man after another raped the poor girl, all while Anna laughed and helped hold the girl down.

"Fuck that slut, she likes it!" Anna shouted.

"No..." Richter whispered, stumbling backward, his face as white as snow. "No!" His voice rose into a desperate shout as he spun away, hands gripping his head, trying to block out the horror. "This can't be real! NO!"

Rose's hand flew to her mouth, stifling a gasp as her wide eyes filled with shock and disbelief.

I stood frozen, my mind struggling to process what I was seeing. The world I thought I knew was ending right in front of me, crumbling into chaos I couldn't escape.

"Stop!" the girl kept screaming as man after man raped her.

"That girl's name is Sunny Loyd," Novak declared. "A high-school student who snuck out at night with her friend Anna to attend a college party. She later committed suicide. It broke her family. Parents divorced. Father is now an alcoholic and lost his job. Mother is in and out of mental institutions."

"You're a fucking liar!" Richter roared, grabbing Novak by the suit, his fists clenched tightly. "This video is fake!"

Novak didn't even blink. "Play video two hundred and two," he said calmly.

Another video started, this time showing Mr. Mauser, one of the first train track victims. The image flickered on the screen, horrifyingly real.

Video 202 looked like store security camera footage. Mauser was in a parking lot, pulling a little girl into his car.

Richter's grip slackened. He let go of Novak and stepped toward the table, his eyes fixed on the phone as if he was seeing the truth for the first time.

Then another video played, showing Mauser in a different parking lot, guiding a different girl into his car.

"He liked them young," Novak remarked coldly as another video of Mauser played. This scene was similar. Mauser and a little girl disappeared into his car, though this time Mauser was carrying a princess balloon.

"Turn it off," Rose demanded, her voice trembling with barely contained rage.

Novak, unfazed, adjusted his jacket with an eerie calm. "Already had enough? I've got plenty more. Considering the work you three do, I thought you'd appreciate my collection a little more. Personally, I admire what you bring to this world."

"I said *turn it off!*" Rose screamed, lunging forward. She snatched the phone and hurled it to the ground. The screen shattered with a sharp crack, but the videos kept playing, their flickering glow casting eerie shadows over the room as Rose collapsed to her knees.

I stood frozen, my gaze locked on the broken phone, unable to look away.

Then Richter snapped. His fury boiled over as he grabbed the edge of the table and flipped it with a thunderous crash.

"Fuuuuuuuuuuuuuck!" he bellowed, his voice echoing through the hollow factory.

I wanted to move, to place a hand on his shoulder, but something held me back. Instead I turned my attention to Novak, locking eyes with him. His stare was steady, unshaken. "As I said, I'm not who you think I am."

And he wasn't.

That was why I'd never seen the monster in his eyes. That was why the rage I should've felt toward him had always been absent.

Jan Novak wasn't a monster.

He wasn't the Train Track Killer—despite placing those bodies on the tracks.

He was ... *a version of me.*

A dark justice dealt to those who did wrong. Maybe not serial killers but clearly people who deserved justice in one way or another.

And Jan Novak administered this dark form of justice. As dark as mine, just less selective in his targets.

For all those years, I'd hunted myself.

The distant drone of helicopters resonated through the hall as the lines between good and evil blurred into a morally indistinct haze.

They were here.

Novak's allies. They'd found us.

But none of it mattered anymore. We'd sacrificed it all.

And all for nothing.

"Well, this was fun," Novak said, his tone as steady as ever. "But I think my ride's here." He walked past me, then paused. "I really enjoyed our dinner the other night. Let's meet again. Maybe we can have, well, a bit more fun next time." Novak strode confidently toward the door. He was almost there when Richter sprang to his feet, his gun aimed at Novak's back. Richter's hands shook. His face was a twisted mix of rage and despair.

Novak stopped but didn't turn around.

"There were other ways to handle Anna," Richter shouted, his voice cracking. "She didn't have to die. And her grandmother … you had Patel kill her grandmother!"

Novak slowly turned, just enough to glance over his shoulder. "If it had been the first time Anna had drugged a girl at a party, maybe. And if it were the first time her grandmother had lied to protect her, maybe. But you see, Agent Richter, the world isn't as black and white as your simple law enforcement perspective might suggest. There are layers to this, complexities you can't begin to grasp. Most people can't even be honest with themselves." Novak shrugged, his voice smooth. "They hide behind lies and convenient stories, burying the truth so deep they forget it's even there. You think you're getting to the bottom of this? You're barely scratching the surface. It's best to leave those matters to people who understand them. People who know everything about them."

Richter's aim stayed locked, the barrel trembling ever so slightly.

"Liam," I said softly, stepping closer. I placed my hand on his outstretched arm, slowly guiding it down. "Liam," I repeated, my voice gentle and steady.

He resisted at first, but then, like a man crushed by the weight of the world, he gave in, his arm lowering as if in defeat.

I squeezed his arm in silent support, then turned to Novak. "What about Emanuel?" My voice was level, controlled. "Why did you kill him? What could he possibly have done to deserve that death on the tracks?"

Novak's eyes locked onto mine. "That," he said, "is a question you'll need to ask someone else."

His words hit me like a gut punch. Novak hadn't killed Emanuel? But if he hadn't, who had?

Without another word, Novak walked out, disappearing through the door.

The three of us stood there, staring after him, the weight of the revelations pressing down like a suffocating fog.

We waited for the storm to crash down on us. Gunmen, army, helicopters, something. Any second now, I expected armed men to burst in, arrest us, or worse, open fire. It made sense to get rid of us. It was what I would have done.

"Are they gonna kill us?" Rose asked. Her voice was calm, almost eerily so, as if she'd already accepted that this was how it would all end.

"Probably," I said, glancing over at Richter. I wanted to say something to him, something meaningful. Maybe that in all this darkness, meeting him somehow made it worthwhile. But the words never made it past my lips.

Seconds ticked by. Then a minute. Maybe two, maybe three.

No gunmen came. The thudding of boots and the hum of helicopters faded into the distance until there was nothing but an empty, unnerving silence.

We stood there, frozen in place, as if time had stopped. Trapped in this crazy limbo, unable to move or speak.

Finally, Rose pushed herself to her feet. "I guess we're gonna see tomorrow after all. What ... now? What the hell are we supposed to do?"

Richter's eyes locked onto mine, searching for answers I didn't have.

At that moment, all I had were questions.

Who was I, really?

I'd already diverged from hunting serial killers when I'd attacked the Night Stalker. Was I really so different from Jan Novak? Did my two wrongs actually make a right, especially now that the man I'd hunted and wanted to kill had turned out to be another version of myself?

It had all seemed so clear when I'd thought Novak preyed on the innocent and I hunted the guilty. But who decided what made someone a monster? Me?

And then there was Emanuel. Who killed him? Why?

"What now?" Richter asked. "What do we do now, Leah?"

"I..." My voice faltered, the words dissolving into the space around us, echoing off the factory's cold, lifeless walls. "I don't know."

CHAPTER NINETEEN

Liam

Rain pounded against my SUV, which was parked in the empty lot of a hiking trail. Lieutenant Colonel Lewis and Chief Murray yanked open the doors and climbed into the back seat. The storm outside matched my dark, brooding mood. It had been a few weeks since Jan Novak's arrest, and after weeks of tense texts, this meeting had finally been called.

Chief Murray slammed the door shut. "What the hell is going on?" he barked. "I'm tired of sitting around like a goddamn caged animal. Are they coming after us, or are we going after Novak again? I'm sick of doing nothing. Something has to happen soon, or I'll lose my damn mind."

Murray had risked everything to arrest Novak. But that was before we'd known what Novak really was—a monster similar to us.

Killing men like Harvey Grand and Carl Carr had been simple. Black and white. But this? Novak was a puzzle with no clear answer, and that moral gray area gnawed at me. It made everything murky, filled with questions none of us could answer.

"They found him before we could extract anything useful," I lied, keeping my eyes on the rain streaking down the windows. "Nobody's come for us so far, and we all still have our jobs. My gut says there's a silent deal in place. Pretend it never happened. Stay quiet, act normal, don't release any footage of the arrest, and in return, we keep our freedom and jobs."

Murray snorted. "Sounds like a lot of guessing to me. There's been nothing on the news about the arrest. But that makes him even more guilty, if you ask me. If he were innocent, they'd have formal investigations so far up our asses, you'd see it in our eyes."

Guilty. Murray was right. Novak *was* guilty. But of what, exactly? Killing a child molester like Mauser? Or a rapist like Anna? How could I justify protecting Leah after she'd taken down the Night Stalker but condemn Novak for doing something eerily similar?

Since that day in the factory, my mind had been spiraling with questions as dark as the night. I didn't have the courage to dig into the details of Novak's other victims—what they'd done to deserve their fate on the tracks. After Mauser and Anna, I just wasn't ready. Or maybe I was simply scared. Scared I'd stop judging Novak for the monster he was. Scared I'd stop judging him at all.

"I still have the footage from the arrest," I said. Luca had secured the phones from his people who'd recorded the event. "As long as we hold onto that, we're safe."

"I don't give a damn about my safety," Chief Murray growled, his eyes blazing with fierce determination. "I'm not a coward. I want Jan Novak gone. Arrested. Dead. Whatever it takes. He's a killer hiding behind powerful friends and a mountain of cash. He's my enemy now. Enemy number one. And I'm not the type to let scum like him shit all over justice. I'll keep pushing until things are set *fucking* straight. I'm the Massachusetts State police chief, for Christ's sake. Novak doesn't walk!"

Lewis nodded. "I'm with Chief Murray. We can't let Novak live like a king while he's out there playing Jack the Ripper."

Innocent people.

I sighed. For a moment, I thought about telling them everything. About Leah, me, Novak. But then what? It was a lot to assume they'd be willing to follow me down that path. Leah's pursuit of dark justice was one thing. But Novak? His story was murkier, much harder to justify. And as of now, I wasn't even sure I was on board with the things he did.

Outside, the rain pounded against the roof, its rhythm relentless.

"For now, we keep our heads down," I said, staring at the drops streaking down the SUV windows. "They haven't come after us, and jumping into another mission would be reckless. Novak didn't give us anything during the arrest. But I promise, I'll find something—something significant. If we rush this, we'll all get locked up. And if that happens, Novak will shit on justice ... and on us."

Chief Murray's eyes narrowed at me. I recognized that look. He could see right through me. He'd spotted my stalling tactic like a gambler spying a neon Vegas sign. Lewis was likely aware as well, but unlike Murray, he was the patient type, accustomed to military strategies that simmered over years.

"You'd better," Chief Murray said, reaching for the door handle. "Because if you don't, I will. And this time, Novak will be taken care of. Maybe even get hit by a stray bullet during an arrest. Wouldn't be the first time it happened. Wouldn't be the last."

He left.

Lewis lingered a moment longer. "You'd better come up with something fast. When you asked Murray for help, you dangled a blood-soaked cloth in front of a bloodhound. Can't call him off the hunt now." He hurried out of the car, disappearing into the rain as he dashed to his SUV. I watched as both vehicles pulled away, leaving me alone with my thoughts.

I pulled out my flip phone.

After the silence that we both needed, Leah had texted me a few days ago. She wanted to meet. I told her soon. And soon was now.

I stared at the screen, my fingers hovering over the keys. I started to type, asking when she wanted to meet. Then, second-guessing myself, I deleted the message and snapped the phone shut with a frustrated click.

I leaned back, my mind drifting.

Jan Novak had changed everything.

He'd made me question my partnership with Leah. Question myself. And that scared the hell out of me.

Rose had pretty much taken time off, said she'd let things play out for now and thrown herself into other cases. I wanted to do the same, but the memory of Anna's cold, blue body clashed violently with the video of Sunny Loyd's rape.

What Anna had done was unforgivable. Inexcusable. But had Novak truly delivered justice by killing her? Deep down, I wasn't sure.

Leah didn't seem to be wrestling with the same doubts, and that worried me as well. She'd already crossed the line when she'd gone after the Night

150

Stalker. Now, with Novak in the picture, this could spiral into something far worse.

I had to talk to her. Now.

I grabbed the flip phone again, ready to text her. Before I could, my work phone rang. Cowboy was calling.

"Special Agent in Charge," he said cheerfully. "You won't believe this. But the red truck you made me look into?"

I'd completely forgotten about that. Carl Carr was already dead, but Cowboy didn't know that. He must have continued going through thousands of hours of surveillance footage from the area where Nathalie had disappeared.

"About that—" I began.

Cowboy cut me off. "I found his truck on footage. On the fucking night Nathalie disappeared."

I rubbed my temple with my free hand. "Cowboy, Nathalie is back home. She said she ran off with a man who promised to marry her, but he dumped her. Surprise, surprise. Now she's back home."

"I know that. But leave it to Cowboy. Bang-bang!"

"Cowboy, not now, I—"

"Thanks to Nathalie's disappearance for whatever reasons, I was able to connect his truck to three other sites where prostitutes disappeared. And those women are still missing."

I straightened in my seat.

"You know how you always tell me to be more independent and think outside of the box?" Cowboy continued. "Well, I did. And hit the jackpot. That guy Carl Carr ... I think it's time to pay him a visit."

Shit. Shit. Shit.

"Richter?"

"Yes, yes, of course. Good work."

"Bang-bang. Leave it to Cowboy."

"Um, hey, listen. Let's not jump the gun quite yet. He might just be some pervert. We don't have anything that makes him a real suspect or anything. Not in the eyes of the court, and we're too busy right now to bust consensual sex. Prostitution or not. That's a cop problem."

"I think there's more to it. I think we really need to pay this guy a visit. I already called him, but his mom said he's not home right now."

I ran my hand through my hair. "You ... spoke to his mom?"

"She answered the phone. A strange woman, if you ask me. Talked a bit with her. Gives me 'College Snatcher mom' vibes. Remember? The crazy one with the dead stuffed cats all over her place?"

"Taxidermized, not stuffed."

"Yeah, whatever. Creepy as fuck."

Shit. This was bad. I couldn't let Cowboy get any closer. "All right. Keep trying to get a hold of Carl Carr to get him in for an interview. But that's it. We can't waste time on this right now, you hear me? Your uncle is breathing down my neck." I knew that would go nowhere. Carl Carr was gone. For now, this was good enough.

"Got it. You can count on me."

"Good."

"One last thing," he said just as I was about to hang up.

"Yes?"

"The Night Stalker."

"What about him?"

"He got out on bail. His mom sold her condo and paid the $200,000."

"Are you fucking kidding me?" I said. "I told the state's attorney that $200,000 was a joke for what that piece of shit did."

"You and every woman in this country."

Could the day get any worse? Fuck! If Leah found out, she'd make sure the Night Stalker was dealt with. It would be ugly. It would be messy. And the fact that Cowboy was sniffing around might complicate things.

"I need you to go over his bail conditions and meet with the state attorney first thing tomorrow," I said, my frustration roaming free. "Until he's found guilty and locked up, I want everything: ankle bracelet, daily check-ins with the police, passport surrender, drug testing, no-contact orders. Throw the damn book at him. And make it hurt. You hear me?"

"Loud and clear. I'll give him hell."

"Good."

He hung up, and I slipped the flip phone back into my coat pocket. I'd text Leah later. Right now, I needed to devise a plan—a plan for Novak. Cowboy. Murray. And now the fucking Night Stalker.

I had to figure out where I stood before I talked to Leah, especially on the matter of killing. After all, she was at the root of all this. At least on my end. But she was likely my only solution too.

CHAPTER TWENTY

Liam

As I pulled into my reserved spot in the condo's underground garage, my headlights swept over a figure standing just outside the parking space. The brief flash of light revealed a woman. Instantly, I recognized her from the picture my sister had sent months ago.

It was my half-sister—the child my father had conceived behind our backs with another woman.

I cursed under my breath. Of all the days for her to show up, it had to be this one. The last thing I needed was to deal with family drama after the kind of day I'd had.

With unsure movements, she stepped aside to let me park. I killed the engine, sat there for a moment, and then opened the door and stepped out.

"Liam?" Her voice was small, trembling with insecurity. Instinct from the bureau kicked in, and I found myself scanning her from head to toe.

There was no mistaking the fact that she was my half-sister, but the woman standing in front of me wasn't the same as the one in the photo. The picture showed a fresh-faced, hopeful girl. But now? Red, swollen hands from years of drug use and a missing tooth told a story of a hard life. Her makeup was caked on as if in an attempt to hide the damage, but it only amplified the contrast between her appearance and the church-like outfit she wore. It seemed that she was desperately trying to make a good impression.

It hurt to see her like this. To see her trying so hard. For me, of all people.

"Hey," I said, locking my car. The beep echoed through the garage, hanging in the awkward silence between us.

"I..." she started, her voice faltering, "I'm Lucy, your half-sister. I'm so sorry for showing up at your place like this. I know our sister said you both didn't want any contact right now. But..."

I pinched my lips. This was true. I had enough on my plate without family drama, especially with Josie's court case having just wrapped up. I couldn't—didn't want to—get involved in this. Not now. Maybe not ever.

"How did you find me?" I asked.

"A coworker at your office gave me your address when I mentioned I'm your sister."

"Cowboy," I mumbled in annoyance. How could he just hand out my address like that?

Frustration must have been written all over my face, as Lucy took a step back, her gaze dropping to the floor. "If now isn't a good time, I could come back another day," she offered.

I sighed. "Yeah. I'm really sorry, but now is actually not a good time." I tried to keep my voice kind, hide the exhaustion of the chaos in my life.

She nodded. "I'll come back—"

"It might be better if I reach out when I have more time," I interrupted.

Disappointment washed over her face, visible even beneath the heavy makeup. It hurt me to see her hurt, but this was exactly the drama I couldn't handle on top of everything else right now. Goddamn Cowboy. Goddamn my cheating asshole father.

"It's not you. Really," I said. "I'm busy at work right now. Please don't take this personally. Karma treats me like shit sometimes. I'm not one of her favorites. Never was, never will be."

She smiled faintly. "I know all about that. Karma don't like me too. She's a sneaky bitch, that one."

I nodded. "Well, I'll catch you later, if that's alright?" My tone was sweet, honest.

"Yes, yes, of course," she said, brightening slightly. She handed me a paper with her contact information. "I work nights at the nursing home, but I'm free during the day. Call me anytime."

"Thanks," I said, pocketing the paper. Then I watched as she left through the garage entrance and disappeared around a corner.

I didn't have much time to dwell on the encounter. My eyes locked on a black BMW in an employee parking spot.

My heart started racing as I headed over, each step faster than the last.

No need to text Leah.

The dark angel of justice was already here.

CHAPTER TWENTY-ONE

Leah

Richter climbed into the driver's seat and shut the door with a heavy thud. Dark circles hung under his eyes, and his hair was a mess. He looked like a man who hadn't slept in days.

"I didn't mean to intrude on something personal," I said, nodding toward the spot where he and his half-sister had been talking.

He rested his head against the seat. "Leah, you and I have faced things darker than my half-sister showing up out of the blue. You didn't intrude."

I nodded. "I'm not an expert on family matters. I don't really have a family. But a lost sibling trying to reconnect ... isn't that a good thing?"

"I don't know." His gaze shifted to the window. "At first, I thought she'd just add more chaos to my life. Add fuel to the fire. But now that I think about it..."

"About what?"

His eyes turned back to me. "Now I think I might be the mess. I'm the fire. And anyone who gets too close is going to get burned."

I let his words settle for a moment. "We have that in common," I admitted. "Now more than ever."

Our unspoken fears filled the silence between us.

"What are we supposed to do now, Leah?" Richter finally asked, his voice low. "Keep going like nothing's changed? Take him out? Or worse ... join him?"

I'd been dreading that question. The truth was, I didn't have an answer. Not one that would satisfy him, anyway.

"I mean," Richter continued, "our mission. Are we really so different from Novak? Or have we become monsters too, playing judge and jury, blind to the fact that we're only human?"

I shook my head firmly. "No. We're not like Novak. The people we've taken down were serial killers—pure evil." My voice faltered as the memory of the Night Stalker crossed my mind. Quickly, I pushed it aside. "If you're questioning what we did, try to remember Harris and those college girls. The frozen head at the crime scene. Or Harvey Grand. The bastard poisoned a baby. An innocent baby."

"I do remember them," Richter shot back.

"Good. Make sure those memories stay with you for the times when you doubt yourself." I sighed. "I never told you what I found in Carl Carr's basement, but trust me, it was pure evil. The kind of evil you can feel in your bones. And Nathalie? She's alive because we stopped him. Does that mean nothing?"

"It means everything," he said, his gaze locking with mine. "It's the one thing that keeps me going through all this. And I don't regret Carr, Harris, or Grand one bit. I sleep just fine knowing we got rid of them."

"But?" I asked.

Richter exhaled slowly, running a hand through his hair in frustration. "But what Novak did ... if I'm honest, Leah, how is it any different from what you did to the Night Stalker?"

That question hit harder than I'd expected. It was the one I'd been dreading, worried that Jan Novak would wedge himself between us like this.

"I didn't kill the Night Stalker. That's the difference," I said firmly.

Richter seemed somewhat satisfied with that answer, though doubt lingered in his eyes.

"No, you didn't. And thank God for that. Because as much as I wish I could stop thinking about it, there's something about Anna's death that doesn't sit right with me. She deserved to rot in a cell, but killing her?"

I nodded, knowing exactly what he meant. Not because I felt the same way about it but because I'd chosen Richter for this very reason—for his empathy. His unwavering moral compass.

In moments like this, I needed him. To justify why I was alive, doing what I did. To keep me on the right path. But though I trusted his judgment, I was incapable of feeling the way he did. Of feeling much of anything.

"Anna was underage at the time of the rapes. She most likely wouldn't have gone to jail," I said. "Not even received a fine."

"So are you saying her death was justice?" Disbelief filled his voice. "Like Grand and Carr? Are we really comparing serial killers to a girl who did something terrible but never killed anyone?"

"I'm not saying that. But Sunny Loyd is dead because of what Anna did. Isn't that a form of murder too?"

Richter's eyes shot to mine. Something sparked in them—agreement? Or was it disbelief?

"Don't you feel the slightest bit of sadness over the whole thing with Anna?" he asked. "Nothing at all?"

I looked away, unable to meet his intense gaze. If I answered him, I'd be honest, and I knew he wouldn't like it.

"Richter, what's done is done. Why do the details matter?"

"They matter to me, Leah. Novak is out there playing God, handing down Old Testament judgments, and that should scare you as much as it scares me. So I'll ask again: Is there anything you can muster for Anna? Sadness? A sense of injustice? Goddamn pity for the pathetic girl she was? Anything?"

I stayed silent.

"Leah!" His voice rose, frustration boiling over.

"No," I said firmly. "No, Liam, I don't. I don't feel anything for her. Anna didn't just watch the horrors that happened to Sunny Loyd that night. She held her down while man after man violently raped that poor girl. Now Sunny's dead. Suicide. And her parents will probably join her soon. So no, Liam, when I think about Anna lying at the foot of that river, blue and stiff, I don't feel sadness. I feel justice. And a bit of relief that it wasn't me who got to her first. And you'd do Sunny Loyd's family—and yourself—a favor if you saved your tears for the victim."

The silence in the car was suffocating. We stared straight ahead.

"I'm not saying you're wrong," he finally said. "But I don't know if I can continue like this. Something about this feels different, no matter how hard I try to convince myself that it isn't. Novak ... I don't know if he's right or wrong, but I do know I can't keep going like this if we end up following his path."

A wave of panic shot through me. Was he considering quitting?

Suddenly, I realized I'd called him Liam again, just like I had in the factory when he'd almost shot Novak. Sitting here now, I wished he'd pulled the trigger. Or that I had.

As if my body weren't my own, my hand moved, resting on top of his. The warmth of his skin sent a toxic rush of excitement through me.

The realization struck me like a live wire: I cared for Agent Liam Richter.

He didn't pull away. His eyes softened, calming as they finally lifted to meet mine.

"What does it matter if Novak's right or wrong?" I asked. "We don't have to be him. We can keep doing what we've always done. Let him go his way. Maybe Anna's death weighs on your conscience, but what about people like Mauser? After you watched him drag little girls into his car. Do you feel bad about his death too?"

Liam didn't hesitate. "Fuck no. I'm a dad, for Christ's sake. If one of those little girls had been Josie..." His voice cracked.

I nodded.

"The Night Stalker..." he said. "You never told me why you did it."

The memories flooded back. That night, alone with my thoughts and slightly intoxicated.

"I was up late again, going over the train track murders. It's all I did most nights back then. The news was playing in the background, and they aired an interview with one of the Night Stalker's victims. The terror in her eyes, the tears ... I felt so powerless against Novak. That feeling turned into rage. And then ... it became a voice. For her and for all the others he hurt."

Liam placed his hand over mine. There was nothing romantic or sexual about it—at least not on his end. It was a gesture of understanding, sympathy, friendship, and support. It meant a great deal to me when almost nothing else in my life mattered.

I wondered if that was all he needed from me—to see the human side of me every once in a while.

"I'm not mad about what you did to The Night Stalker," he said. "But I'm relieved you didn't kill him. Our work with serial killers is so black and white. But Novak ... I'm not convinced, Leah. And I need you to promise me that what happened with the Night Stalker, that attack—it won't..."

"It won't happen again," I interrupted, knowing what he needed to hear. To keep our work going. And to keep him in my life. "After that day in the factory," I continued, "I wasn't sure who I was anymore. Am I just another monster like him? Or am I the monster, and he's the justice the world needs? But now, sitting here, I realize it doesn't matter. I need to continue my work. If you're with me on this, I'll take that as a sign that I'm still on the right path."

He looked at me, his eyes searching for something in mine. Then the tension in his face eased as he sighed. "As much as I hate it, I think we need to talk to him."

"Novak?" I asked.

"Yeah. We need to find out what the other victims did to end up on those tracks. I might not agree that Anna deserved to die, but people like Mauser... that's a different story. Novak's methods are brutal, but if we want to figure out what to do with him, understanding his reasoning could help. Don't you think?"

"You want to find out if we should go after him or not," I concluded. I honestly had no feelings toward killing Novak if that was what Richter really wanted. "Has it ever crossed your mind..." I trailed off.

"What? To ask Novak if he knows of any other serial killers still out there? His company possesses almost god-like powers."

I nodded.

"Sure did. But I'm worried that would force us into making him an ally," Richter said.

"Not a bad trade-off if we catch them faster."

"Not bad at all. Until he kills someone innocent. For now, I have to treat Novak like any other psycho time bomb. Maybe some guy cuts him off in traffic. Dead in a river. Then what? Are we responsible for that? For not stopping Novak when we had the chance?"

Liam pulled his hand away from mine. The shift in conversation was clearly unsettling him. I regretted steering it in that direction.

"Well, for now, let's stay away from him as much as possible," I said. "Until we find out more about the other victims from the train tracks. I'll talk to him at the next shareholders' meeting."

Richter nodded slowly. "Yeah. That would help a lot. Thanks." He reached for the door handle.

"Wait," I said.

He paused, turning back to me.

"I actually came here to invite you to my Christmas concert. You and Rose. I've got a ticket for McCourt too, just to keep things from looking suspicious."

His eyebrows lifted in surprise. "I heard it was sold out. Tickets are going for record prices after all the cancellations."

I smiled. "It's my concert. I think I can financially weather the loss of three ticket sales."

A small grin tugged at his lips. It was a glimpse of the Richter I used to know—before Novak, before everything changed on the day of the arrest.

"It would defiantly make the FBI look good. And we need that right now," he said softly. "Might bring some normalcy back. Maybe even help with Rose. Help her move on ... or smooth things over."

"We could also go over some new items on the agenda," I said casually.

He cocked a brow. "New items on the agenda?"

My attention drifted to a couple stumbling into the garage, drunk, kissing wildly, unable to keep their hands off each other. "I've been paying hackers to surf the dark web for me. It's tedious and time-consuming work because these perverts are extremely cautious, and websites pop up and disappear daily. But it's showing promise."

Liam tilted his head. "Dang. Is that how you found the Night Stalker?"

I nodded.

"And you think we could use that to find other serial killers?"

"At the very least, it could help us follow up on leads faster. We could access sensitive information like Jan Novak does. It's illegal without a warrant, obviously, but building our own network could be useful, especially if we decide Novak is an enemy, not an ally."

Richter smirked. "Hackers. That actually could be a game-changer. Like having our own FBI cyber unit, but without all the red tape—no warrants, no rules."

"It would definitely trample on privacy rights," I said.

"Well," he shrugged, "those perverts lose those rights the moment they surf the dark web for murder porn. Not exactly 'green flag' guys, don't you think?"

I couldn't help but smile at that.

Our eyes shifted back to the drunk couple, now practically having sex against the side of their car. Richter shook his head, amused.

"What?" I asked, teasing. "Not proper?"

He laughed. "Nah. It's not that. Just thinking back to when I was still that carefree and fun."

"You're still fun," I said with a faint smile.

"Oh yeah? You mean between the murders, shootouts, and mental breakdowns? When I don't look like a walking piece of burnt charcoal?"

I laughed. "Some women find men who carry the world attractive. I think they call them 'well-seasoned.'"

He threw me a sarcastic smirk.

The drunk couple clumsily climbed into their car, and the engine roared to life.

"Oh, hell no," Liam said, tearing open his door. "I'd better stop them before they kill somebody."

"You do that," I said, watching as he rushed over and pressed his badge against the driver's side window.

I watched their exchange from a distance—the man stumbling out of the car, apologizing, practically begging. The woman, trying to prove she was sober, attempted to jump on one leg only to lose her balance and fall to the ground.

Then it hit me again.

The strange feeling I'd had earlier when Richter's hand had rested on mine.

It was comforting, soothing, like a wave of warmth and relief washing over me.

Maybe I was a monster, like Novak. Maybe I had been all along. But standing there, watching Richter, I realized something. As long as he kept me walking that fine line in the twilight, just one step from falling into complete darkness, it didn't matter anymore.

Novak.

Good.

Evil.

Me.

None of it mattered. Not as long as Richter was guiding me through the shadows like the first light at dawn.

CHAPTER TWENTY-TWO

Liam

The rapid-fire clicks of camera shutters echoed around the cramped, run-down bedroom. Cowboy stood beside me, chewing gum obnoxiously loud. The two-bedroom apartment in Dorchester looked like a bomb had gone off inside it. Clothes and dirty laundry were strewn across the floor like discarded memories.

In the center of the room, a large mahogany-framed bed dominated the space. On it, a woman lay motionless, her faded T-shirt and sweatpants soaked in blood. Her eyes, wide open, stared into nothing.

Next to her, slumped against the bed frame, was a man. A bullet hole gaped in his skull, a gun still loosely hanging from his limp hand. His head drooped forward like that of a rag doll, his chin resting on his chest.

I knelt beside the woman, my gloved fingers just inches from her vacant blue eyes. The sour stench of blood and sweat clung to the air, thick and oppressive. I leaned closer, meeting her empty gaze. "You get a shot of her face yet?" I asked.

A forensic tech, wrapped in a white coverall and booties, snapped his camera once more and nodded. "Got it."

With a slow, deliberate movement, I closed her eyes. The finality of it settled in the room like a weight. For a moment, she almost looked peaceful—if one ignored the exit wound on the side of her head, where the bullet had torn through her skull.

I stood, my gaze shifting to the man on the floor. He wore boxers and a wife-beater. The blood-soaked fabric clung to his skin.

Taking a deep breath, I glanced at Cowboy. His jaw worked the gum as if he were a cow chewing cud. Rose was tied up in a meeting. That left the two of us to represent the FBI here.

"Lie to me," I muttered, already knowing this wasn't going to be clean.

Cowboy cracked his neck, gum still popping between his teeth.

"Just tell me it's not the Night Stalker," I clarified.

Cowboy shrugged. "All right, it's not the Night Stalker."

I sighed, my frustration mounting. If Leah found out about this...

"Fuck," I muttered, placing my hands on my hips.

"Thirty-six-year-old Caucasian female," Cowboy read from his notepad. "Regina King. Worked the register at a local grocery store. Around one a.m., an unidentified white male in his thirties—"

"Cowboy, I know damn well it's the fucking Night Stalker."

"Oh. Right. Okay. So around one a.m., a not unidentified white male called Terry Patterson, AKA the Night Stalker, entered with a key and argued with the victim. Neighbors didn't call it in 'cause apparently arguing wasn't out of the ordinary for those two."

"Did anyone hear the gunshots?"

"Nope. Probably 'cause he didn't shoot her until morning. Jackhammers and trucks from the construction site outside drowned out any noise."

I'd noticed that on the way in. It was loud as hell.

"Still waiting on some tests," Cowboy continued, "but looks like he shot her around ten a.m., then turned the gun on himself."

Suddenly, Rose burst into the room, her strides quick, her gaze sharp as it landed on the Night Stalker's body. She caught her breath.

"Shit," was all she said.

Cowboy shot her a frown. "What're you doin' here? Thought you were filling in for Miller over at Violent Gang?"

"I am. But McCourt wants another pair of eyes on this."

"Why?" Cowboy's brow furrowed.

"Because this shitshow happened a week after he got out on a two-hundred-thousand-dollar bail," Rose said, her tone clipped. "For violent rapes."

"Yeah." Cowboy nodded, lips tight. "That."

I shook my head, disbelief churning in my gut. "Fuckin' hell. A violent rapist. Two-hundred-thousand-dollar bail. Did we make sure our recommendation to deny bail got to the judge on time?"

Cowboy nodded. "Yep. All on file. We even objected after the bail was set."

Rose clenched her jaw. "I hate to stab the DA in the back, but we'll need to leak our objections to the press."

Both Cowboy and I turned to Rose, eyebrows raised.

"Let me guess," Cowboy muttered. "My uncle's idea?"

Rose nodded. "Yup. He tried to get a hold of you," she said, looking at me. "Wants to see you, now."

I nodded, understanding perfectly. This was bad. Every drug addict in the streets got held longer than this guy, and now an innocent woman was dead because the system screwed up.

My gaze drifted to the bedroom across the hall. It was lined with movie posters and skateboards. Cowboy followed my stare.

"The kid. Where is he?" I asked.

"He's with his biological dad. Shared custody with the victim," Cowboy said.

"Thank fuckin' God he wasn't here when it happened," I muttered.

Cowboy's expression darkened. "Don't thank the Lord yet. The kid is the one who found her. With his dad. When he dropped the kid off."

A heavy weight pressed on my chest, and my lungs struggled to fill. As I stared at the woman's pale face, a knot tightened in my gut. "Jesus. What a shitshow."

Cowboy's face twisted into a frown. "Feels like we failed her, doesn't it? This didn't need to happen."

"No, it didn't. But it's not on us," I said firmly. "We didn't pull the trigger. We tried to stop him. Told the court to hold him. We did what we could."

"Not everything," Cowboy muttered, locking eyes with me. I knew what he meant. "If that woman in the park had just kill—"

"Stop it," Rose snapped.

Silence fell between us. It was broken only by the click of cameras and the voices of officers securing evidence.

"If you keep going down the 'what-if' road, Theo, it'll eat you alive," I said, my voice soft.

He nodded slowly, letting it sink in. "I'll talk to the neighbors, make sure the witness statements are solid. The family's gonna sue, no doubt, and when shit hits the fan, the FBI better be squeaky clean on this."

"Good," I said, feeling a sense of pride in how far he'd come. "Smart thinking."

Cowboy smirked. "Don't tell me you're starting to like me, boss."

"Let's not get ahead of ourselves," I joked, but everyone at headquarters, including Cowboy, knew how fond I'd become of the little prick.

He chuckled but lingered.

"Is there something else?" I asked.

"Remember the guy with the red truck you asked me to look into? Carl Carr?"

"Not that again," I said.

"Wait. Hear me out," Cowboy said. "I talked to a prostitute who swears she saw him the night Nathalie disappeared. She said—"

"Jesus." I sighed loudly enough for him to get the message.

"All right, maybe not now," Cowboy said. "We'll talk later."

"Thanks," I muttered.

Cowboy nodded and left.

Rose stepped closer. "Can I talk to you outside for a minute?" she asked.

We moved down the hallway, where it was quiet. Both of us glanced around a few times, making sure the coast was clear.

"What are we gonna do now?" Rose asked, hands on her hips, worry written all over her face.

"What do you mean?"

She stepped closer, right in front of me. "Don't do this, Richter."

I exhaled sharply. "What do you want me to say?" My voice was a harsh whisper, my eyes flicking around to ensure no one overheard. "That I feel like we failed this poor woman? That she'd still be alive if Leah had just killed that piece of shit? Like Novak does?"

Rose took a deep breath, her gaze dropping to the floor. "I ... feel lost, Richter."

I blinked, caught off guard by how quickly she'd surrendered. Deep down, I wanted her to fight me on this, tell me it was good that Leah hadn't killed the Night Stalker. Give me some reason to believe in the system again—a reason that I currently couldn't see.

But she hadn't. Maybe she couldn't. Just like me.

Yet, it was my job to lead, not to crumble into doubt. I had to stay strong—or risk breaking beyond repair.

"Listen." I placed a hand on her shoulder. Her eyes snapped up to meet mine. "We saved Nathalie, didn't we?"

She nodded, though the weight on her face remained.

"And God knows how many more are alive because Grand and Harris are dead. We need to focus on those victories, not the losses."

The tension in her shoulders eased just a little.

"We saved a lot of people, Rose. Mothers like Nathalie, families who deserve to survive a glass of water from their taps because assholes like Grand are dead." I paused, my eyes locked on hers. "Can I count on you?"

Her expression tightened. I had to offer her a way out too. Forced loyalty was a ticking time bomb.

"If you're not up for this, it's okay," I continued, my tone gentle. "Go back to being a regular agent. Let me and Leah handle the ugly side of things. No shame in that. Honestly, part of me wants you to walk away, Rose. Save yourself. One more life saved."

"No." The answer came sharp, with no hesitation. "You can count on me."

I searched her eyes. Then I nodded and pulled my hand away.

Rose turned, checking the hallway again, making sure no one was close. "What about Leah and Novak?" Her voice was low, but it carried the weight of the million-dollar question.

I exhaled through my nose. "I'll handle Leah. I'll talk to her. She won't do anything reckless. She's the smartest person I know. The Night Stalker won't change that."

"And Novak?"

"Well," I exhaled. "We'll dig into his victims. Find out who they really were. Until then, we lay low."

Rose nodded firmly.

Suddenly, Cowboy stumbled around the corner. "You're still here?" He blinked at us.

Rose and I exchanged glances. Fuck. Had he heard anything? The construction noise outside was loud, but still...

"Did you talk to the neighbors?" I asked.

"Yeah. Mrs. Jones, down the hall, didn't hear anything. But I'll keep working my way through the damn building. Make sure nothing ugly shows up later."

"Good. Agent Rose, I'll see you at the concert tomorrow?" I asked, loud enough for Cowboy to catch.

"Yes, I'll be there."

Cowboy frowned. "Wait. What concert?"

"Leah Nachtnebel," I said.

"The ... pianist?" He raised a brow.

"Yup," I confirmed. "McCourt thought it'd be smart for us to show up. Strength in numbers after what went down."

Cowboy's frown deepened. "And nobody invited me? That woman's a ten!"

Rose rolled her eyes. "Maybe that's exactly why nobody asked you. After what happened, we have to look professional, Cowboy, not collect a harassment complaint from Leah Nachtnebel. I'll see you guys at the office."

She turned and strode down the hallway.

"What the hell!" Cowboy called after her. "You think I'm some out-of-control dog? I know how to make a smooth move on a woman! I'm a green flag guy, Rose! *Green!*"

I shook my head. "I'll see you at the office."

As I walked past the victim's apartment, I stopped and stared into its short hallway. Another motherless child. Another innocent woman, gone. Her life snuffed out because of the Night Stalker—a violent rapist whom the courts had let walk free.

Leah was still on my mind, too.

I had to tell her about this. Sooner or later, she'd find out, but the real question was, what were the consequences of all this? We'd agreed to stick with serial killers and let the courts handle the other scum. But where had that gotten us?

The world wasn't just upside down anymore. It was twisted beyond repair. Chaos had become the new baseline, and insanity was its weapon of choice.

And then there was Novak. If he'd been handling the Night Stalker, Terry Patterson would be dead, either strapped to the train tracks or floating face-down in a river. An ankh symbol—Novak's signature—carved neatly beside him.

But was a lunatic killing people on train tracks really a better choice, let alone justifiable?

As I made my way down the hallway, the voice in my head was loud and clear. No matter how hard I tried to drown it out, it kept repeating the same damn thing.

If Leah had killed him, Regina King would still be alive.

CHAPTER TWENTY-THREE

Rose

I tugged at the collar of my suit, trying to get some air. This whole situation felt off. McCourt and I sat in the VIP box next to Luca Domizio. Both of us were here for Leah's Christmas concert. It was the spectacle of the year. Across from us, the biggest names in politics and commerce filled the seats—people like the newly reelected Senator Wheezer, who shot us a hateful glance.

We looked ridiculous, sitting in suits with our badges hanging from chains around our necks. Then there were Luca and McCourt, who exchanged glares like two kids about to fight on the playground.

"Can we at least pocket these damn badges?" I muttered. "Feels stupid wearing them like we're at a crime scene."

McCourt shifted in his seat. "You think I enjoy this? I'd rather be dealing with an active shooter. But orders are orders." He popped a pain pill just as another reporter called his name. We both forced a smile as the camera flash went off, temporarily blinding us.

I glanced at the empty seat beside me—the seat where Richter should've been.

"He'd better get his ass here soon," McCourt grumbled.

"He said he's finishing something at the office. He'll be here," I assured him.

McCourt let out a sharp laugh. "Yeah, he'd better. This? All of this? It's his mess. And they damn well know it."

I leaned forward, intrigued. "You hear anything about the arrest?"

McCourt rolled his eyes. "Kid, I've been doing this for over thirty years."

"So? Spill it."

Silence had hung over the Novak situation ever since the arrest. No firings, no inquiries—nothing.

McCourt leaned back, a smug look crossing his face. "Doesn't matter. If you think we're not gonna pay for this down the line, you're too stupid to wear that badge."

His ability to piss people off was impressive.

"Can you skip the drama and fucking talk?" I asked, my patience thinning.

S. T. ASHMAN

McCourt's eyes flicked toward a reporter approaching us.

"Or else I'll make a scene," I threatened, nodding toward the journalist. "Let's see how your masters like that after all the effort to make the FBI look good tonight."

We both flashed fake smiles for another picture. Once the reporter left, McCourt muttered curses under his breath. "Novak," he finally said.

"What about him?"

"I heard he's the one who saved our asses."

I blinked. "Novak? Why the hell would he do that?" My thoughts started racing. I'd assumed the silence was due to the video evidence we had of the arrest. I thought people were avoiding a scandal. "Is he scared we'll leak the arrest to the press?" I asked.

McCourt snorted. "Scared? Novak? Of what? We don't have shit on him. His lawyers and allies would chew us up and shit us out like a laxative. You ever hear of the Billmart heiress? Killed people driving drunk—fucking twice, that alcoholic cunt. Didn't face a single charge. You think anyone cares about some trailer trash dead girl in a river when the killer's a billionaire funding half the politicians in DC?" He chuckled again, this time with a provocative edge.

I brushed off his insult. "So why did Novak stop us from getting fired?"

McCourt shrugged and popped another pill. "How the hell should I know? Word is, he stopped the formal hearings—or, more likely, a bullet in our heads."

Shit.

I had to talk to Richter and Leah. Novak had something cooking. No way was he protecting us out of kindness. He had a plan, and whatever it was, I wasn't going to like it.

My gaze drifted back to Richter's empty seat. The concert hall was filling up. People were taking their time, chatting.

My eyes wandered over to Luca Domizio. Dressed sharp, champagne in hand, he oozed arrogance. He wasn't watching the crowd. His focus was locked on the stage. I followed his gaze.

And then I saw her.

Leah.

Just a shadow, blending into the backstage darkness near the velvet curtain, but I knew it was her. No doubt about it.

Fuck.

Was she looking up here? At the empty seat where Richter should've been?

I yanked out my phone and dialed Richter's work number. Straight to voicemail. I tried his personal number. Same.

"Where the hell are you?" I muttered, my eyes flicking back to the stage just as Leah's shadow disappeared.

This concert was her olive branch, the chance to get things back on track. If Richter didn't show up, who knows what would happen? The man she'd spared had just gotten out on bail and shot his fiancée.

When I grabbed my burner phone, McCourt sneered at it with obvious disapproval. It rang a few times before I got a generic text: *Can't talk right now. Call you right back.*

"Trouble in paradise?" McCourt smirked.

"Just pop another pill and shut the hell up," I snapped, forcing a grin for the latest journalist to take a picture.

That smile was harder to fake. Something felt off.

But as long as Richter showed up before the curtain dropped and Leah spotted him here, we'd be fine.

No need to panic.

Not yet.

CHAPTER TWENTY-FOUR

Liam

I was wrapping things up at the office while constantly checking my phone, making sure I left on time. The whole floor was dark except for the light spilling from my office. I was the last one left.

But it was the weekend, and Regina King's ex-husband and parents had already hired a lawyer. While I wanted justice for them as much as they did, the focus now was ensuring that everyone understood the FBI had fought tooth and nail against releasing the Night Stalker on bail.

I shut down my computer, grabbed my jacket, and was ready to head out when my personal phone buzzed.

I expected it to be my mom or Josie. But no—Lucy's name flashed on the screen.

"Shit," I muttered, pocketing the phone. I'd told her I'd call when things settled down.

I turned off the light, stepped into the hallway, and started for the stairs. It buzzed again. Lucy.

Pushing the call aside again, I started wondering if it was important. When I'd met her, she hadn't seemed like the pushy type.

The phone rang for a third time as I reached the stairwell.

Lucy.

"Damn it," I grumbled. I hesitated, then answered. "Hello?"

"Liam?" Her voice was so soft, I barely heard her.

"Yeah, hey. Everything okay?"

There was a short pause. "Yeah ... sorry for calling you like this, but I just wanted to say, well, thank you for the other day."

My alarm bells went off. I'd been on this job long enough to hear the weight behind those words. I could feel the crisis hiding in her tone.

I leaned against the wall, feeling the tension building. "Thank me? For what? What's going on?"

She sniffled.

"I'm so sorry to call. I just didn't have anyone else." She paused. "No. This is unfair to you, I'm sorry I ca—"

"It's fine, Lucy. Really," I said quickly before she hung up. "What's going on?"

A long silence hung between us before she spoke, her voice cracking. "My mom ... she passed. The funeral was today. She was the only person left in my life."

"I'm ... so sorry."

"No, don't be. I know what she did to your family. The woman who had an affair with a married man. She knew all about you and your mom. She kept trying to get your dad to leave. Maybe that's why I was the only person at her funeral today. But it still hurts, you know?"

"Of course it does." I swallowed hard. "I mean, I didn't know her, but my dad ... he must have seen something special in her to have an—"

My voice trailed off. For some reason, I couldn't finish. A heavy silence followed.

"Where are you?" I finally asked.

"It doesn't matter. I just wanted to say thank you for being kind to me."

"Lucy, whatever you're feeling now, it can get better."

Another heavy pause.

"Did you know you have a niece?" I said out of the blue. "Her name is Josie. She's amazing. You two would get along."

Lucy's laugh was bitter. "Funny, isn't it? You think the world's this messed-up place, and then you look in a new direction and see true kindness. That direction was you, Liam. I'm sorry for everything my mom did to your family. God. My brother. My mom. Me. Maybe it's fair that a family that wasn't ever supposed to exist doesn't anymore. Thank you, Liam. I hope life will treat you kinder soon. You really deserve it."

"Lucy, wait—"

The line clicked dead.

My heart pounded as cold sweat slicked my forehead. I tried calling her back, but it went straight to voicemail.

"Fuck!"

I sprinted back to my office and flicked the computer on. Each second it took to load felt like a lifetime. Finally, I was able to do a quick search on her. As soon as her address popped up, I called 911.

"There's a possible suicide attempt at twenty-three Gulp Street," I said into the phone as I left my office. "Lucy Folbs. Send an ambulance now."

I hung up and leaped to the stairs, hitting the garage in record time.

"Please, God, please."

I jumped into my car just as my phone buzzed. It was Rose. Shit. The concert. But this was more important.

I ignored the call, turned on the siren, and sped out of the garage. Another call from Rose. I quickly shot back a standard text: "Can't talk right now. Call you right back." Then I dialed Lucy again.

Nothing.

"Goddamn it, Lucy!" I shouted to no one as I floored it, racing against time.

I slammed my hand against the steering wheel, frustration boiling over. This was exactly the kind of drama I didn't need. And yet, maybe it wouldn't have happened if I'd let Lucy into my life when she'd asked.

I grabbed my phone and called the police again to make sure they were on it. Relief hit when the dispatcher confirmed a unit was on the way.

Each turn felt like slow motion. My mind spun, and questions pounded in my brain. Was any of this real? Leah, Lucy, Carl Carr?

By the time I pulled up to the scene, there was just one cop car. The officer inside was likely finishing up paperwork. I screeched to a halt in front of him, then practically jumped out of the car before it had fully stopped.

"Where's the ambulance?" I yelled, rushing toward his open window.

The officer glanced at my car, its flashing lights still on, then back at me. "Already on the way to the hospital," he said calmly.

"Was she alive?"

"Yes."

I froze. My head tilted back, and I stared up at the cloudy night sky. The weight lifted off my chest.

Thank God.

I could breathe again. The tightness in my lungs was finally releasing.

"Which hospital?"

"I think they said Hyde Park General," the officer said.

"Thanks."

I didn't waste another second, just dove back into my car and punched the hospital into the GPS. The concert had probably already started, so there was no point in calling to interrupt it.

I'd wait until it was over and apologize to Leah. She'd understand. She had to.

This was more important right now.

CHAPTER TWENTY-FIVE

Leah

The final notes of my improvisation on *O Come All Ye Faithful* echoed through the sold-out concert hall. I'd chosen a few classic Christmas pieces for tonight's crowd, adding my own signature touch, and the crowd's reaction didn't disappoint. The applause thundered. Chants and whistles filled the room. People wiped tears from their eyes, and the ovation lasted longer than any I could remember. Tonight wasn't just a performance—it was my return after the shooting.

As I stood under the spotlight, bowing to the crowd, my eyes drifted to the seats reserved for Rose, McCourt, and Richter. Rose and McCourt were there, but Richter's seat remained empty.

A pang of disappointment hit me. Why wasn't he here? I caught myself overthinking it, telling myself it didn't matter. But it did. It was ridiculous how much it bothered me.

After forcing a few more bows and smiles, I left the stage and walked quickly toward my artist's suite.

After everything that had happened, tonight was supposed to be a symbol for the three of us—a reaffirmation of our work and how we had to adapt to keep going. The plan was to talk in my dressing room right after the concert.

"Leah, Senator Wheezer and the mayor want to congratulate you in person," Crystal said, hurrying after me as I strode down the hallway.

Of course Wheezer did. He had no idea about my connection to the arrest. Novak had kept quiet—for reasons I still didn't understand.

"I'm tired. Tell them another time," I said, my tone final.

Crystal knew better than to argue. She nodded, slipping away.

I entered my dressing room and closed the door behind me. My eyes went to the flip phone on my golden vanity. Any messages from Richter? I grabbed it and checked.

Nothing.

Then a soft knock came at the door.

"Crystal, I said I'm tired," I repeated.

"I ... I know," she stammered through the door. "But there's a man. He insists that you want to see him."

Richter?

I rose quickly and made my way to the door. When I opened it, I found a confused Crystal—and a face I recognized: Jan Novak's driver. He wore a crisp, dark suit with a neatly pressed white shirt. His face was lined, with thinning gray hair combed back, and a quiet, stoic expression.

My eyes narrowed. "Where is he?"

"Waiting for you outside," the driver answered.

I glanced at the flip phone on my makeup table, then back at the driver. Novak had been silent for weeks. In fact, he'd never made direct contact before. But considering he held more cards than we did, hearing him out seemed wise.

I grabbed my coat from the hanger by the door and slipped into it. "Let's go," I said, brushing past Crystal, who stood frozen in confusion.

The driver, dressed in a crisp suit and cap, led me out the back door of the concert hall and into a quiet alley. Parked there was a sleek Maybach, its polished surface gleaming under the streetlights.

The driver opened the back door, and there he was: Jan Novak, dressed casually in jeans and a wool sweater. Beside him lay a neatly folded pile of women's clothes: jeans, a sweater, and boots, all looking eerily similar to his outfit.

I hesitated, surprised by his appearance, but then regained my composure. "I take it you didn't attend the concert," I said as I stepped closer to the car.

"No," Novak replied smoothly. "When I told you I don't care for classical music, I meant it."

"Fine by me," I muttered.

But something made me pause.

I turned once more, looking back at the concert hall's door. I was half-hoping, half-expecting to see Richter burst through, to come and stop this. Stop me from walking into something dark, something inevitable.

But the door stayed shut.

I nodded and stepped into the Maybach. The door closed behind me with a weighty thud as if sealing a new chapter in my life.

"So," I asked, meeting Novak's gaze, "where to?"

A confident smile played on his lips. "I've got a surprise for you."

"I don't care for surprises."

"Oh, you'll care for this one. Believe me."

CHAPTER TWENTY-SIX

Liam

I rushed up the concert hall's stairs, dodging the few remaining elegantly dressed attendees. Almost everyone had left.

When I reached the balcony, I found Rose. McCourt was gone.

My eyes scanned the empty hall, then flicked back to Rose.

She gave me an accusatory look. "Where the hell were you?" she demanded as she followed me into the hallway and down the stairs toward the backstage area.

"Busy," I said, my voice heavy with exhaustion as I tried to shake off the lingering memory of the night's events.

I tugged at the backstage door. Locked. But then a violinist stepped out, and I quickly flashed my badge, slipping through without a word.

"Richter!" Rose called after me, struggling to keep pace as I charged ahead.

When I noticed she had stopped, I turned.

She approached slowly, arms crossed. "Where were you? McCourt was unbearable, and Leah wasn't happy you didn't show."

"I know," I muttered, taking a deep breath. My eyes met hers briefly before they dropped to the floor. "It was my sister."

"The one in college?" Rose asked, her face softening.

I shook my head. "It's complicated. But anyway. My sister. She ... she tried to kill herself."

Shock spread across Rose's face. "What? When?"

"Right before the concert. She called me to say goodbye."

She blinked slowly, the weight of the words sinking in. "Jesus."

"Yeah."

"Is she okay?" she asked quietly.

"She's alive," I replied. "I went to the hospital. But she said she didn't want to see me. I'll try again tomorrow with Josie."

Rose remained silent.

"Come on," I said, motioning toward Leah's room. "Let's talk to her so I can go home. I'm really fucking tired."

"Of course," Rose said just as Crystal appeared. I would have recognized her red hair and glasses from a mile away.

"Agent Richter!" Crystal greeted me with a huge smile, a light blush coloring her cheeks.

Rose rolled her eyes.

"Good to see you, Crystal," I said, forcing a polite smile.

"What are you doing here?" she asked.

"The FBI director wanted us to personally thank Ms. Nachtnebel for hosting us tonight," I explained.

"That's sweet of you," Crystal said, "but she's already left."

"Left? Already?" I asked. Rose and I exchanged glances. Leah usually remained after concerts, making sure no fans lingered for autographs or photos. "Where did she go?"

Crystal shrugged. "Some limo driver picked her up right after the concert. She seemed to know him. They left together."

My stomach twisted. I exchanged another glance with Rose.

"Thank you," I said, forcing a smile at Crystal before turning to walk with Rose toward the entrance hall.

Once Crystal was out of sight, Rose stepped in closer. She kept her voice low. "Please tell me it's not who I think it is."

I cursed under my breath and pulled out my phone. It rang, but Leah didn't pick up.

"Nothing," I muttered, hanging up.

Rose let out a sharp breath. "We could head back to the office, track the limo with traffic cameras."

I shook my head. "Won't get us far. He's probably taken her out of Boston by now."

Her forehead creased with worry. "He won't hurt her, right?"

I hesitated. "I don't think so."

Murder didn't seem like Novak's move when it came to Leah, at least not tonight. Picking her up with his driver in front of witnesses felt too bold, too sloppy. He could've tried to kill her quietly a dozen times already. She was safe—for now.

Rose nodded slowly, absorbing my logic. "So what now?"

"As much as I hate it, all we can do is wait."

She exhaled through her nose, then tried a smile. "Get some rest. You need it. I'll let you know if I hear anything."

"I'll do the same."

She leaned in, smirking. "Who knows? Maybe we'll find Novak face down in a river tomorrow. If anyone can pull it off, it's her."

I let out a dark chuckle. As messed up as it sounded, it would make things easier. "Don't give her ideas," I muttered.

Rose threw me an innocent look, her grin not fading. She placed a hand on my shoulder. "Let me know if you need anything."

I nodded and watched her walk away.

Today had been a shitshow, like most days since Harris had been killed in those woods over a year ago. But if this was my life now, the only thing I could do was keep moving forward—*falling* forward was more like it—until things got better. Or until my head was next on the railroad tracks.

CHAPTER TWENTY-SEVEN

Leah

We hit Route 1 North and left Boston behind. The car had been mostly quiet. I had questions, of course, but Novak answered only when he wanted, so I remained quiet.

"You're not scared?" he asked as I stared out the window, watching the closed businesses blur by.

"No."

He grinned. "I expected a million questions by now."

"Why bother? You seem to talk when it suits you."

Silence fell over the dark limo until he shifted in his seat. "Fair enough. I feel chatty now. Ask away."

I turned to face him, doubt creeping into my expression.

"I mean it," he said, catching the look. "Ask whatever you want. I'll answer truthfully now that the secret's out."

"Anything?"

He nodded. "Except one question."

"What's that?" My brow furrowed.

His hand tightened briefly around an object in his hand. It was the first crack I'd seen in his confident facade since I'd known him. He shoved the object into his jeans pocket. "I won't talk about the meaning of the tracks or the ankh. They're connected."

Just like that, he'd admitted he was the Train Track Killer. I already knew that, of course, but it was strange to hear the confirmation this way.

"All right," I said, straightening up. "How long have you been entertaining your ... hobby?"

He frowned, thinking. "About fifteen years now."

Longer than I expected.

"How did it start? Your first murder?"

"I don't call it murder, but fine. Let's not argue over labels." He took a deep breath. "Back then, I'd just secured a big contract with the largest home security company in the world. It was the investment I needed to make my company the largest cloud storage firm in the nation. But soon after that, people at Obligato started reporting crimes caught on the security camera footage we stored on our cloud. The company that rented the storage didn't want to report them after we reported the incidents. They were afraid it'd hurt business. Lead to the loss of customers. People wanted protection from other people's crimes but not their own. So they stayed quiet."

"Of course they did. The almighty dollar is hardly a secret."

He nodded. "See no evil, hear no evil. As long as the cash comes in."

"But not you."

He shook his head. "No. Not me. At first, I played along. Couldn't afford to lose the contract. Money talks, not ethics and fuzzy feelings. But then we contracted the biggest online storage provider in the nation. They became a subcontractor under us to cut costs. The cloud is expensive. Soon after that, one of my IT techs flagged a violent rape at a man's home. The man had recorded it and stored it on his computer, which synced its data with online storage on our cloud. We'd seen bad things before, but this one..." Novak's face darkened, disgust and anger mixing in his expression. "This man raped a woman he'd paid for from a sex trafficking ring. And he did it ... with a knife. Somehow, the poor thing lived for over an hour, enduring this horror over and over again. Then she finally died. I was never so relieved to see somebody die."

I narrowed my eyes at Jan, watching him relive the memory. He looked distant, disgusted, but mostly angry.

"I paid the guy a visit at night. Shot him straight in the head while he slept. It was so easy. I knew everything about him—his routine, where he ate, even the church he went to, singing songs to Jesus before he went home to rape and kill women." Jan shrugged. "I felt nothing but justice as he lay there, motionless in a pool of blood. My only regret was that he left this world too quickly. Without pain."

Was that why he'd chosen the train tracks? To squeeze out every ounce of fear? To inflict upon them the horror of being tied down and staring at an oncoming train? But something told me there was more to the tracks than that.

"I've always had this feeling of disgust," he continued, "this rage toward people who do wrong." He balled a fist. "Something in my childhood burned it into me, like branding cattle. You must feel it too, right? This thirst for justice. Your work's close to mine."

I thought back to my first kill: a man who'd plowed his car through a crowd to avoid jail, taking innocent lives with him. The satisfaction I'd felt driving that shard of glass into his neck was undeniable. The peace his family would feel once the tears dried and they realized they were finally free.

We left the highway, and the road darkened as we turned onto a more rural stretch. We had to be about an hour north of Boston. Houses became sparse, blending with farmland.

"I understand why you use men like Patel to do the dirty work," I said. "If they get shot, no loss. Genius move. But what about Kirby? He wasn't a monster. He was the sad result of a corrupt and failing system. Why groom him for something so dangerous? That bomb could've killed innocent people."

"Kirby was a troubled soul. When I first noticed him, he was already planning a mass shooting."

"Before you met him?" I raised an eyebrow.

Jan nodded. "My software flagged his texts to a friend about shooting up a mall. Anything suspicious—whether it's a message, phone call, or video—gets flagged and sent directly to me."

"You go through all that? For the entire nation? That's impossible."

"I work day and night, but even then, I barely make a dent. The darkness in this world is beyond imagination."

I couldn't help but feel a strange sense of admiration. The cold-blooded monster I'd always thought Jan Novak to be didn't exist. The more I saw of him, the more the puzzle pieces fell into place. They revealed an operation far beyond anything I could've imagined.

"So you redirected Kirby's anger into a bomb attack?"

Jan's jaw clenched. "Not at first. When I found Kirby, he was ready to leave this world in all the wrong ways. But I gave him purpose. Showed him glimpses of what the world could be."

"You fed him targets from your system?" I asked.

"I did. Every one of those targets deserved it in one way or another. And the more people Kirby stabbed, the more he believed in the mission. Like he forgave himself for the terrible things he'd done in the name of our government. He started using his skills to cleanse the world, like something out of an action movie."

"And the bomb attack?"

"It was planned for a meeting of high-profile pedophiles on a private yacht docked near Boston. All of them are tied to human trafficking. Names you'd never hear in that context but faces you'd recognize from TV and government. Kirby was willing to sacrifice himself for something that meaningful."

For a moment, it felt like Richter and I were the villains, stopping Kirby from wiping out those predators. But then...

"Nice story," I said, locking eyes with Jan. "But Kirby was a ticking time bomb himself. He didn't need a mission. He needed therapy. A chance to rebuild his life. You could've stopped the shooting and gotten him committed to a psychiatric hospital. Instead, you sent him on a suicide mission. Trapped him in the hell he was trying to escape."

"He volunteered. It was his idea," Jan shot back.

"And yet, he shot Agent Rose when she confronted him. Almost killed Richter and me too. You can justify my death, sure, but Rose and Richter? They're not like Anna, Carr, or Mauser. They're nothing like you and me."

Jan's eyes narrowed, and a flicker of betrayal crossed his face. Of course he wouldn't agree. A few moral arguments meant nothing when his methods were so efficient, so effective.

"Fighting fire with fire only makes the flames bigger," I said. "What other outcome is there?"

"Then how do you exist?" he asked as the car pulled into a dark, empty parking lot. He turned away, looking out the window. "Don't you fight fire with fire, Leah? You don't seem to mind the scorched earth you've left behind so far. Why question mine?"

I reached for the pile of clothes next to him. "I assume these are for me?"

He stayed silent as, unfazed, I slipped out of my concert dress and into the jeans and sweater. Then I stepped out of the car and into the cold night air. Whatever he wanted to show me, I knew it was waiting somewhere in those dark woods.

"The difference between my scorched path and yours," I said, turning to face him, "is that what I burn to ash never deserved to exist in this world. You, on the other hand, are a wildfire—swallowing everything in your path without mercy."

I caught myself speaking like Richter. Did Jan notice? I never felt remorse for people like Anna or Kirby. But I understood the logic behind Richter's doubts, and I defended them like they were my own.

"What if Kirby's bomb had killed the innocent waitress on that yacht, just trying to make a paycheck while serving rich pedophiles? How do you justify that?" I asked.

Jan Novak got out of the car. His flashlight cut through the dark as we stepped onto a narrow, overgrown trail. The path was rough. Tangled roots and damp leaves made it barely visible under the beam's flicker as we moved deeper into the woods.

"Some things can't be justified," he said, "but they're sacrifices for the greater war. Like friendly fire between allies. Shooting down a helicopter because you thought it was the enemy. A mistake, sure. But do you stop the war on terror over one misstep? Or is the greater good too important to count every single life?"

"I'm familiar with the Doctrine of Double Effect," I said. "Allowing harm as long as it's an unintended consequence of achieving a good outcome, as long as the harm isn't the goal and the good outweighs the bad."

"I live by it. So do you, even if Agent Richter tries to pull you away from this destiny."

The trees and brush closed in around us. The night was dense and silent. Not a single house was in sight. Rocks and branches crunched under our boots as we passed several "Private Property" signs.

"You're wrong about Richter," I said firmly. "And the doctrine is flawed because it lets people justify morally questionable actions just because they claim good intentions. The harm is the same, whether it's deliberate or not. Richter and I live by a much simpler doctrine: the one where monsters are taken out, no innocents harmed. Smaller-scale justice. But even a bathtub fills if the drops keep coming."

Jan stopped and looked at me. His flashlight pointed at the leaf-covered ground. "And who's going to tell that to Regina King?"

My eyes widened. "Regina King?"

"Yes. Or her son," Jan continued, "who'll never see his mother again, except for the image of when he found her? Brains splattered across the bed every time he closes his eyes."

I fell silent, feeling the icy sting of betrayal creep into my chest.

"What?" Jan asked, feigning surprise. "Richter didn't tell you that the Night Stalker shot his fiancée yesterday? He got out on bail, courtesy of the justice system we're all supposed to trust. Then he shot her hours later."

My fists clenched, nails digging into my palms. Was this true? Why hadn't Richter told me right away? Was he afraid of the rage he knew I'd feel, the justice I craved? Was that why he hadn't shown up to my concert?

Was I shaking? Surely, it was just the cold.

"How much longer will you lie to yourself?" Jan pressed. "This hope that you and Richter are meant to be? I get it—creatures of the dark crave the light. But night is night, and day is day. You can't change that."

I started walking again, ignoring him. If Jan thought he could bring me out here and manipulate me like he'd done with Kirby, Patel, and Carr, he was dead wrong. I lived by my own choices. My thoughts, my reasoning—

they were mine, not shaped by anyone's mind games, not even someone as cunning as Jan Novak.

We walked in silence for another twenty minutes or so until we reached a small, decaying wooden hut in a clearing. Moonlight bathed the rotting boards, highlighting the two broken steps leading to the porch.

"What's this?" I asked.

"My surprise, of course," Jan replied with a smile. "Come on, you'll like it."

I followed as he stepped over the crumbling stairs and onto the porch. Without hesitation, he moved straight to the door, which was locked with heavy chains. One by one, he unlocked them with a set of keys. The chains clattered to the floor.

He pushed the door open and disappeared inside.

I froze.

That hut.

Something told me that whatever was inside could change my life forever.

Instinctively, I glanced back at the trail, half hoping—no, almost expecting—that Richter would appear, grab my arm, and pull me back to his world.

But why was I putting so much hope in him?

I'd always been alone. From my first breath to this one, standing on this rotting porch. No one was forcing me to stay. I could turn around, walk away, and return to my own mission, my own sense of justice.

And yet, as if something beyond my control was pushing me, I stepped inside.

The stench of feces and mold closed in around me.

Jan's flashlight swept across the room. It revealed a row of people tied to chairs, their mouths taped shut. Six men and one woman. Their clothes were dirty, some torn, and the stench of sweat and piss hung heavy in the air. The horror in their wide, pleading eyes was unmistakable. Their bodies trembled as they struggled against the ropes. They moaned and shifted in their chairs. But I didn't flinch as I met their gazes. Their fear sank into the darkness that already lived within me.

I felt nothing for them. Nothing.

"Remember that chat on the dark web? The one the Night Stalker held so dear?" Jan asked, approaching an older, bald man who was bleeding from the forehead. He wore cargo pants and work boots. A badge identified him as a school janitor. "This is the one who liked to brag about the baby porn."

Jan's eyes gleamed as he pointed to the next man. "And him? He's the one who said he had a little girl at home whom he did things to at night, things his wife doesn't know about."

The skinny man was in his thirties and had a long, scraggly beard. He blinked rapidly and shook his head, denying everything with an almost believable enthusiasm.

"They're all here, the men from the chat. Coordinating everything was a bit interesting, as we had to retrieve these people from all across the US, but as always, where there's a wallet, there's a way. Do you want me to introduce them all to you?"

I shook my head. My eyes landed on the woman all the way to the left.

"And her?" I asked. "What about her?"

Jan nodded. "Ah, yes. Carole Traylor. She helped the cartel set up fake photo shoots for kids. She pretended to be a photographer and told the parents to leave so the kids could act 'more natural.' When the parents came back, they'd find an empty room. Kids gone, sold into human trafficking."

I narrowed my eyes at the woman. Her bleached-blonde hair was greasy and unkempt. She rocked back and forth as she watched us, tears streaming down her face, smearing her mascara into dark streaks like shadows of guilt. She was begging for her life, trying to scream through the tape. For a moment, I saw Nathalie again—when I'd found her in Carl Carr's basement. But then I remembered the innocent horror in Nathalie's eyes—that of a victim. Carole's eyes lacked the same innocence.

Jan swung the flashlight to the corner of the room, where red canisters of gasoline glistened in the beam.

I didn't need to ask questions. It was obvious.

Novak grabbed the first canister and began pouring gas over the woman. Then he moved to the old man beside her.

I just stood there. Silent. Watching.

The man's T-shirt read "Spread the Love."

"Him, I actually know," Jan said, grabbing another canister and dousing a man in silk pajamas. "From a fundraiser. He works in Senator Wheezer's office. Small world, huh?"

The man thrashed in his chair, desperate, but the ropes held him tight.

The room reeked of gasoline as Jan emptied several canisters over the group, soaking them. Then he grabbed one more and walked over to me. "You ready?" he asked. Unfazed. Cool. Almost jolly.

I stood there a moment longer, then nodded and stepped outside.

Jan followed, trailing gasoline out of the hut, down the steps, and toward me.

I stopped about thirty feet from the hut.

We stood together in silence, listening to the branches swaying in the wind, an owl hooting somewhere in the distance—and, of course, the muffled screams coming from the hut.

I should've run. Maybe even killed Jan with the gun I'd slipped from my coat and into my back jeans hip trim. But aside from knowing I wouldn't stand a chance in a physical fight if he grabbed my wrist in time, I realized I didn't want to run.

I didn't want to stop this.

The rage over Regina King's death at the hands of the Night Stalker was still too raw. I felt responsible. In some way, I even blamed Richter. It was his voice in my head that had stopped me from killing the Night Stalker when I'd had the chance.

My leg twitched as if some part of me was still telling me to run. To return to the moral compass I used to follow. The one that Richter carried for me like a torch in the dark. To kill monsters. Serial killers. Not just people who did horrific things.

There was a difference, wasn't there?

At least, according to Richter.

And yet...

My eyes locked on the silver lighter that Jan had pulled from his pocket and was holding in front of me. His hand was steady, waiting. For a moment, I stared at the lighter. Then I grabbed it and flicked it open. The small flame danced in the wind. Without another second of hesitation, I dropped it onto the gasoline trail.

In seconds, the flames ignited and raced toward the hut. They crept inside and onto their targets. The muffled screams grew louder as fire burst through the windows, then up through the roof. Raging flames swallowed the house in a violent blaze that ascended to the sky.

It was almost incredible how long it took for the screams to die down.

And still, we waited. Watching. Until Jan pulled out a pocketknife and started carving the ankh symbol into a nearby tree.

I watched, fear lingering in the back of my mind.

Richter.

His name tore through my mind, and a sharp sting of loss stabbed deep into my chest. I hurt. Real pain. Shocked by the intensity of the emotion, I almost checked for a blade.

But then that familiar feeling washed over me—the same twisted satisfaction I felt when I killed killers. And in that moment, I realized my dark prophecy had at last come true.

To be fair, it had probably been a hopeless task from the start. And I'd just been too sentimental to see it. Like the little girl in the library all those years back, hoping she'd feel something one day.

In the end, Richter had failed to save me.

I'd become the monster I'd always been.

CHAPTER TWENTY-EIGHT

Liam

I sat in my office, empty eyes fixed on the flip phone in my hand. It had been a week since the concert, and after four messages and several calls, Leah still hadn't gotten back to me.

When I heard a knock at the open door, I shoved the phone into my pocket.

"Got a minute?" Rose asked, stepping through the door. The way she quietly shut it behind her told me nothing good was coming.

She sat across from me and dropped several manila folders on the desk.

"Violent Crimes Unit got a call a few days ago about those bodies in the woods. Remember?"

"Yeah. A hiker and his dog got lost in Bear Brooke State Park and found an old hut that had burned to the ground. Six men, one woman inside. Our Violent Gang force supervisor thinks it was arson." We were the largest FBI office around, so my desk was littered with crimes from all over New Hampshire, Maine, and Massachusetts.

"Yes. Ellis also thinks the La Mano Roja cartel is behind it," Rose said, flipping open a folder.

"Burning snitches and people in debt is their calling card," I said. "Last year, we found five burnt immigrants in that factory in Boston."

Rose nodded. "Well, I was just wrapping up a meeting about the incident at Bear Brooke State Park with Ellis down at Violent Crimes when the DNA results of the victims came in."

I leaned back in my chair, my eyes narrowing at the folders. My gut tightened. I hoped her next words wouldn't confirm what I was now thinking.

"The problem is..." she continued, flipping open one of the folders. A mugshot of a bleached-blonde woman in her twenties stared back at me next to a charred pile of what might've been a living body at some point. "This one. Carole Traylor. She has a history of human trafficking."

I tensed. It was cartel-related, so there was still a chance it wasn't what I feared.

"Cartel crime," I said, almost convincing myself.

Rose opened another folder, revealing a bearded man in his thirties. "Then there's this guy, Roger Miller. Registered sex offender from Nebraska."

I stared at the images, feeling the hope drain out of me. My tie suddenly felt tighter. "What about the others?" I asked.

She opened another folder. "Three are still unidentified, but this one? Daniel Justling. He's got several violent rape charges. All of the victims were minors." Rose looked at me, her eyes sharp. "Three victims with criminal records. Burned alive in the middle of the largest state park in New Hampshire, in a hut nobody even knew existed. What I need to hear from you now is"—her voice dropped—that you've heard from Leah. That everything between you two is fine, and this is just a cartel hit. That these victims having a record is just a coincidence."

Silence hung between us. I leaned back, staring at the folders. "I can't," I muttered, the words slipping out before I could stop them.

"Yeah," Rose said. "That's what I thought."

I leaned over the table and flipped open the other three folders. Charred bodies labeled "John Doe #1," "#2," and "#3" stared back at me.

"We don't know who they are yet?" I asked.

Rose shook her head. "Our forensic odontologist and anthropologist are on it."

I kept my eyes on the photos. The images almost carried the stench of burnt flesh.

"We should have their names soon," she added. "The new databases should help speed that up, thanks to the cloud."

I shot her a look, my brow furrowing.

"So let me just state the obvious," Rose said, her voice lower. "I'm guessing these other three bodies have a record too or some sick hobby nobody knows about yet. Child porn, murders, rapes, who the fuck knows? But you know where I'm going with this, right?"

Of course I did. This had emerged shortly after Jan Novak had picked up Leah from a concert.

Rose pointed at the folders. "I think they did this. Together."

I leaned back, my gaze still fixed on the pictures. "Anyone at Violent Gang suspect anything out of the ordinary?"

"No. Everyone's convinced it's La Mano Roja. Even if all the victims have skeletons in their closets, it still fits the cartel's signature. Human trafficking and burning people alive are classic La Mano Roja. Like they did in Boston last year. And with the buses of immigrants arriving in the city from the south..."

I nodded slowly.

"So?" Rose raised an eyebrow. "Do you want me to do anything about all of this?"

I thought about it for a moment. "Like what?"

Rose threw her hands up and leaned in closer. "I don't know, Richter! Why are you asking me?" She dropped her voice even further. "This isn't what I signed up for."

"So what do you suggest?" I asked. "Opening an investigation on Novak and Leah?"

"On what grounds? We've got no evidence whatsoever. We'd go down. You and me. People would think we're crazy. Taking Novak down without Leah would be harder than taking down the president. And Domizio might kill us the moment he saw us turn on her." She took a deep breath as if bracing herself for what she was about to say. "So why even bother? I mean, do you even think what they're doing is that bad?"

I opened my mouth, then shut it again. I didn't know what to say. I wasn't even sure where I stood anymore. Should I care that they'd burned some perverts who'd molested kids? Did anyone?

"If I'm honest," Rose whispered, her eyes dropping to the folder. "I don't feel bad for any of them. Not even the woman. Her record ... she got only four years for helping traffic kids because there were only witness statements and no hard evidence. When she was arrested, no kids were found at her residence. She probably went right back to it after she got out. Just look at her assets. The Porsche. The house. All cash-bought. So if you ask me"— Rose looked up at me, her eyes glinting—"let Leah and Novak do their thing. Like some twisted couple from hell. And you and I ... we go back to being agents, ignoring the occasional weird cases with their signatures all over them. Nobody will question a thing. They don't know what we know."

I just listened, her words pulling me in like a cobra swaying to the movements of a flute.

"We're in pretty deep, Richter. But if there was ever a time for us to stop this, it's now. I'm ready to be a real FBI agent again. Get the bad guys. With what we've got here at the bureau." She leaned back in her chair, her gaze still locked on mine. "Let's be the good guys again."

Maybe Rose was right.

And maybe Leah was right too.

Maybe we could exist with similar missions but in different ways.

Maybe I'd been riding that high horse for too long, looking down with my morals like some wannabe saint. Regina King had changed everything for me. We'd left it to the system, and now she was dead. I had no doubt that she'd still be alive if Leah had killed the Night Stalker when she'd had the chance. And God knows how many kids had been spared now that these sick bastards were reduced to ashes.

But I couldn't just move on, pretending nothing had happened. Who knew what Novak had told Leah, what methods he'd used to pull her into this mess? She'd trusted me, and I wasn't the kind of man to let her down. Especially not after she'd saved my life. I'd stop by her house as many times as it took until I got the chance to talk to her.

Slowly, I nodded, then closed the manila folders like they weighed a ton. The moment they snapped shut, the temperature in the room seemed to drop back to normal.

"You're the Special Agent in Charge of the Boston FBI," Rose said.

She wasn't wrong. I spent most of my time with the BAU and trusted my unit supervisors to run things their way without my assistance. But I was in charge, after all.

"You could keep me in Violent Gang a little longer, just to make sure everything stays quiet around this case," she added. "They could use the help."

"We could too, with Heather on maternity leave." God bless her. She was having another baby, and she was greatly missed.

"Violent has Higgins and Moore out on long-term disability. Higgins got shot on the last mission, and Moore had a stroke at a barbecue."

I knew all that. We were short on agents everywhere right now, but Violent Gang was definitely feeling the blow harder.

"Yeah," I said. "You might be right. Stay there for a bit."

She nodded, then stood, leaving the folders on my desk. As she reached the door, she paused. "One more thing," she said before turning back. "Cowboy met with Carl Carr's mother."

I stiffened. "He fucking what?"

"I heard him talking to Martin about it. He's got this whole theory about Carl Carr being a serial killer."

I let out a loud, annoyed breath. "For Christ's sake."

"Martin didn't bite. Told him to drop the crap and focus on the job. But you remember what happened the last time an FBI agent went rogue chasing a serial killer nobody else believed in."

Of course I did. Back then, I was Cowboy, and Larsen ... he was sitting right where I was now. The sense of déjà vu was eerie. "Shit," I said. "I'll think of something. In the meantime, can you babysit him for a bit?"

Rose rolled her eyes.

"Take him to Violent Crimes. Partner up with him on BAU cases," I said.

"Oh, come on. Like cop partners?" Rose protested.

"Yep, like cop—"

The door flew open without a knock, and Cowboy stuck his head in.

"...partners," I finished.

"Did I hear 'partners'?" Cowboy asked.

"Jesus Christ, ever hear of knocking?" I asked.

Cowboy grinned and knocked on the wide-open door.

I sighed. "What do you need, Cowboy?"

"Oh, yeah." He shuffled some papers in his hands. "Remember Carl Carr?"

Rose and I exchanged glances.

"Good God, Cowboy, no, no, no," I said. "I don't have time for this. From what I heard, Carr's gone. Ran off or something."

"Yeah, that's what his mother told me, but something doesn't add up. Ever since you told me to check the traffic cameras on his red truck, I've had a weird feeling about him."

"Cowboy..." I started.

"And now look at this." He fumbled with the papers. "His truck was parked near the pianist's concert hall, and then near her house, multiple times over two weeks, right after Nathalie disappeared."

"Cowboy," I said again, firmer this time, more aggravated.

"We've got it all on camera. A guy like him? Into classical music? Nah. I think he did something to Nathalie that she won't admit. Too scared to tell us. And now he might be planning to kidnap—"

"McCourt!" I snapped, my voice echoing around the room.

Rose shot me a sharp, scolding look. Cowboy froze, his eyes wide.

But this had to stop. Now.

"I just heard you went to Carl Carr's mother despite me telling you to stay away. Is that true?" Anger edged my voice.

Cowboy nodded.

"And now you're here, showing me days of research on something I told you to drop. Is there really no work to be done in the BAU besides chasing a guy who pays for *consensual* sex? No killers? No rapists? Did the world suddenly turn into all love and gummy bears while I wasn't paying attention?"

The silence was heavy, dead serious. Cowboy cleared his throat. "No, sir. It didn't."

"So there *is* actual work to be done at the BAU, then? Work that your coworkers have been doing for you while you're off on a side quest like this is fucking FBI Zelda Two Point Oh? Regina's family is suing the state, the DA is trying to blame our reports for their failure to keep him in, we've got a guy out there who might be imitating the Night Stalker, Martin just told me about two women found dead in a month, both in doll wigs, and you haven't lifted a finger for any of it?"

I glared. I wanted him to feel my anger.

"Because you want to track down a man who hasn't been charged with a single crime, for the disappearance of a woman we *found*? A woman who told us she ran off with a guy?"

Cowboy's face fell. His eyes were wide, embarrassed, full of doubt. And the worst part? Deep down, I knew he was right. He just wasn't allowed to be.

"I'm ... I'm sorry, sir."

I took a deep breath, trying to steady myself. I saw flashes of Larsen yelling at me for prying into Leah Nachtnebel. Right here, in this same damn chair. Only back then, she was the bad guy, and I was the good guy. Right?

"Good," I said, keeping my voice calm. "You'll work on cases with Rose for a bit."

"You mean supervised like some kid?" Cowboy protested. However, when he saw the shock on my face, he backed down. His gaze dropped and shifted to Rose as if he were a scolded kid ready to leave the principal's office.

"Anything else, sir?" Rose asked.

"No." I felt like a piece of shit, but I needed him to stop. If anything, chasing Leah now was dangerous, especially with Novak involved.

Rose nodded. "All right. We'll talk to the police about the two dead women with the wigs, then see if Violent Crimes needs help with anything."

"No," I said, stopping them. It was better to keep Cowboy away from that crime scene for a while. I had no idea how active he'd been behind the scenes. "Focus on the victims with the wigs. Martin's handling the new serial rapist. We need all hands at the BAU."

If Leah and Novak were working together, we'd have to switch back to our old investigation tactics. Hopefully, they were smart enough to avoid active FBI cases. God knows there were enough other bad people out there for them to hunt—people whom no one would miss.

"Yes, sir," Rose said.

Cowboy nodded, and they both left.

I watched them go, shaking my head. How the hell had Larsen managed this for so many years without anyone finding out?

I grabbed the folder on the burnt woman and opened it. Her mugshot was rough. She looked wrecked.

With a forceful snap, I shut it again.

Maybe it was time to go back to normal, to let Leah and Novak do their thing. But first, I had to talk to her. The decision to break things off wasn't mine—it was hers. And I wasn't ready to let her go. The nagging emptiness in my chest made that painfully clear.

CHAPTER TWENTY-NINE

Rose

It had been almost two weeks since Cowboy and I had started working together—or, more like, since I'd started babysitting him. Things almost felt normal again. The world was still fucked up, and I was still part of the FBI, trying to patch up whatever cracks I could.

We'd just wrapped up interviews with the families of the two dead women. The family of Claudia Wayne, the young nurse found dead while wearing a wig, lived outside Boston. We were driving back to the office when I noticed Cowboy wasn't taking the turn back into town.

I raised an eyebrow. "We heading to a petting farm or something?" I glanced at the rearview mirror as the highway faded behind us. The barren trees looked like skeletons against the gray sky.

Cowboy smirked, but then his expression darkened. "Claudia's family lives close to something I want to show you." He shook his head as if trying to clear the thought. "Weird. Feels like a sign."

I shot him a look. "A sign? What the hell are you talking about?"

Cowboy's grip tightened on the steering wheel as he exhaled. "I ... need to tell you something. But you can't tell Richter."

I leaned forward, the seat creaking. "Cowboy, no. Absolutely not. No. No. No. I don't want to hear—"

"I talked to Nathalie yesterday," he blurted out.

I jerked in my seat and turned to him sharply. "You fucking what?"

He raised a hand as if that would douse the fire rising in me. "I had to. Something's wrong. I feel it in my gut. Richter's always said to trust your instincts, right? That your gut is half the investigation. Well, I did, and I'm on to something big." Cowboy's jaw tightened with frustration. "So I don't get why he won't back me up! He treats me like a child, Rose. That high-profile arrest at the mansion? The one where you guys flew off in a helicopter like James fucking Bond? 'Just forget about it, Cowboy. Top secret—nothing for the kids,' right? 'Fuck Cowboy. He's just here for everyone's amusement.'"

A curse slipped through my teeth as I fought against the pity creeping in. "Don't say that. You're a hell of an agent, and Richter believes in you, Cowboy. He does. He's just under a shit-ton of pressure. This isn't the Wild West, no matter how much we joke about it. Mistakes cost lives."

Cowboy's eyes stayed locked on the road ahead and the landscape stretching out in front of us—bleak fields, dry and empty.

"You trust Richter, don't you?" I pressed, hoping to break through his stubbornness.

"Of course I do."

"Then you know Richter would take a bullet for you. For all of us."

He glanced at me, and our eyes met.

"He's not perfect, but if there's one thing I know about him, it's that he's not in this for himself," I said. "He does what's right for others, always. He's working himself into an early grave to make a tiny difference. That's a unicorn right there."

Cowboy's gaze drifted back to the road. His lip twitched as he bit down. Then he let out a long breath. "Shit. Maybe you're right. Maybe this is all bullshit."

I reached over and squeezed his shoulder. "Doesn't change the fact that you did good work, though. Really."

He nodded slowly, his eyes distant. "Well, we're here anyway. Might as well do this last thing—"

"Here?" I cut him off, my body tensing as we turned a corner on the country road. The land stretched out ahead of us, revealing a large, desolate turkey farm. The grass was withered, the fences sagging and broken. "Theo, no!" My voice was sharp. "Turn around."

"One quick stop, Rose. After this, I swear, I'll stop." He pulled up the road, past outdoor pens crowded with sickly-looking birds, their feathers ragged and barely clinging to their bony frames—products of mass production.

"This is a waste of time, Cowboy. Richter's gonna lose his shit."

He parked in front of the meat processing facility, killed the engine, and looked at me.

My gaze shifted from the rundown white farmhouse with its cracked windows and back to Cowboy.

"That's why you're not telling him," Cowboy said, getting out of the car.

Sweat beaded on my forehead. It dripped down as I rushed after Cowboy into the meat processing facility. The cold, sterile air hit me like a wall. It was filled with the sharp scent of raw meat and disinfectant. Stainless steel tables lined the room. The place buzzed with activity, but the workers—most of whom looked like they were from overseas—kept their heads down, focusing on their tasks, barely noticing us.

"Cowboy!" I snapped, grabbing his arm. "What the hell are you doing? We don't have a search warrant!"

"We don't need one. Mrs. Carr gave us permission, remember?"

"No, I don't remember that. I've never even met her."

"She takes a nap in her house around this time."

"What? How often have you been here?"

"Two, maybe three times. Mrs. Carr always invites me in. Last time, she showed me around until we got to that red door at the end of the facility. She refused to let me see inside. She walked me back to the house with some bullshit excuses."

"What about cameras?" I shot back, hoping to stop him.

Cowboy shook his head. "No cameras. She told me that too. Don't you think that's strange? A large turkey processing plant with no surveillance? What's Carl Carr hiding?"

We stopped in front of a red metal door.

"Looks locked," I said, hoping to end this insanity.

"That's why I had a key made from a picture I took of the lock." Cowboy smirked as he pulled out the key.

I stood there in disbelief as he slid it in. The lock clicked open.

If I'd ever thought Cowboy was all bark and no bite, that was now a thing of the past.

"Oh look," he said, pushing the door open. "It's unlocked. Just like Mrs. Carr told us." He shot me a sly, knowing look.

"Cowboy, they'll take our badges for this."

"Nope." He stepped into the room. "Not if I'm right about what's in here. Old, sweet Mrs. Carr will pretend she had no idea about the red door's secrets. She'll go along with our lie that she gave us permission to look around freely. As a testament to her innocence."

The small storage room looked ordinary—shelves lined with dusty cleaning supplies, and a worn rug spread across the floor. But I couldn't shake the feeling that something was off. That red door—it didn't belong.

"Nothing here," I said, sweeping my arm around the room. "See?"

Cowboy wiped a finger across a dusty bottle of detergent. "Maybe."

"Maybe? What the hell do you mean *maybe*? There's nothing! Let's go before she wakes up." I threw my hands in the air, frustration boiling over.

Cowboy stood still, his hands on his hips, looking defeated. But then his eyes narrowed and locked onto something on the floor. "Wait."

Without another word, he yanked the rug aside, revealing a hatch in the floor. My pulse quickened as he pulled it open and shined a light into the abyss. Instinct kicked in. I drew my gun, following his lead, the tension building in my chest.

I silently cursed everyone: Carr, Richter, Cowboy, Leah. All of them.

It was too late now. Carl Carr's secret was about to hit every news channel in the country.

As we descended the dark, narrow stairs, the smell of feces and rotting meat slapped me in the face, making me gag. Blood stained the walls and steps. At the bottom, Cowboy's flashlight flickered, nearly slipping from his hand.

"Fucking shit," he choked. I followed the beam of his flashlight, and my breath caught—a shelf lined with human heads, floating in jars.

"Shit," I whispered, horror clawing at my throat.

Cowboy snapped out of his trance, swinging the flashlight wildly, as if expecting Carl Carr to lunge from the shadows at any second.

"All clear," he gagged, the flashlight revealing nothing but us and the remains of the women.

I pulled out my phone, already dialing. "Jesus Christ. I can't believe this."

Cowboy lowered his gun and swallowed hard, likely bile.

"Carl Carr," I said, keeping my voice steady. "He's not starting over. He's on the run."

Cowboy nodded slowly. "That piece of shit."

I called in for a search warrant and the arrest of Carl Carr. And for backup.

At least if people thought Carr was on the run, no one would suspect he was dead—by Leah's hands. No body, no evidence. Carl Carr was just ... gone.

"Mrs. Carr must've lied to you the first time you contacted her. Bet he was still here, and she warned him we were onto him. So he fled."

"That makes the most sense. That old, evil hag. Who the hell protects a monster like this?"

"A mother," I said, my voice flat, emotionless.

I stood next to Cowboy, my gaze locking onto the grotesque sight. The heads, with their swollen eyes and lips, suspended in fluid, looked like zombies. It was horrific.

And yet, I couldn't help feeling a sense of dark satisfaction. Carl Carr had left this world in great pain. "Let's call Richter from upstairs," I said, my eyes still on the jars.

Cowboy clenched his jaw and gave a small, resigned nod. "I trusted my gut, just like Richter told me to," he mumbled, repeating the words as we made our way back up the stairs.

"You did," I said, trying to make my voice comforting. "You did."

As fucked up as this whole situation was, and would be, Cowboy had been right. If Carl Carr were still alive, Cowboy would've been the one to have stopped him and saved lives. And at least now, the body parts of those poor women could leave this house of horrors. Just like Nathalie.

It would be a nightmare to clean up, and the real consequences were yet unknown. But Richter would find some comfort in this too.

At least those women could finally rest in peace. Now they were free.

CHAPTER THIRTY

Liam

It was an overcast day, and the Boston Zoo was nearly deserted. Lucy, Josie, and I stood by the wombat enclosure, watching as the fluffy animal climbed a branch.

"Oh. My. God!" Josie gasped. "This is the cutest thing I have ever seeeeeeeen!"

"It's cute as buttons," agreed Lucy. They both broke into high-pitched murmurs as they tried to contain themselves over the furry, walking teddy bear.

"Dad!" Josie called, spinning toward me. "You don't think this is cute? Are you made of ice or something?"

I couldn't stop thinking about Leah. It was constant. I didn't eat. Sleep. I'd stopped by her house and even the concert hall a few times, and each time, her maid or Crystal had turned me away without a word from her. My texts, my calls—ignored. Every damn one.

"Daaaaaad!" Josie insisted.

I cracked a smile. "It's pretty damn cute."

"I heard wombat poop is cube-shaped," Lucy said, her tone casual.

"No way." Josie laughed, her eyes wide.

"Seriously." Lucy nodded. "So the poop doesn't roll away. It helps mark their territory."

Josie almost doubled over laughing, then caught the look on my face as I watched the wombat in its enclosure.

"I'm sorry," Lucy said, looking unsure. "Was that inappropriate?"

Josie rolled her eyes. "It's not you, Aunt Lucy. Dad hates zoos. We don't usually come here. He feels sorry for the animals, you know, being stuck in cages."

Lucy nodded. "Looking at it like that, it is kind of sad, especially for the big cats and elephants."

"Yeah," Josie agreed, her voice quieter now.

"Oh no," Lucy said, glancing between us in horror. "Did we come here because I suggested it, and you didn't want to say no? I'm so sorry. I—"

"It's a zoo, not a cigar lounge," I cut in, trying to ease her nerves. "Don't worry about it. We got to see cube-shaped poop."

Josie and Lucy grinned. It had been a week since Lucy had been allowed to leave the residential mental health facility during the day. This was good for her.

"Dad, can I get a pretzel?" Josie asked, eyeing the food truck down the path.

"Of course," I said, handing her a ten. "You want anything?" I asked Lucy.

She shook her head. We both watched as Josie sprinted off.

"How are you holding up?" I asked, turning back to Lucy.

"Pretty good," she said, glancing down. "I feel awful that I did this, to be honest. It's so embarrassing."

"Don't say that. There's nothing to be embarrassed about."

She nodded, though her gaze stayed distant. "They drill it into your head that suicide is a permanent solution to—"

"Temporary problems," we both finished. We shared a knowing smile, both of us amused at how overused the phrase had become.

"Thank you, Liam," Lucy said, her voice soft. "For being here for me. For letting Josie into my life."

"Nah, nothing to thank me for. You belong with your family, even if it's a bit of a fucked-up one."

Lucy laughed, but it faded quickly. "I didn't always deserve to be here with you and Josie." Her face tightened as if old demons were clawing their way out of the past. "I did some pretty bad things when I was using. It was hard growing up with a mom who resented us. She blamed us for our dad never being around, like his screw-ups had taken the shape of two kids. We were constant reminders of his mistakes. It was too much for David—our brother. He died of an overdose right before I went to rehab and quit. I've been sober over ten years now, but the past"—she let out a sharp breath—"it still haunts me."

"We've all done things we're not proud of," I said, a wave of guilt washing over me. If she only knew what I was wrapped up in with Leah.

"Not like me," she muttered. "You've probably pulled my record? It's fine if you did, I just—"

"I didn't," I interrupted. "I thought we'd start fresh. If there's anything you want to tell me, that's your call."

"Do you believe people can really change?" Her eyes found mine. They were glassy with unshed tears, filled with doubt, shame, and sorrow.

For a moment, I wasn't sure. But standing there, looking at my sister—someone who'd been the tragic product of our asshole dad, the pain and regret so clear in her eyes, yet fighting to be better—I knew the answer.

"I do," I said quietly.

She held my gaze for a beat longer, then wiped her eyes. "You're a good man, Liam. If the world had more of you, it wouldn't be so fucked up."

I was about to make a joke when Josie stomped back, her face red with frustration. "Fifteen bucks!" she fumed. "He wants fifteen bucks for a pretzel." The ten I'd given her trembled in her hand. "Fifteen, Dad!"

"Jesus," I muttered, reaching for my wallet to hand her another five.

She pushed the ten back at me. "No way. I'm not buying into that rip-off. Told him I wanted a pretzel, not a share in the pretzel company."

Lucy and I exchanged amused glances as Josie crossed her arms.

"Let's go to the goats," Josie announced.

"She's so much like you," Lucy said, a grin tugging at the corner of her mouth.

"Yeah." I shook my head with a smile. "That train's left the station. Sarcasm's in her DNA now." Just then, my phone rang. I answered. "Richter."

Rose didn't waste time with pleasantries. Cowboy. Carl Carr. It was bad, and I had to leave—*now*.

I hung up, rubbing my temples. My life was a circus, and every day was a new act.

"Everything okay?" Lucy asked, concern crossing her face.

My mind raced. How the hell was I going to handle this? If Nathalie didn't talk, we could frame it as Carr on the run. Rose probably already had. The way she'd mentioned Carr's arrest warrant suggested that she was around others and was giving me our way out.

"Is everything okay?" Lucy repeated, snapping me out of it.

"That was work," Josie said, stepping in. "Happens when your dad's in the FBI, saving the world." Pride filled her voice. She had so much understanding for a kid her age. I couldn't help but grin at her. "He's about to tell us that he has to leave," she continued, grabbing my hand. "And that's okay." She looked up at me, her eyes shining. "He's tired all the time. But he still does so much with me. When I'm an adult, I wanna be just like him."

I squeezed her hand back, the lump in my throat rising.

But if she knew where I was headed—off to a crime scene to cover up the brutal murder of a serial killer by Leah Nachtnebel—would she look at me the same way?

"I'll drop you both off," I said, clearing my throat. "Sorry about that."

"All good." Lucy smiled. "This has been one of the best days of my life."

CHAPTER THIRTY-ONE

Leah

I walked out of the concert hall through the back door. Once I was outside, my breath hung in the winter night air. Novak's Maybach sat idling by the curb. It was parked in front of my own limousine, where Mark waited behind the wheel. My steps slowed, then picked up again. Piles of dirty snow, left by last night's storm and the snowplows, lined the sidewalk like forgotten barricades.

Novak's driver, dressed in a sharp wool coat and suit, opened the door. I climbed in, pulling my cashmere coat tighter around my waist as I settled into the seat. It was our first meeting since the hut incident in the woods. I'd known he'd reach out again, but I hadn't expected it to happen like this— just as before. I sent a quick text to Mark, telling him to follow us.

Exhaustion weighed on me. I hadn't slept in days, my mind tangled with thoughts of Richter. I'd watched from the window as Aida had turned him away. I'd hoped—*wished*—he'd ignore her, storm the house, and find me. But then what? It would probably be our last conversation, filled with accusations and disappointment. He'd finally see me for what I really was.

And that look would haunt me forever.

"Can I ask you something?" I said.

"Of course," Jan replied smoothly.

"Do you know who killed Emanuel Marin?" I asked. Maybe, at least, that haunting mystery could be solved.

"No," he answered, a little too quickly.

I narrowed my eyes, unconvinced. He had eyes and ears everywhere—including on me. Was this just another one of his games?

"If you're planning another mission like last time, I'll have to cancel," I said, my voice icier than the night outside. "This way of communication doesn't work for me. Neither does our collaboration if this is how you picture it."

Novak nodded. "Fair enough. But there's no mission today. I want to show you something else."

I raised a brow.

"Nothing like last time," he added. "I promise."

I smoothed a wrinkle in my black evening dress. "I'm too tired for this, Jan."

In those dark woods, Jan Novak had handed me an opportunity, a way to truly make a difference in this twisted world. But it had also taken something from me, something I hadn't realized I held more dear than my thirst for justice.

Richter.

"It won't take long," he assured me.

I thought about it, then nodded.

"Has Richter contacted you yet?" he asked, his gaze locking onto mine.

I held his stare. It was none of his business, and my silence made that clear. "What is it you want to show me?" I finally asked.

The car cut through Boston's narrow streets before heading into the quieter outskirts. Trees thickened on either side as we left the city behind. The sound of commercial freight trains rumbled somewhere in the distance. After a brief drive, we arrived at a secluded stretch of commercial train tracks cutting through the forest on Pine Street near Wilkers Manufacturing.

We both stepped out, and Novak, ever the gentleman, offered his arm. I reluctantly took it as we made our way toward the tracks. My heels sank slightly into the soft earth, and the crunch of fallen leaves underfoot echoed in the stillness. The faint smell of damp moss and pine lingered in the air. We walked along the tracks, passing a few weathered wooden benches that seemed out of place in the wilderness. Ahead, a rundown station waiting house loomed in the darkness, its roof collapsed—a relic of an old commuter station long forgotten.

Jan came to a stop near one of the wooden benches, positioned by a small clearing along the tracks.

"Remember when I told you not to ask about the train tracks and the ankh symbol?"

I nodded.

"Well, tonight, I want to tell you a story about a poor immigrant family from Slovenia," Jan said, gesturing toward the benches. It felt like an invitation to his own home.

I sat down. Through my cashmere coat, the cold wood pressed against my legs.

"They had two boys," he continued, his eyes fixed on the darkened tracks ahead. "Mojca and Anton. Both often wished they'd never been born, at least not to those parents. The drinking, the beatings, the screaming… endless fights." He paused, the memories darkening his expression. "Anton, the older one, he could've escaped. He was smart and kind. Had that rare something about him that drew people in. He could've run off and started a better life. But he stayed. For Mojca. He took care of his little brother. Made sure he had shoes, a coat for the cold weather, and food. When things got bad at home, Anton took Mojca to playgrounds in the summer and museums in the winter. He loved his little brother with all his heart."

I watched as a faint, bitter smile tugged at the corner of Jan's lips. It was like he could see the boys playing in front of him.

"Their favorite place in the world was the Egyptian exhibit in town. At night, before the nightmares came, they'd talk about the stars and the old gods, just like in ancient Egypt." He still didn't look at me, his gaze now locked on the tracks. "One day, after another bad fight between their parents—knives were involved, which wasn't unusual—Anton found Mojca outside in the bitter cold. Barefoot. Anton rushed inside and grabbed his brother's shoes and coat. They spent the day wandering, waiting until it was safe to go home."

His voice cracked. He walked toward the edge of the tracks, his hand slipping into his coat pocket, clenching into a fist as if he were holding onto something.

"They were on tracks just like these," Jan said quietly, "when Anton had a seizure. He had them occasionally. Their mother smoked and drank through both pregnancies. But Anton, selfless as always, had grabbed Mojca's shoes and coat that day instead of his own jacket, where he kept his medicine."

His voice grew tighter, strained.

"During his seizure, he collapsed onto the rails at the station. Mojca screamed for help as he leaped onto the tracks, desperately trying to pull his brother off, but Anton was too heavy. He tugged and strained, tried and tried. The train wasn't even in sight yet. There was enough time to help. But people ... they just stood there. Staring. Watching. Like heartless statues."

He pulled out a silver ankh necklace. The pendant dangled in the dim moonlight. His eyes—filled with sadness and hate—stayed on it.

"When the train hit, only one boy survived. The boy and his brother's favorite possession." Jan slipped the necklace back into his pocket, then turned to meet my gaze.

I sat there, feeling the weight of his story sink in. Anton and Mojca. The accident on the tracks. The meaning behind the ankh. "You ... are Mojca," I said quietly.

Jan didn't answer right away. His expression was cold. "It's horrific what a train does to the human body. Especially one so small," he finally said. The sadness in his eyes faded, replaced by flickers of pure hatred. "People ... most of them are rotten inside. No soul. No heart. They need to face that truth. Confront their demons and leave this world knowing that they've been seen for who they truly are."

I held his stare, the tension between us almost tangible. "The Ankh. It's a mirror," I murmured. "But instead of reflecting what people want to be seen, it reveals their true selves. Their darkest sins."

Jan's hand slipped from his coat pocket. The movement was slow and deliberate. "I told you I wasn't who you thought I was. But now that you know the real meaning of the ankh, maybe I can be."

I stood and took a step toward him, but my phone buzzed in my pocket, pulling me back to reality.

Richter.

I should have ignored it, but my hand had already moved to retrieve the phone. Under Jan's watchful gaze, I opened it and read the message. *Can we talk now?* A picture of Nathalie sitting alone in an interrogation room was attached.

Jan's voice cut through the silence. "Why does he hold such power over you? I see it every time I look into your eyes. Him. I see him in them."

I slipped the phone back into my pocket. "I apologize, but I have to go. I'll call my driver. No need to drop me off."

Jan stayed motionless, his eyes fixed on me as I turned to walk away. I didn't need to look back to feel his gaze; it was heavy, lingering. He must have thought I was cruel for leaving so abruptly, especially after he'd opened his heart to me. Should I have said something, pretended to feel something for him? But how could death itself ever become anything more than a messenger of misery?

I was who I was.

And yet, the timing of the text couldn't have been worse. Jan would surely take this personally—maybe even as a rejection.

But I had to meet Richter.

It was time.

Time to face him.

Time to make him see or lose him forever.

CHAPTER THIRTY-TWO

Liam

As I slipped the flip phone back into my pocket, my eyes shifted to the screen. Nathalie was there, sitting in the FBI interrogation room, waiting under the harsh lights. Leah wouldn't talk to me about the hut in the woods, so maybe this would add some pressure.

It was after 10 p.m., but Cowboy had arranged this meeting with Nathalie, marking it as *urgent*. To him—and everyone else—Carl Carr, suspected serial killer, was still on the run.

To Cowboy, Nathalie was a key witness, just too scared to talk while Carr was "out there." Sometimes, a lie made as much sense as the truth. The heads in Carr's basement, linked to missing prostitutes, were enough to fuel that narrative. One surveillance clip from a liquor store camera even showed him with a woman from his basement—proof that Cowboy had latched onto. I couldn't block this interview, especially not when Nathalie had agreed to talk again.

I leaned back in my chair, my gaze on Nathalie through the screen. She looked so different now. Short hair. Clean. Wearing a decent coat. Her file said she was working at a local grocery store, and she had enrolled in online classes to become a teacher.

It almost made me grin. A former prostitute and serial killer survivor teaching kids? Finally, someone with something useful to teach about this world: how to spot the real monsters. How to survive.

My eyes drifted to the manila folder on my desk. I opened it for what felt like the thousandth fucking time.

Carole Traylor.

Her bleached-blonde hair. Blue eyes that had gone from haunted to accusing in the past few days—and I couldn't explain why.

No.

That wasn't true.

I knew exactly why.

My sister.

Her suicide attempt. The zoo.

After we'd talked at the zoo, I'd decided to look her up in the system. I had to make sure she hadn't been involved in anything that could hurt Josie. And she hadn't lied about her dark past. She'd been the getaway driver in an armed robbery. An elderly woman was stabbed and later died in the hospital from a heart attack. The DA cut her a deal. Rehab instead of jail if she identified the others. She took it.

And here I was.

Staring at the burnt remains of a woman with a past. Just like my sister, whom I'd somehow found it in my heart to forgive. She'd turned her life around—sober for ten years, working at a nursing home where she was known for her kindness and loving treatment of the residents. Many of them would be all alone without her. Now guilt ate her alive. There was a genuine desire for redemption.

If I'd found it in my heart to forgive her, how could I condemn Carole Traylor?

Some digging had revealed that Carole Traylor had been a victim of human trafficking too. How much of a choice had she really had when the cartel had told her to get those kids? Who was I to decide her crimes were worth a death sentence while I granted a second chance to someone I cared for?

I tilted my head back and stared at a dried leak in the ceiling.

"SAC?" Cowboy's voice broke the silence as he knocked on the open door. "Nathalie's waiting in the interrogation room."

"I'm coming," I said, standing.

If Nathalie talked, this would go from fire to a full-blown inferno. She'd never seen Leah's face, but she'd heard her voice. And we already had footage linking Carl Carr to Leah—him stalking her. If Nathalie mentioned a mysterious woman killing Carl, it wouldn't be long before Cowboy's gut would lead him on another trail. The same one I was on. The one that had led me to Leah. And now right back to me.

"I'm coming," I repeated, hiding the dread that threatened to creep into my voice. Part of me almost wanted it all to come out. To end this mess. At least then, I'd know who I was again. Know right from wrong. The burden of judging over life and death lifted off my shoulders.

It was heavy.

Maybe too heavy for any human to carry so easily.

CHAPTER THIRTY-THREE

Nathalie

Once the agents entered, the FBI interrogation room felt small, as if the walls were creeping in. The flickering overhead light didn't help. It cast an uneasy glow that I'd seen too many times before.

I'd been in rooms like this plenty of times. But this time was different. This time, they were after *her*. The woman who'd pulled me from the pits of hell. The one who'd killed that monster.

I had to stay strong. For that angel God had sent me.

I'd never been arrested, but I'd been questioned, and I'd lied to cops more times than I could count, always covering for the other girls. I could do it again. I had to.

I took a sip of the coffee I'd brought with me. Street smart. Never take a drink from cops.

We all knew that trick. They'd swipe my DNA and tie it to something from Carr's basement.

Across from me sat two agents. One was in his late thirties. He had brown hair and even darker eyes. Agent Liam Richter. His presence was odd—calm and comforting.

Next to him was Agent Theo McCourt, the one I already knew. Blond. Younger. Restless energy radiating from him. Ready to make things happen right now.

"You're not hot?" McCourt asked, nodding at my gloves.

I shook my head.

"You want another drink?" He glanced at my coffee.

Another head shake as I put the empty cup into my coat pocket. "I recycle," I lied. "Global warming."

His sigh gave away his frustration. "So..." McCourt started. "You know why we called you in?"

Richter glanced at him before turning back to me, his voice warmer. "Thanks for coming in so late, Nathalie. I know you have little ones at home. And just for the record, this isn't an arrest. You're not in any trouble. We just want to chat. See if you can help us save lives."

I shifted in my chair. "I guess it's about that serial killer again? The one Agent McCourt said is on the run?"

Richter nodded. "Carl Carr."

Agent McCourt slid a picture across the table—the monster who'd kept me locked in his basement for weeks. The man who'd done things to me even the devil would flinch at.

My chest tightened, and my heart pounded as I stared at him. The bastard who'd carved out chunks of my flesh while I was still alive. To eat them.

My gloved hands clenched in my lap. The taste of bile crept up my throat. Was I about to throw up?

"I know you're scared, Nathalie," McCourt said, watching me closely. "But there are other women out there who could be next. We need your help to stop him. Now. Before he can hurt anyone else."

If Carr were still alive, I'd have sung like a bird. But I knew he wasn't. Thanks to her. The woman who'd done what no one else could: saved me. I owed her everything. There was no way I'd betray her.

I leaned back, keeping my voice steady. "I really hope you find him," I said almost casually. "But I don't know how I can help."

McCourt's eyes narrowed, and he slid another picture onto the table. A red truck parked in a dark alley.

"Know this place?" he asked.

Like the back of my hand. Fergy Avenue. The alley where clients parked to find us.

"No," I lied. "I don't think so."

His lips pressed tight. "Let me help you out. This is Carl Carr's truck. Parked right around the corner from where you were working that night. The night you disappeared."

"Ran off with a man," I corrected. "Another loser, promising the world, delivering nothing but a pile of shit."

"Mm-hmm," Agent McCourt mumbled sarcastically. He added another picture—me at a convenience store, buying coffee and a chocolate muffin, right before it all went down. "That you?"

I shrugged. "I don't remember." Pulling my hair aside, I revealed the scab where Carl Carr had slammed me with an iron bar. "I tripped that night. Freak accident. Hit my head. Things were blurry for a while after."

The room was charged, filling the space like an invisible weight.

"Did he do that, Nathalie?" Agent McCourt asked.

I shook my head.

"I know you're scared, but lying to a federal officer is a crime, right, Nathalie?" Agent McCourt said, turning "bad cop."

"Agent McCourt..." Richter's tone was a quiet warning.

"And lying to me means Carl Carr keeps doing what he's doing, Nathalie. To others."

"McCourt." Richter's voice was firmer now.

McCourt took a deep breath, barely holding it together. "So let me ask you again." He tapped the photo of Carr. "Have you ever met this man?"

I refused to look at the monster's picture again. Instead, I stared straight at McCourt.

"Why protect him?" he continued. "If you're scared, we can help. Help you get that college degree. Help you provide for your kids. Help you keep them all safe."

My heart pounded, and my gaze dropped to the table. For a moment, I thought about telling them. What if they found out, and I got a record for lying? I'd stayed off the system for years, working the streets, and now things were finally falling into place. Could I risk it all?

"Nathalie," McCourt said, softer now. "I'm here to fight for you. Let me help you and your family." His finger hovered over Carr's picture. "Please. Have you ever met this man?"

Silence hung in the room. Maybe I wasn't as strong as I thought. Maybe it was okay to let someone else fight this battle. Carry the weight of this dark secret.

My mouth opened before I could stop myself.

"No," I said, my voice steady. Its strength surprised me.

McCourt's hand slammed down on the metal table, rattling it. "You're lying!" he snapped. "I can see it in your eyes."

Richter's voice cut through the tension. "Theo! A word." He nodded toward the door as he stood and opened it wide.

"I'm really sorry, Nathalie," Agent Richter said, his voice softening. "It's been a rough few days. We just need to find this man before he hurts anyone else."

I forced myself to meet his eyes. "I understand. Don't worry."

His lips pressed together in a brief acknowledgment as he stepped aside. "It's late. I'm sure you're tired."

Without hesitation, I hurried out into a dimly lit hallway. My mother stood there, her face etched with worry, arms open and waiting. Her coat hung loosely around her as she pulled me into a warm hug. Tears burned behind my eyes. I tried to hold them back, but the horror of seeing Carl Carr again was too much.

"Let's go, my little Peanut." Her words were soft and comforting as she led me toward the elevator.

We stepped inside. As the doors began to close, I glanced up for the first time since leaving the room.

Standing at the end of the hallway was Agent Theo McCourt, watching me like a hawk, his eyes narrowed. He didn't even look at Richter, who was still lecturing him.

The doors shut, and a chill ran through me.

He knew.

He fucking knew.

And he wasn't going to give up easily.

CHAPTER THIRTY-FOUR

Leah

When I opened the front door and saw him standing in the pitch-black night, I turned and walked into my study. I didn't know what to say.

Liam quietly shut the door behind him and followed me.

The fireplace was burning, its flames casting orange shadows across the walls. I switched on the desk lamp so I could see him better—his face, his eyes.

He made his way to the fire and stared into it.

"Nathalie's sticking to her story," he said, his voice low.

I moved around the desk and sat down. For a while, we remained silent. I watched him stand by the fireplace, his gaze lost in the flames. The quiet between us felt like a wall. It was as if we were both afraid of what would happen once the words were spoken.

"They say," he began, his voice low, "when your body's on fire, you might pass out in a minute or two from inhaling hot air or toxic gases like carbon monoxide. Your lungs get scorched, or the smoke suffocates you. But before that happens, your skin starts to melt—every nerve ending screaming as the flames eat you alive. And death? If you're really fucked, that can drag out for five to ten agonizing minutes." He turned to look at me, his eyes dark. "Five to ten minutes. That's a hell of a long time to burn alive, don't you think?"

"Definitely one of the more painful ways to die," I agreed. "If those rapists didn't want to burn, they shouldn't have worn flammable clothes."

"Nice one," he said, his tone dripping with sarcasm.

He pressed his lips together, then pulled a thin, rolled-up manila folder from his coat pocket and dropped it onto the desk in front of me. I glanced down and opened it to reveal the mugshot of the woman from the hut.

Caroline Traylor.

I braced myself for one of our usual arguments. For his anger. But instead, he just stood there, his eyes locked on the picture of the woman.

"I ... don't know what's right or wrong anymore," he said, his voice steady but quiet. "However, I do know I can't keep going on like this. Won't keep going on like this."

The room felt heavier with the silence that followed.

"You're not like them, Leah," he finally said, shaking his head. His gaze found mine. For a split second, I thought I'd see disappointment, maybe even disgust. But instead, there was only sorrow. And as twisted as it was, hope. Was that for me?

"You're not a monster like Grant, Harris, Carr, or ... Jan Novak." His hand reached across the table, landing gently on mine. The warmth of his touch burned deeper than the flames in the fireplace ever could. With his eyes on me, his gazed pierced into shadows that I didn't want anyone to see.

"We don't hurt good people, Leah. You and I, we save them."

His hand lingered, heavy with meaning. Then he hesitantly pulled it away and stepped back.

A soft meow broke the tension. Liam looked at the cat that was rubbing against his leg. A faint smile curved his lips as he crouched to pet it. "Does the cat have a name yet?" he asked, his tone lighter.

I shook my head. "No."

He straightened up. "Josie thinks Hope would be a good name."

I almost laughed. "Hope? In this house? Living with me?"

He shrugged. "She's a kid. Whatever hell they go through, they usually hold onto the good in the world ... until they grow up."

I frowned. "A remarkable strength," I said.

His brown eyes glanced at the folder, then caught my gaze again. "I'll ... talk to you soon," he said.

I knew what he was really saying. He was giving me time to think.

I stood as he left. His figure disappeared down the hallway before the front door clicked shut.

For a moment, I stared at the picture of the woman in front of me. What was it that Richter saw in her that I didn't?

Pushing the photos aside, I sat and started reading through her file. Her story was anything but ordinary: a teenage girl running away from an abusive home only to fall into the clutches of sex traffickers. By the time I'd finished the first few pages, I could sense the darkness in every chapter of her life.

Sure, I understood her life hadn't been easy. She'd been a victim once. But did that excuse her choices? What did her past matter when she'd gone on to harm others? Kids had gone missing because of her, and they would've continued to disappear if she were still alive. She had a choice: her life or theirs. What kind of argument was Richter trying to make? I knew he'd rather die than harm an innocent child.

"Of course I would," I could almost hear him say. "But that choice isn't so easy for people who've been trapped in hell their whole lives."

And he had a point, logically. I didn't feel anything for Caroline Traylor, but it made sense that people who hadn't experienced her kind of suffering couldn't easily judge her actions by their own standards.

I shut the folder with a snap and leaned back in my chair.

The way he'd talked to me. Even the way he'd tried to appeal to my humanity with ... this. He hadn't given up on me, not even after the hut incident. He might never work with me again, but he still believed I was something more than a psychopathic killer.

Though he'd shown me this courtesy, I wasn't sure I could extend the same grace to myself. That night in the woods—it had changed me. My work with Jan meant something. With his power, we could make this world better. Save thousands of innocent lives.

I could set boundaries with Jan. For Richter. Focus on serial killers and psychopaths, just on a larger scale. Would Richter really oppose that? Was I missing something? Was my inability to feel and think like a normal person clouding my judgment again?

I felt like that little girl in the psych ward all over again.

I'd learned to feel a few things, thanks to Richter, but I still didn't understand them. Like rain trying to explain to fire how it nurtured life while drowning out the flames at the same time.

Maybe rain and fire both had a place in the world—just not together.

I grabbed the folder on Carole Traylor and walked over to the fireplace. Without a second thought, I tossed it into the flames. The paper curled and darkened as the fire devoured it.

I felt nothing when I looked at that woman's picture. Her file was also full of missing girls she'd lured in. Witnesses had seen her with the kids, but there hadn't been enough evidence to send her away for life. Four years. That was all she'd gotten. Four. Years.

And then she'd gone right back to it.

Richter's point about her tragic past left a bitter taste in my mouth. Sure, she might've been a victim once, but when she burned, she was the predator.

When I'd burned her in that hut, all I'd felt was justice.

Nothing else.

If Novak came back to me after how I'd left him at the station, I'd have killed for him again. Over and over.

This was who I was.

This was Leah Nachtnebel.

CHAPTER THIRTY-FIVE

Liam

Three months later

I stood in my office as agents milled around. Dead silence filled the air. I was on hold with the Trace Evidence Unit within our Laboratory Division. A witness had come forward on the tip line, reporting a man who'd backed into her car in the parking lot where Claudia Wayne had gone missing. The witness said she'd seen a woman matching Claudia's description in the man's car. The woman's head had been resting against the window, and her eyes had been closed. She'd been either sleeping or passed out.

We'd tested paint scrapings from the witness's car against those of a van that a neighbor had called in after we'd released a picture of the offending vehicle—and the offer of a reward—to the media. The van belonged to Gerald Smith, a middle-aged landscaper from Roxbury.

My gut told me we were close—so damn close—to catching the sick bastard who'd raped and killed two women and put doll wigs on them.

"Lab just confirmed it," the voice on the other end crackled. "The paint. It's a definitive match."

A surge of adrenaline shot through me, and my heart pounded against my ribs. "Good work," I said.

"Go get him."

I slammed the phone down a bit harder than necessary. The agents nearby turned to look at me, anticipation on their faces.

"Gerald Smith. It's him!" I announced. "The lab confirmed the paint match. We've got our guy!"

A ripple of excitement swept through the room. In an instant, the team sprang into action.

"Everybody to the equipment room to gear up," I commanded. "Matin, get me a warrant. We move in ten!"

As everyone hurried to prepare, I grabbed my FBI jacket. Despite the electric energy rushing through me, my hands were steady. This was it: the moment we'd been pushing toward for weeks.

We pulled up to Smith's house just as the midday sky cast a gray, dark winter hue over the dilapidated neighborhood. The house stood out even among the other worn-down homes. It was a sagging two-story structure with chipped paint that might have once been green. The lawn was overgrown, weeds choking what remained of a cracked walkway leading to the front door. A battered van—the one that had hit the witness's car—was parked in the driveway next to an old pickup loaded with rusted landscaping tools.

We moved in silence, fully geared with FBI vests and identification jackets. Firearms drawn, we advanced toward the house, each step deliberate. An FBI agent trained as a locksmith crouched by the front door. His tools glinted faintly in the dim light.

As I waited for the door to be unlocked, I scanned the surroundings. The neighborhood was eerily quiet. My eyes drifted to the side yard. Something caught my attention: a rusty swing set behind a leaning fence.

A knot formed in my stomach. I prayed the kids weren't here. They were supposed to be with their grandmother this weekend, but she hadn't picked up when we'd called on our way here.

I glanced at Rose, who caught my eye and faintly shook her head. She was thinking the same thing.

A soft click signaled that the door was unlocked. Rose turned the knob slowly and pushed the door open inch by inch. We slipped inside, where the worn carpet muffled our footsteps.

The stench of stale cigarettes clung to the room, with something even fouler lingering beneath it. Discarded pizza boxes and empty beer cans littered the floor, mingling with dirty clothes and broken toys. The dim lighting cast long shadows, and every corner was a potential hiding spot. I swallowed hard, fingers flexing nervously around the gun's handle.

I signaled to the team to spread out. Rose and Cowboy took a left toward what looked like the kitchen while I moved straight ahead down a narrow hallway.

Suddenly there was gunfire.

Wood splintered near my head as bullets tore through the wall. I dove behind a large closet in the hallway.

"FBI! Hold your fire!" I shouted.

More shots answered.

I pressed myself tighter against the wall behind the closet, my mind racing.

During a moment when the gunfire had paused, I heard the sound of crying from a room farther up the hallway to my left. It was most likely the living room. The kids—they were here!

"Your kids are in the house!" I yelled. "Gerald, stop shooting!"

A brief pause, then another round of bullets. He wasn't listening.

I locked eyes with Cowboy, who was waiting down the hallway near the front door, close to Rose. She peeked out from behind a doorway, her expression grim. We were pinned down, and any aggressive move could put the children at risk.

Taking a deep breath, I steadied myself. "I'm going for the kids," I said to Rose. "Hold your fire."

She nodded slightly, her eyes conveying both trust and concern. "Hold your fire!" she shouted to the other agents.

I launched myself from the cover and sprinted up the hallway to the living room. Bullets whizzed past. One slammed into my vest with a force that knocked the wind out of me. Pain exploded across my ribcage, but I pushed through, adrenaline fueling me like a jet.

I burst into the cluttered living room and spotted two small children huddled together on a stained couch. The boy, around three years old with tousled brown hair, clung tightly to a slightly older girl. They held each other close as the flickering glow of the television cast an eerie light over their tightly shut eyes.

"Sh-sh-sh. It's okay," I whispered, forcing calm into my voice. "I won't hurt you."

Their eyes met mine. A flicker of hope pierced the fear as I scooped them into my arms.

"Close your eyes again and hold on tight," I instructed.

Without wasting a second, I moved toward the nearest exit: a large window next to the TV. Hugging the kids close, I turned my back to the glass and kicked it out with my heel. The window shattered outward. Shards rained down as I shielded the kids with my body.

Behind me, gunfire erupted anew. Splinters flew as bullets tore into the wall against which we'd just stood. I leaped through the opening and landed hard on the unkempt lawn.

"Agent down!" voices shouted nearby.

"Get the kids!" I yelled back.

Hands reached out, and I quickly transferred the children to waiting arms. They were rushed away to a spot behind a vehicle.

I pressed myself against the exterior wall, breathing heavily. The pain from the bullet impact throbbed dully. Blood trickled from minor cuts, but nothing felt serious.

Inside, the chaos continued. Sharp cracks of gunfire echoed through the house, then abruptly fell silent.

"Suspect down!" Rose called out.

"House clear!" Cowboy added moments later.

Relief washed over me. I closed my eyes, giving myself a second to regroup.

"Call for an ambulance for the kids!" I shouted as I pushed off from the wall.

Rose and Cowboy emerged from the front door. Their faces glistened with sweat. Rose's usually neat ponytail was disheveled, with strands of hair sticking to her forehead. Cowboy's eyes were bright, and his cheeks were flushed.

"You okay?" he asked, eyeing the torn fabric of my vest.

"Another day, another dime," I replied with a wry smile. "I'll live."

Rose glanced at the cluster of vehicles where the kids were being tended to. "The children?"

"Scared but okay," I assured her. "Just some scratches."

She nodded. "I'll arrange for social services and a trauma counselor."

"Good."

Cowboy stretched out his twitching hand. "Adrenaline's wearing off," he said with a shaky laugh. "I'm getting soft. Too much desk work lately."

I held up my own hand, a faint tremble visible. "Keeps us on our toes."

He checked his phone and grimaced. "Ah, man. I gotta bail."

I raised an eyebrow. "What the hell? Seriously? Forensics will get here soon."

"Got a ... thing," he said, a mischievous glint in his eye. "Didn't expect to be playing hero this morning."

I smirked. "Date?"

He shrugged.

"Go on, get out of here before I change my mind," I said, waving him off.

"You're the best, boss." He grinned and clapped me on the shoulder. "Except for that time you—"

"Already changing my mind," I said.

He laughed. "Don't let him die before he approves my PTO," he said to a group of agents coming out of the house as he headed off.

"He has to approve mine first!" one of the agents hollered after him.

As I watched Cowboy jog toward his car, a small smile tugged at my lips. Then, turning back, I surveyed the scene. The forensic team was already arriving as the police put up tape to section off the home from nosy neighbors.

My gaze drifted to the kids. They were sitting in the back of an SUV, wrapped in blankets. Rose was speaking to them softly. Their faces were pale and their eyes wide, but they were alive. And safe.

A heaviness settled in my chest. Their mother had passed away from cancer not long ago. Now, their father was gone too. They had a grandmother who cared, who'd been fighting for custody, claiming that Gerald was abusive to her daughter and the kids. Maybe now they'd get a chance at a better life.

But the road ahead would be hard. Trauma like this didn't fade quickly.

I sighed and removed the vest. A sharp pain flared where the bullet had hit. I'd have a hell of a bruise tomorrow.

Then suddenly, in all of this, Leah's face flashed in my mind.

It had been two months since we'd last spoken. Two months of silence, yet not a day had gone by that I hadn't thought of her. The unresolved tension between us followed me like my shadow. So far, there had been no bad surprises. No burnt bodies in the woods or floating in the river. Not that this couldn't happen again soon, but today, for a brief moment, the world felt a little safer. Today we'd made a difference. The FBI had saved lives. And maybe, just maybe, there was hope for finding a way forward. Both with Leah and within myself. One without Novak. Something more sustainable. More bearable.

I took a deep breath. The cool winter air filled my lungs.

"Agent Richter," a voice called out.

I turned to see one of the medics approaching.

"Let's get you checked out," he said.

I nodded and followed him toward the ambulance. As I walked, I cast one last glance at the kids.

This was why I did what I did.

For moments like this.

Despite the chaos, despite the pain, today was a win. And that was enough for now.

CHAPTER THIRTY-SIX

Leah

I stood in the dark alley, the winter air biting at my bare legs and arms. My wig felt tight, hiding the real me beneath shoulder-length brown hair. Blue contacts masked my green eyes.

The muffled thump of club music pounded through the walls, but out here, in the cold night, the world felt as lifeless as a graveyard.

Marcus, my escort, pressed me against the brick wall. His hands slid around my waist. "You're so beautiful," he whispered, his breath warm against my neck.

But all I could think about was Richter: his brown eyes, the way he'd watched me as the flames from my study's fireplace had flickered across his face, his gaze heavy with something I couldn't name. It haunted me. Every second.

I shoved Marcus off. His confusion was immediate. "What's wrong?"

I reached into my purse and pulled out an envelope stuffed with cash. Two thousand dollars. High-class escorts didn't come cheap, but they were clean and well-educated. The agency was picky for its wealthy clientele. "Here," I said, my voice cold. "You can go now."

"What? But—"

"I said you can go." The finality in my voice left no room for discussion.

His eyes darted from my face to the money. After a brief pause, he snatched the envelope and disappeared into the night.

I turned and walked back into the club.

The noise hit me like a wave. The bass pounded in my chest, and the strobe lights flickered, casting quick shadows over the sea of bodies moving to the beat. I slipped through the crowd, blending into the chaos, and headed straight for the bar.

A man in his mid-twenties, with messy brown hair, sidled up next to me. "Can I buy you a drink?" he asked, barely audible over the music.

I shook my head and signaled the bartender for a drink.

The brown-haired man didn't waste time, just moved on to the next woman—stumbling, drunk, barely able to stand. I narrowed my eyes. I'd seen him before. No. I *knew* him.

His name was Rhodes Walker. I'd read about him in police reports, deep dives into the dark web. He was the reason I was here tonight. Women had accused him of drugging their drinks, but the police had dismissed it. Not enough evidence. Just a bunch of "claims," they said. Case closed.

But I wasn't the police.

Watching him, I felt a familiar spark of anger. At one time I'd hunted real monsters. Now I played with scum. It wasn't the same, but it made a difference. And after the meeting with Richter, no matter how certain I'd felt when I'd burned Caroline Traylor's file and body, I was here. Lost. Confused.

Both Jan and Richter had made their cases. Now what?

Both had tried to reach out. One with roses, daily. The other with silence, then a single text.

I saw Rhodes slide a drink under the bar just long enough to spike it before handing it to the stumbling woman. His movements were casual, practiced.

Before she could take a sip, I was there. I shoved her aside, ignoring her annoyed protest, and stepped up to Rhodes. "I changed my mind," I said, stepping in close with a slow, deliberate smile. "I'd love a drink."

I took the glass from his hand and pretended to take a long, slow sip. My eyes were locked on his.

He grinned. The predator, oblivious to his own trap.

We spent the next hour together, blending into the crowd, talking about nothing, just like people in clubs do. His conversation was insufferable: sex, women's bodies, endless crude remarks.

Each time he handed me a drink, I excused myself to the bathroom and dumped it down the sink. He kept watching me, waiting for his drug to take effect.

Eventually, he leaned in, his voice low and sleazy. "You wanna fuck? In my car?"

Of course, the pig didn't even bother to offer a real bed.

I swayed a little, pretending to be tipsy and out of it. "No," I slurred. "I wanna go home."

"Alright, let's go," he said.

We slipped out of the back entrance. Our breath hung in the cold night air, visible in misty clouds.

I staggered a few steps ahead, feigning a stumble, when Rhodes grabbed me roughly and slammed me against the same wall where Marcus had pinned me earlier. His hand shot to his zipper, and he yanked it down. In seconds, his hard cock was pressing against my stomach.

"Bitch, suck it!"

He grabbed me by the head and pushed me onto my knees. I scanned the dark alley to confirm we were alone, then quickly reached into my purse and pulled out plastic gloves.

Along with a plastic tube of hydrofluoric acid.

Rhodes glanced down as I slipped on the gloves and twisted off the cap.

"What the fuck is this?" he asked.

"Well, Rhodes..." His eyes widened when I called him by his real name. Sober. "Let's not drag this out, you disgusting prick."

He froze, realization dawning in his eyes. "What the hell are you talking about?" He tried to zip his pants back up, but I grabbed his limp cock tightly.

"All those drugged women. I have the drugs in the drink. Your prints. Enough to send you to a prison where they kill rapists like you."

His face paled, and his cocky grin faltered as panic took hold.

"Now listen carefully. You'll tell the police that a crazy homeless attacked you and did this to you," I hissed.

"Did ... what?" he whimpered, paralyzed by fear like a frightened child. A coward, through and through.

"Trade your weapon for your life," I said coldly, dumping the acid on his exposed cock. I quickly took a large step back and closed the plastic container before any acid could hit me by accident.

Rhodes's hysterical screams came almost instantly as the acid began eating away at the flesh of his dick. His hands shot to his crotch, only spreading the burning to his fingers, making it even worse.

I watched as Rhodes collapsed to his knees, screeching for help.

It felt good. Not as satisfying as killing would feel but sufficient for now.

I slipped away into the night, his desperate cries echoing behind me. A cold wind hit my face as I rounded the corner.

Richter crept into my thoughts again.

Would he approve of this? Was this what he wanted from me— a tame version of the monster?

Jan would accept me for who I was. We could thrive together, fueled by rage.

But out here, in the biting cold, with the distant echoes of panicked shouts, I realized justice wasn't what I craved anymore.

The feelings I'd been searching for since I was a little girl weren't about justice at all. It dawned on me that killing killers—this relentless pursuit— had just been a distraction from my own lonely, pathetic life. A desperate way to make myself feel *something*. Anything. In helping people, even through dark means, I'd found just enough to force myself out of bed each day.

But now it all seemed almost foolish compared to what Richter had stirred in me. Rage and murder couldn't hold a candle to the depth he'd unearthed.

Liam Richter could make me feel sadness—real sadness—and that strange warmth that might even be joy.

And now I'd lost it all.

Sacrificed it to the fire of rage that had fueled me for so long.

Was it too late?

Had I already pushed Richter beyond the point of forgiveness? I knew his moral compass, how high his standards were. He'd warned me after the Night Stalker incident, but I'd kept pushing, letting Novak pull the strings to manipulate me like a puppet master.

Like Kirby. Like Patel. Even Carl Carr.

By the time I reached my townhome, looking like I'd just come back from a Symphony Hall rehearsal, I'd decided to contact Richter.

But I didn't make it past the kitchen.

My eyes landed on a small tablet that Ida had left on the counter with a note.

This was left for you. Thank you, it read.

A cold weight settled in my chest.

Jan Novak had taken my silence for refusal.

He'd reignited the games.

And this time, I didn't have a choice about joining his deadly dance.

CHAPTER THIRTY-SEVEN

Liam

I lay in bed, wide awake at 2:30 a.m., staring at the ceiling. It was completely silent. Josie was with her mom this week, and sleep wasn't an option. My mind was a mess of racing thoughts.

It had been a few days since Gerald Smith's arrest—or, rather, his shooting. Things were running smoothly, and the FBI was getting praise nationwide for wrapping up the case so quickly. *Well, who gets a gold star for this masterpiece?* I thought wryly.

The kids were with their grandmother now. Maybe, with enough love, time, and therapy, they'd be okay.

But Leah was a different story.

I'd reached out to her on the day of the incident at Smith's place, but she'd never responded.

Suddenly, my flip phone buzzed on the nightstand. I shot up and grabbed it.

It was Leah. As if she knew she'd been on my mind again.

We need to talk. Now. Bring Rose. Don't meet me at the house. Meet me at Gerald Smith's place. Avoid main roads with traffic cameras.

I stared at the message. This wasn't good. Something was off.

I jumped out of bed, threw on sweatpants and a sweater, and slipped into my shoes before racing out. I dialed Rose as I went.

As much as I hated to admit it, a surge of excitement rushed through me at the thought of seeing Leah again. Maybe we could finally sort out some of our issues. Maybe she was ready to work with me. Ditch Novak. Dial things back.

Or maybe she wasn't. But I couldn't let my mind go there yet.

CHAPTER THIRTY-EIGHT

Leah

I waited inside Gerald Smith's residence, dressed in boots and a coverall to avoid leaving any trace of DNA. The kitchen was a mess. Old takeout boxes and empty beer cans littered the countertops and floor. Light from the street poured through the window, casting long shadows across the room.

At around 3:30 a.m., I heard a car pull up and park outside. Moments later, Richter and Rose entered the house, flashlights in hand.

"Leah," Richter called in a sharp whisper.

"I'm here," I answered from the kitchen.

They walked in, their faces tight with worry and anticipation.

"What's going on?" Rose asked. "Why are we meeting here?"

"It won't raise his suspicion if you're seen visiting a recent crime scene," I explained.

"Whose?" Richter pressed. "Novak's?"

I nodded. "We can't be seen together right now."

"What happened?" Liam asked.

"Hard to say. The last time I spoke to him was the day we met in my study," I said. "He told me about his past—his childhood and how his brother died on the train tracks while everyone just watched."

Rose sighed, her shoulders slumping. "So the ankh is some kind of twisted punishment symbol? To make people pay?"

"There's more to it, but we don't have much time." I set the tablet on the counter. Its glass screen reflected the dim light from the street outside. A green indicator flashed, signaling that it was charged. Ready for games, videos, news—or, in our case, something far more sinister.

"What's this?" Liam asked as they moved closer.

"Ida found this tablet on my doorstep today," I said, tapping the screen. The display lit up with a serene mountain background. I quickly navigated to the video gallery and hit play. "I texted you right after I watched what's on it."

Security footage from a coffee shop began to flicker on the screen. Its light reflected off Liam's and Rose's tense faces.

We watched as Agent Theo McCourt stepped into a farmhouse-style coffee shop. He ordered a coffee, then sat and scanned the room with caution. About a minute later, the door swung open, and a blonde woman walked in.

"Shit," Liam muttered, his eyes widening.

"Please tell me that isn't Nathalie," Rose said, her hands planted on her hips.

The video cut out and transitioned to another: McCourt and Nathalie at a Chinese restaurant—chatting, laughing.

A third video loaded, stitched together like a cheap, hastily made trailer. This time, we watched Theo McCourt and Nathalie strolling through a park. McCourt was giving it everything he had—smiling, flirting, throwing out jokes, showing empathy in every glance and gesture.

The video skipped ahead to show McCourt buying Nathalie a drink and fries from a food truck. Then the tone shifted. Their conversation grew tense. Nathalie stood there, her arms crossed, her face uncertain. She wasn't being defensive—just on the verge of revealing something, clinging to a thread, barely holding back a dark secret that was ready to spill.

Then she said something. There was no audio, but it didn't matter. Cowboy planted his hands on his hips, his face tilted upward, and paced in front of her. We all knew what Nathalie had confessed.

The fucking truth.

"Goddamn it!" Richter snapped.

The weight of everything—her confession, the videos, and what it all meant—crashed down around us.

"Why the hell did Novak send you this?" Rose demanded in a tight, tense tone.

I chose my next words carefully. "I think you need to get a hold of Agent Theo McCourt and Nathalie as soon as possible. Right now, in fact."

"Goddamn it," Liam said again, pulling his phone from his coat pocket. "I'll call Nathalie. You contact Theo."

Rose pulled out her phone. Her fingers moved swiftly as she dialed.

"Hello?" came a woman's voice through Liam's phone.

"Mrs. Moore, I'm so sorry to call you this late, but is Nathalie at home?" Liam asked.

"Yes, why?" Mrs. Moore's voice had a worried edge to it.

Liam let out a long breath, gathering himself. His tense shoulders eased a little as his eyes met mine, then flicked to Rose. "We might have had a sighting of Carr," he lied smoothly. "I'm going to arrange for a local patrol car to be stationed outside your house. Don't be alarmed if you see them there for the next few days. Just make sure all the windows and doors are locked at night."

"Okay," Mrs. Moore responded calmly. It was clear she wasn't worried about Carr. She likely knew he was dead. Yet she played along, just as her daughter had. Only she didn't know how deep this all went. That her daughter might have placed herself on the hit list of other psychopaths.

"I'll keep you updated," Liam assured her.

"Thank you."

Liam ended the call, then dialed his contact at the local police department. His voice shifted into formal business. "This is Special Agent in Charge Liam Richter. I need a patrol car stationed at fifty-five Exeter Street tonight to cover the Moore residence. Please coordinate with me on this."

He paused as the officer on the other end responded.

"Yes, thank you," Liam said. "I'll send my contact information for follow-up." Liam hung up and turned to us. "It's set. They'll have eyes on the house tonight. Anything on your end?" he asked Rose.

She shook her head, her expression tightening with worry. "No answer. He's not picking up."

"Fuck," Liam muttered, his frustration simmering.

"Why the hell is Novak doing this?" Rose snapped, dialing McCourt's number again.

"There could be many reasons, but the most obvious would be to protect the work," I said.

"Just like Larsen did," Liam muttered, his jaw tightening as if he could barely stomach the words.

"The work?" Rose asked. "I thought Novak was killing only bad people. Theo isn't a monster. He's one of the good guys."

"We don't have time to make sense of a psycho's twisted mind," Liam said, his voice taut with urgency. "We have to find Theo. I'll check his house."

Rose didn't hesitate. "I'll check the office. He's been working nights lately."

They darted toward the hallway, their footsteps quick and urgent.

"Wait," I said.

Both of them froze mid-step, then turned to face me.

"I'm afraid you won't find him at home," I said. "Or the office."

The weight of my words settled in the room. Liam strode toward me, eyes wide, searching for answers.

"You should check the hospitals," I said. "Or the morgues." I added the last part quietly.

"What?" Rose's brow furrowed.

"Theo McCourt's death wouldn't carry symbolic value for Jan Novak," I explained. "It would ... look like an accident. To Jan, it would be more of a necessary casualty. Quick. Humane. Something that wouldn't raise questions."

They both stared, but it was Liam's gaze—cold and full of blame—that pierced through me. His hand hovered over his phone while his brown eyes bore into me. They flickered with panic tangled with sadness and something heavier: regret.

Regret directed at me.

I hadn't pulled the trigger on Agent Tony Russo or Theo McCourt, but pulling Liam into my dark world had demanded more of him than he could bear.

Or maybe it was more than I could bear to watch him endure.

Jan Novak had stripped away the one thing I held dear, and I'd realized it too late. It was Liam Richter.

A cold knot tightened in my stomach as this truth hit me like a wrecking ball.

There was no turning back. No salvation for me.

Maybe two wrongs could make a right. But who decided what that right was?

My mother's face flashed in my mind as Liam spoke frantically into the phone, instructing someone to search for Theo McCourt in every hospital across Boston—no, all of Massachusetts.

A childhood memory flashed in my mind. My mother's long, sharp nails dug into my small shoulders. I was just a kid, soaked to the bone, and I had accidentally tracked mud onto the rug.

"When you play in shit, you get dirty, you stupid girl," my mother yelled before slapping me across the face. Back then, I'd thought she'd meant the mud. But now, as crude and simple as those words had seemed, I finally understood.

How could I have ever denied such a simple truth?

No matter how hard you tried, when you played in shit, you got dirty.

Rose had already left, her focus entirely on dialing hospitals. She didn't waste a second on me.

Liam lingered, phone in hand, as if he wanted to say something but couldn't. We stood there, trapped in a silence that felt like an eternity.

I took a tentative step toward him. "Liam—"

"Don't!" His hand slammed against the counter. The sound cut through the tension like a whip.

The silence returned, heavier this time. It felt like torment.

That little girl from the psych ward had finally found what she'd been searching for her whole life—only to destroy it.

To destroy him.

"I swear," Liam's voice trembled, "if Novak hurt—" He broke off, his anger barely contained. After a steadying breath, he tried again. "Killing someone innocent like Theo goes against everything we've fought for, Leah. Don't you see that?"

"I do," I replied quickly.

His gaze darkened. "I hope so, because I swear on everything I hold dear, I won't stand by and let Novak slaughter innocent people for his twisted vision of a better world. If Theo gets hurt, I will kill Jan Novak. And when I look into his dead eyes, it won't feel any different than with any other serial killer we've taken down. Because at the end of the day, Leah, that's what he is—a ruthless killer who hides his twisted mind beneath a polished exterior, like poison wrapped in silk.

The pain in his eyes left no doubt—this wasn't just a warning. It was a promise.

I couldn't hold his gaze any longer. My eyes dropped to the floor. The weight of his disappointment was too much to carry.

"Next time you see him, tell him I'm coming for him," Liam growled.

Without another word, he spun around and rushed out the door.

I stood there, rooted to the spot, my chest tight with a pain so sharp it nearly stole my breath.

I'd done all this. Played God and paid the price as a human. And now there was only one solution. Two wrongs had to make a right one more time. Just one more time.

It would take some planning. It would take everything I had. But the puppet had to become the master.

I owed it to Richter.

I owed it to the world.

And I owed it to myself.

CHAPTER THIRTY-NINE

Liam

I floored the gas of the FBI SUV, its siren screaming as I tore through city streets. Leah had probably been right, but I had to see it for myself. A flicker of hope kept me pushing. Maybe Theo was just asleep, his phone off.

The GPS guided me through the winding roads of Newton. Each turn cranked up the tension. My chest tightened as I pulled up to a modest condo complex. The SUV screeched to a stop.

I stormed up the walkway and pounded the front door so hard, the small frame rattled. "Theo!"

Nothing. No sound, no movement.

Without thinking, I rammed my shoulder into the door, then followed up with a barrage of kicks. Adrenaline overrode all reason. "Theo!" I shouted, my voice bouncing off the quiet street as lights flicked on in neighboring homes.

I didn't give a fuck.

"Theo!" I yelled again. Each kick sent splinters flying as the door frame started giving way. With one final hit, the door cracked open and slammed against the wall. Wood chips scattered across the floor.

I charged inside, where a suffocating silence hit me. Dark, quiet, spotless. It was too perfect, too homey. Typical Theo—everything was always over the top. An FBI agent through and through.

"It's me!" I called, pushing into the living room. "It's Liam!"

I swept through the kitchen, then the hallway, scanning the two small bedrooms.

Empty.

He wasn't there.

The frustration drained out of me, replaced by an overpowering dread. I staggered back, my body hitting the hallway wall, my legs buckling as I slid to the floor. Hands pressed against my head, I fought for breath.

"Goddamn it, Theo," I muttered, my voice cracking.

This was on me.

What the hell had I thought would happen? Playing God, deciding who lived and who died, challenging the most powerful man in the nation.

Self-loathing crashed over me like a king tide. And yet, even now, I couldn't bring myself to hate Leah.

Despite everything, I found a way to hope she wasn't the monster that even she thought she was.

Was this insanity? Had I finally crossed the line into madness?

The scream of sirens yanked me out of my head. Lights flashed through the cracks in the door. My heart sped up as an officer shouted, "Police! Hands where I can see them!"

A flashlight blinded me, and I squinted as the beam stabbed through the hallway.

"FBI!" I said, forcing calm into my voice. "Agent Liam Richter. This is Agent Theo McCourt's residence. I'm reaching for my badge, alright?"

"Richter, is that you?" A familiar voice echoed down the hall. Another flashlight found my face.

"Thompson?" I called back, trying to place it.

"Yeah," Officer Thompson replied. He switched on the light to reveal his stocky frame and thinning hairline. Three other officers stood next to him, guns lowered. "It's alright, boys. He's FBI."

I stood up, shaking off the adrenaline. "Good to see you, man." We exchanged a quick handshake. Thompson and I had a history from a murder case years back. "We're looking for Agent Theo McCourt," I explained, urgency creeping into my voice. "Carl Carr's still out there. Someone called in, said they saw him around Boston tonight."

Thompson's face darkened. "I'll make sure everyone's on alert for that bastard."

I nodded and was about to ask if there had been any accidents involving an agent when my phone buzzed.

Rose's voice came through, panicked.

"We found him! Mass General Hospital!"

"I'm on my way!" I snapped, cutting her off before she could tell me if Theo was dead or alive. I didn't want to hear it. Not yet.

I bolted out the door and jumped into the SUV.

Sirens blared as I floored the gas and sped toward the hospital.

There was still hope. And, by God, I held on to it.

I found Rose waiting in the large entrance hall. Silence pressed in from every corner.

"What happened?" I demanded, nearly colliding with her in my rush.

"Car accident. It happened around nine p.m."

"At fucking nine? Why didn't anyone call us? He had his badge on him."

Rose's face tightened. "He just came out of surgery," she said, her voice strained. "They think his brakes failed—while going seventy-five on the highway. The trauma team fought for hours. His heart stopped twice, but they shocked him back both times."

I stood there, words choking in my throat. The frustration, the guilt, it all crushed me. I fought against the tears burning in my eyes. My chest tightened with every breath.

"So he's alive?" I said.

Rose's eyes flickered with hope for a second, though her expression remained tense. "Yes. But he's in a coma. They said it's serious. Really serious."

The brief relief that had sparked inside me died out, replaced by a sinking weight in my stomach.

"Come," Rose said softly, "I'll take you to the doctor. He'll explain everything."

I followed her, barely aware of the people and nurses we passed, their faces a blur. The sterile scent of antiseptic hung in the air, making everything feel colder.

"We have to call his mother," I said.

"I already did." Rose's voice was quiet but firm. "Before I called you. I thought his mom should know as soon as possible. In case..." She didn't finish the sentence. She didn't need to. "She's on her way. So is McCourt."

"Good. Well done," I said.

Rose dipped her head in acknowledgment, though her eyes stayed ahead.

We met up with Dr. Goldman on the ICU floor. He looked fresh out of his residency—mid-thirties, still wearing blue scrubs and a surgical cap. Fatigue lingered in his expression.

The hallway was quiet except for the steady beeping of machines from nearby rooms. The smell of disinfectant was stronger here, almost suffocating.

"Liam!" A woman's voice echoed down the hallway. I turned just as Bonnie, Theo's mom, rushed toward us. Tears streaked down her pale cheeks, and her short, tousled hair looked like she hadn't slept. Dressed in a loose sweater and jeans, she crashed into me, her sobs muffled against my chest.

"He's still alive. There's hope," I said, though the words felt hollow in my mouth. It was as if I was saying them more for myself than for her.

She nodded, trembling in my arms.

"You'll be able to see him soon," Dr. Goldman said, his voice calm—almost too calm for the gravity of the situation. "He took a significant hit to the head. It's honestly a miracle he survived the impact. We managed to stop the bleeding, but there's one artery we're monitoring closely. Once we're sure it's stabilized, you can go in."

Rose's head dropped into her hands. For a moment, she stayed like that, her shoulders shaking slightly. Then she straightened up, forcing herself to hold it together, to stay strong. "Will he wake up?" she asked, her voice tight, barely above a whisper.

Everyone turned to Dr. Goldman.

"We'll have to wait a few days and see," he said. "Right now, it's too soon to say. But he's a fighter, that much I can promise you. Don't lose hope."

I swallowed hard. My hands were shaking. I realized I hadn't stopped trembling since I'd gotten the call.

Dr. Goldman glanced down at my leg, his brow furrowing. "Come with me for a minute," he said. "Let's get that stitched up before it gets worse."

I glanced down, only now realizing that my pants were torn. A large, dark bloodstain had spread across my shin. I must have cut myself kicking the door in.

"I'm fine," I muttered, but Dr. Goldman's raised brow made it clear he wasn't buying it.

"Go with him, Liam," Bonnie insisted, her voice strained. "Rose and I will grab some coffee and call my brother."

I nodded and watched them walk away.

"Just follow me," Dr. Goldman said, gesturing ahead. "This won't take long."

"Thanks," I said, trailing behind him.

My head throbbed, and nausea churned in my stomach. What the hell would I do if Theo didn't make it? The thought pressed down on me, but I shoved it aside. I couldn't afford to go there—not yet.

As long as he was breathing, there was hope.

But hope in itself wasn't enough. Not without fuel. It had to be fed and sustained, like everything else in life.

And this hope would last only if Jan Novak was taken care of.

In any way possible.

CHAPTER FORTY

Leah

I was parked near Josie's school. The rain fell steadily against the windshield. It was the day of her school play—some adaptation of *The Three Little Piglets*.

The bare trees lining the street stood like eerie shadows against the gray sky. Their twisted branches waved like skeletal arms in the wind.

I sat in the driver's seat of the Beamer—Emanuel's Beamer, the one I'd bought him. The leather was cold under my skin, and the dashboard cast a soft glow in the dark. I'd never gotten rid of the car. It was as if I'd known it would serve a purpose again someday.

And that day was today.

I glanced at myself in the rearview mirror. I was dressed to be seen: an evening dress, black and sleek, clinging to my body. The fabric shimmered subtly with each shift, and the deep neckline revealed just enough to be both sexy and classy. My lips were a defiant shade of crimson, vivid against the paleness of my skin. My hair fell loose over my shoulders. I never wore it like this, but today was different. Today I chose to be free.

The rain stopped, and I kept my eyes on the entrance to the school. It had been two weeks since Theo McCourt's crash. Two weeks since the investigation had claimed that there was no foul play, that the brakes on his car had failed.

But I knew the truth.

So did Liam and Rose.

We hadn't spoken since. Theo was still in a coma, fighting for his life. But I knew that Richter was devastated about it. I saw it in his face every time I closed my eyes, and I promised him that I would make things right. That Jan Novak would be taught a lesson—in a language he understood.

Then I saw them—Liam and Josie—walking out of the school, hand in hand. They looked happy. Josie, in her little piglet costume, beamed up at him, her cheeks flushed from the excitement of her performance.

For a fleeting moment, I wondered what it would have been like to have watched the show with them.

Would I have sat next to Richter in the school auditorium, the warmth of his presence grounding me? Would I have smiled as Josie performed, my chest filling with that quiet, aching joy? I could almost hear Richter making a joke about the school orchestra's awful music, and I'd whisper back that it was indeed an assault on the senses. We'd laugh quietly only to be shushed by some annoyed parent sitting nearby.

For a moment, I let myself feel it: the life I could've had, the one I'd always craved. But then the familiar, hollow emptiness returned, sharp and cold.

Gray nothingness.

I was never meant to walk that path.

No.

That wasn't true.

People could choose to change, to do the work needed, and then walk any path they wanted. But I'd chosen something else. There was only one road left for people like me. Monsters.

And tonight, Jan Novak would learn that too.

I watched as Richter and Josie got into their car, still talking, still laughing. I sat there even after they'd driven off, long after the last parents and children had left. The school was empty now, the brick walls darkened by the clouds.

I wanted to stay in that moment for as long as I could.

But I had to acknowledge that it was gone.

That it was time.

Time to face Jan Novak.

CHAPTER FORTY-ONE

Leah

I sat across from Jan Novak in his grand dining room. The long mahogany table gleamed under the soft glow of crystal chandeliers hanging high above. Egyptian artifacts adorned the walls alongside priceless paintings, one of which looked like an original Monet. The air was filled with the scent of polished wood and subtle traces of exotic spices from the kitchen.

Jan's mansion, nestled on the outskirts of Boston, overlooked manicured gardens that faded into the dense forest beyond. The sky had cleared, and a silver moon shone through the tall, castle-like windows. It cast a cold, ethereal light across the room. In the enormous stone fireplace, a fire crackled softly, sending warmth through the air.

Unlike our last encounter, we weren't alone. A server dressed in a tailored vest moved with quiet efficiency, setting plates down with care. Everything about tonight screamed luxury ... and control.

Jan, of course, looked impeccable. His black suit—sharp and flawless—fit like it had been stitched to his skin. His crisp white shirt stood in stark contrast, and not a hair on his head was out of place. His calm demeanor bordered on icy, though I could sense the subtle tension in his posture. Beneath the polished surface, he was wondering if I'd truly chosen him after what he'd done to Richter.

"You can go now," Jan instructed the waiter as the man poured wine into our glasses. The waiter nodded, then left.

The salad in front of me was artfully arranged: thin slices of heirloom tomatoes, vibrant reds and yellows, topped with microgreens and delicate edible flowers. It looked perfect, like everything else in the house.

"I'm glad you decided to join me tonight," Jan said, picking up his fork and taking a bite.

I picked up my wine glass but didn't drink. Jan's eyes flicked up, and a faint crease formed between his brows.

"So you're upset with me after all," he mused, dabbing his lips with the white napkin that had been resting on his lap.

I set down my wine glass deliberately and met his gaze. "I am." My voice was cool but firm. "Very much so."

He leaned back, studying me. "You disapprove of the handling of Theo McCourt, then? Sacrificing one life to save hundreds?"

I shrugged. "Not really. I see the logic. McCourt's accident itself doesn't bother me much."

He nodded, his eyes darkening. "But..."

Silence settled between us. My gaze held his.

Tonight wasn't about emotions. I felt no rage toward him. No hate. I'd meant every word when I'd said that McCourt's death was a logical solution to the problem. And that McCourt himself meant nothing to me.

But McCourt meant everything to the one person I cared about—and protecting that person from the reckless spiral that would follow Jan's attack was what tonight was really about. That recklessness could get him killed, and I couldn't allow that.

"Ah," Jan finally said, the corners of his mouth lifting in a cold smile. "My bad. How dare I upset Agent Liam Richter."

I kept my voice level. "It's more than upsetting. What you did to him—"

"Yes, to *him*, indeed." His expression turned grim. "And I hated it. Every moment of it. McCourt didn't deserve that. He was on our side. But you understand that my hands were tied, don't you? If anything, I did it for you. McCourt would have hunted you relentlessly." He shook his head. "You and I, we don't live by Richter's naive code of morals. We can't afford to. No. Not people like us. You and I, we're soldiers in a war."

I nodded slightly and picked up my fork. I couldn't disagree with him—not now. Not when he had to believe I was on his side.

Luckily, I agreed with the things he said. Most of them.

"Promise me you won't hurt Richter," I said, keeping my tone measured. "And I promise you, I'll never see him again. End whatever childish hope there had ever been between us." I took a bite of the salad, though my attention never left him.

Jan paused, watching me closely, searching my face for any hint of a lie. After a tense moment, he picked up his fork again. "I promise as long as he leaves me alone."

"He will," I replied quietly.

Jan's eyes lit up, and a wave of excitement washed over him. "Now that we've resolved that … unpleasant matter, I have something for you."

I glanced down at the plate, surprised by the abrupt change in tone.

"We'll finish dinner in a moment," he said, his voice light. "Come, don't make me wait. I'm quite excited to show you."

He reached out, gently took my hand, and guided me through a door that led from the dining hall to the library. The room was like something out of a historical movie—bookshelves stretched to the ceiling, filled with antique volumes that had probably never been touched. Egyptian artifacts filled this room as well—golden figurines, a scarab amulet, and several busts of pharaohs. A fire crackled in the large stone fireplace, casting flickering shadows across the luxurious space.

The life of a billionaire. As beautiful as it was absurd.

Jan stopped in front of an exhibit case, his grin almost boyish in its energy.

My eyes widened when I saw the necklace—the same ankh necklace I'd admired at the Smithsonian Museum during our first meeting. It was golden, inlaid with lapis lazuli gemstones, and shaped like a T crowned with a loop. On its crimson silk pillow, it glittered like stars against the night sky.

"The Eternal Kiss," I whispered, awe creeping into my voice.

Jan moved behind me, his breath warm against my ear. "It belonged to Agathoclea, the favored mistress of the Greco-Egyptian Pharaoh Ptolemy IV Philopator," he murmured. "His obsession with her was legendary. He built temples for the gods, hoping they'd allow her to join him in the afterlife. Stunning, isn't it?"

"Agathoclea…" I echoed, watching as Jan lifted the necklace. "She tried to take the throne with her brother after Ptolemy's death. They failed, and she was torn apart limb by limb."

"Most great men's downfall is a woman," Jan joked softly.

"Most great men's downfall is the man himself," I countered.

His grin widened as he placed the necklace around my neck. It felt heavy and cold. Just as he reached to clasp it, I stepped away, slipping out from under his arms.

His eyes flashed with surprise.

"I … I can't accept it," I said.

The enchantment from moments ago dissolved. Jan's face hardened.

"Not yet," I added quickly.

His expression shifted. Curiosity replaced the coldness. He placed the necklace back on the silk pillow, then turned to face me. "Why is that?"

"Because now you'll need to come with me," I said, my tone steady. "Just like you asked me to go with you to the tracks, to show me who you really were. Now it's my turn to show you who I really am."

Jan studied me. Finally, he nodded slowly. "Very well," he said. "Lead the way."

CHAPTER FORTY-TWO

Liam

I stood on my small balcony, staring up at the moon and stars shimmering in the clear night sky. It was almost nine. An icy breeze brushed against my skin. It carried the faint scent of the city below.

I should've been dead tired, considering that I'd been up every night since Theo's accident. But sleep wouldn't come. Not tonight. My mind was too restless, my thoughts racing like a freight train that couldn't be stopped.

Guilt weighed heavy on my chest. Anger too. Yet something else lingered beneath it all.

Worry.

For Leah.

It was strange how things had shifted once the first wave of anger subsided. At first, I couldn't even look at her without feeling regret. After those videos had played in the kitchen, I'd stared at her with pure frustration, wishing I'd never met her. In my mind, she was the reason for all this chaos. I'd blamed her for everything. Larsen shooting Toni. Theo's accident. The bodies that piled up as our lives spiraled further into darkness.

But if I was honest with myself, none of that was her fault.

She hadn't pulled the trigger on Toni, nor had she tampered with Theo's brakes. Leah was just another pawn in the same deadly game I found myself trapped in. The difference was, she'd been playing it much longer. When I'd joined, it wasn't because she'd dragged me in. I'd chosen this path. And time and time again, she'd risked her life for me.

I gripped the cold railing, my knuckles turning white. She'd saved me from Patel, risked everything when I'd begged her to save Rose in the woods with Kirby. She'd never asked for anything in return except for my help in hunting down monsters.

Sure, we didn't always agree on the methods. I could never bring myself to kill someone like Carole Traylor. And especially not Cowboy.

Maybe people saw it as weakness, maybe as self-righteousness, but I refused to accept a world where we sacrificed innocent lives for the so-called greater good. Who the hell got to decide who'd be sacrificed? What if it was someone we loved? Would we still feel the same about making that choice if it were their life on the line?

I couldn't sanction that.

But Leah. Leah had a different moral code. She saw the world in black and white: monsters and victims. And though I'd questioned her judgment more times than I could count, part of me understood her.

A sharp jolt twisted in my chest, cutting deeper with every breath.

I had to see her.

Talk to her.

To make sense of it all.

She was the only one who could understand my pain. After all, she carried the same burdens, wore the same scars. And if, in the end, we couldn't see eye to eye on the mission or the lives we took, if our paths had truly split, at least we wouldn't part as enemies. Not like this.

I tilted my head back, letting my gaze linger on the moon a moment longer. Its mystic silver light bathed the world in a strange, ethereal glow as if offering me some kind of strength.

I took a deep breath, letting the cool night air fill my lungs before I exhaled slowly. Then I reached for the flip phone in my pocket. I was ready to call her, ready to bridge the silence that had grown between us.

But before I could type a single word, my phone buzzed in my hand.

A text.

My pulse quickened. Adrenaline surged through my veins as I stared at the screen.

It wasn't from Leah. It wasn't from Rose. It was from an unknown number.

I opened the text, my heart pounding, a sense of unease settling deep in my gut.

When my eyes scanned the message, a chill crept up my spine.

Fucking hell.

The game wasn't over.

It was only just beginning.

CHAPTER FORTY-THREE

Leah

I drove my car down the lonely country roads, the dense forest lining either side like looming shadows. The rhythmic hum of the tires on the uneven asphalt was the only sound that broke the silence of the night. Jan hadn't been suspicious at first, but when I took a sharp turn leading away from Boston, I saw him glance out the window.

His expression tightened. "This isn't the way to your home," he said, pulling out his phone. His fingers flew over the screen as he typed something quickly, then slid the phone back into his pocket.

"No," I replied, my eyes fixed on the dark road ahead.

"Then where are we going?" His tone was calm, but I could feel the unease creeping in, like a chill in the air.

"You'll know soon," I said, my voice cold and detached, as if the decision had been made long ago.

We drove in silence for a few minutes. The forest seemed to close in on us, the trees taller and darker, their branches curling overhead, grasping for the car.

Almost casually, Novak nodded to himself as if he was finally piecing it together. "The tracks," he said softly. "You're taking me to the tracks."

"Yes," I confirmed, keeping my eyes forward.

He nodded again, a faint shadow of a smile pulling at the corner of his mouth. "What for?"

"To show you who I really am."

The unease thickened between us like a fog, but I kept driving until the road narrowed. We turned onto Pine Street, the winding forest path that led to the tracks. The same tracks where Jan had once told me everything about his past.

I slowed the car as we neared the crossing. The pale moonlight cast an eerie glow on the silver rails ahead as if the ground itself were pulling us toward some final, inevitable destination. With a sharp turn, I steered the car directly onto the tracks, then positioned it to face the direction from which the train would come. I turned off the engine.

The sudden silence hit like a blow, deafening in its finality. The trees loomed on either side. The moon hung above us, cold and indifferent.

I reached under the steering wheel and flipped the switch. A loud click echoed through the car as the doors locked, sealing us inside.

This car was built to trap people. The locks, the bulletproof windows, the reinforced frame—I'd had it all installed to make sure no one would get out. Not even Novak. There was nothing he could do to get out of here. Nothing.

We sat in the dark, listening to the soft rustling of leaves in the wind, the calm before the storm.

Jan glanced at me, his brow furrowing slightly. "Not what I expected," he murmured, reaching for the door handle. He pulled, but the door didn't budge. His hand slipped from the handle, and he leaned back into his seat, his face calm, though his eyes were calculating. "The door won't open," he said after a moment. "Even if I were to take the keys from you by force? Or flip that switch again?"

I shook my head. "No."

"And the windows ... if I rammed my elbow into them, the glass wouldn't break, would it?"

"Bulletproof."

He gave a curt nod toward the tracks. "How much did you pay the train driver to hit us at full speed instead of braking?" A hint of admiration crept into his tone.

"He asked for one hundred thousand. I gave him five. I figured the guilt of killing someone might weigh heavy on him later."

A strange calm settled between us—the kind of stillness that comes before a storm.

We sat there, motionless, as the first faint horn of the approaching train echoed through the night. It was distant but growing louder each second. The ground trembled slightly—a reminder of the raw power rushing toward us.

"You said you wanted to show me your true self," Novak said, his gaze meeting mine, cold and unwavering. "Is this it? Your true self?"

His icy blue eyes betrayed disappointment but also a strange sense of relief. Maybe it was the same relief I felt—knowing it was all about to end. Knowing there was no need for pretense anymore.

"Yes," I replied, my voice just as cold as the night around us. "This is me. The real me. You can kill me now if you want. I won't resist. The train will do the same in," I checked my watch, "about a minute. It doesn't matter to me how I die, one way or another."

He studied me for a long moment, his face unreadable. "So this is how it ends?" he asked.

I nodded, feeling the weight of my decision settle heavily on my chest.

He let out a low, humorless laugh. "This ... all of this. It's for him, isn't it? You figured he'd come for me, so you're killing me first. To save him from himself. And from me."

I shook my head, my eyes fixed on the silver rails ahead, gleaming in the moonlight like a path to nowhere. There was something almost beautiful about it—the clarity, the inevitability. And the silence that would follow. The peace of never having to wake up again, never having to force myself to face another day of a hollow, lonely life.

"It's more than just for him," I said quietly. "Don't you see? You and me ... we can tell ourselves whatever we want, but at the end of the day, we're just like them. Like Carl Carr. Patel. Harris. Grand. When you tried to kill Agent Theo McCourt, you revealed a dark part of yourself. Something all monsters carry: the ability to kill innocent people without remorse. You and

I are monsters that don't belong in this world. And the only way to stop a monster is to kill it. I know you understand that."

He remained silent, so I pointed at the tracks ahead. "I carved an ankh on the tracks right over there for you. The mirror. It wasn't just to reveal people's true nature, was it? It was also for your older brother, Anton. To guide you to him when it's time. Like a path to the afterlife. Am I right?"

Novak's lips curled into a faint smile, one of admiration, even respect.

"I wish you would've let me put that necklace on you," he said softly. "It had found a worthy owner again after thousands of years of waiting."

I drew in a deep breath as the train's headlights appeared in the distance. Its beams sliced through the darkness like two enormous stars, growing closer with every heartbeat. The low rumble of the train's engine grew louder, the air vibrating with its approach.

"Just so you know, I'm not angry about any of this," Novak said, placing his hand on mine. "It makes sense, considering who you've always been. To me. To this world. To yourself ... and even to him." His eyes locked onto mine. They were steady and sure. He leaned forward slightly, his voice almost tender. "Do you want to come with me?" he asked as if he already knew the answer. "To meet my brother?"

I shook my head, my gaze never leaving the blinding headlights of the train thundering toward us. The sound of the horn was now deafening in the night.

"No," I said. "I don't want to go anywhere. I hope there's nothing after this. No smiles. No tears. No love. No hate. No afterlife. No rebirth. Just ... nothingness." I felt a sharp ache in my chest as the weight of my lifelong loneliness pressed in from all sides. "I'm not sure I could bear to live another life as lonely as this one."

The train was almost upon us, its light blinding, the sound of metal on metal screeching louder than anything I'd ever heard. My heart raced, but my mind was calm. The ache in my chest sharpened, but I welcomed it—his final gift.

The gift of feeling.

"I guess I'll find out soon enough if peace is finally possible," I said with a bittersweet smile.

Not much longer. Just a few more moments, and it would finally be over. My dark flame extinguished. Black nothingness swallowing my rotten heart and soul.

The end.

Finally.

"Peace," I mumbled, the word barely escaping my lips.

"I'm afraid not quite," Jan suddenly said, his voice cutting through the roar of the train. "I hope, with time, you'll forgive me."

"What?" I asked, confused, my eyes snapping to his as the train loomed just seconds away.

"Sixty." He smiled warmly, squeezing my hand one last time. "I told him if he hit the passenger side of the car at sixty miles per hour, he could get you off the tracks."

I stared at him in shock. The train's blinding lights and ear-splitting horn filled the car, drowning out everything else.

Jan spoke his last words. "I'm not Mojca, by the way—I'm Anton. My little brother somehow managed to push me off just before the train scattered him along the tracks. Never forget what we're capable of when we truly want something, whether out of love or hate. Nothing compares to the sheer will we carry inside us. The ankh... you'll understand it in time."

Then, in the blink of an eye, he shot back in his seat.

Before I could react, headlights from an SUV appeared out of nowhere, speeding toward us on the passenger side.

"No!" I screamed, my voice tearing from my throat as the SUV slammed into the car just as the train collided with the front. The impact ripped the world apart.

The car spun violently, tumbling over and over. The airbag exploded in my face. My head slammed into the side window before whipping back with merciless force. Everything was a blur: metal, glass, darkness. Flashes of images burned into my mind. Novak's side of the car ripped away, the train tearing through metal like paper. Another spin. Another impact. I was certain that I'd die, certain the end had come, until the car finally came to a tumbling stop and slid a few more feet on its side.

I lay there, barely conscious, barely alive.

"Liam," I whispered, the name slipping from my lips before I realized that I'd spoken. My voice was weak, barely audible, each breath a struggle. "No," I begged with the little strength I had left.

I wasn't afraid to die. I wasn't even afraid of living another life of utter loneliness again. But right now, the only thing I feared was that the train might have killed Liam.

And I'd die never knowing.

The one thing I'd tried to protect might be gone.

What a tragic and pathetic ending.

Even for a monster like me.

Then the world began to spin, and everything faded to black in the blink of an eye.

CHAPTER FORTY-FOUR

Liam

The pain was unbearable. I hung with full force against the seatbelt, my car flipped upside down, the world a twisted mess of smoke, fire, and darkness. Blood dripped steadily from my forehead, smearing against the airbag as I struggled to focus. My breathing was labored. Each shallow inhale sent a stab of agony through my ribs. The coppery taste of blood filled my mouth.

I coughed, wincing as I fumbled for the seatbelt buckle. My hands were trembling, clumsy, and the world spun as I hung upside down. The buckle seemed to weigh a thousand pounds. No matter how hard I pressed, the damn thing wouldn't budge. It was jammed—or maybe I was just too weak to force it open.

Every movement sent fresh waves of pain through my battered body. My vision blurred as I turned my head, and the muscles in my shoulders screamed in protest. Through the haze, I saw that the train had traveled a good distance before stopping. It was now a monstrous silhouette in the far distance.

Then I saw Leah's car—or what was left of it.

Flames engulfed the vehicle, creeping toward her like a predator closing in on its prey. The fire hissed and crackled, flapping from the wreckage like a large tongue. Thick, dark smoke swirled into the cold night air.

"No," I mumbled through the pain, panic settling in my chest.

I pushed against the seatbelt buckle again, this time gritting my teeth in frustration. My hand slipped. I tried once more, pressing down with all the strength I had left. Finally, with a loud click, the buckle released.

I slumped down onto the airbag, collapsing in a heap. My entire body felt like it had been beaten with a sledgehammer. Broken ribs? Probably. My legs wobbled as I rolled out of the car and hit the cold ground. Every breath burned, but I forced myself to stand. My vision swam as I stumbled toward Leah's car.

The impact with the train had sheared off the passenger side where Novak had been sitting. The flames were spreading fast, hungrily crawling from the undercarriage toward the hood.

Without hesitation, I reached for the door handle, only to yank my hand back as the heat from the metal burned my skin. I hissed in pain and shook my hand, the skin already blistering. But I couldn't stop.

"Leah!" I shouted hoarsely. My chest felt like it was collapsing, but I didn't care. I had to get to her.

Ignoring the pain, I grabbed the door handle with both hands and pulled with everything I had. The heat was unbearable, the fire growing, turning the car into a furnace. My hands were shaking, the skin peeling as I yanked at the door again and again. Then it hit me—the entire passenger side of her car was gone. Dazed and barely thinking, I stumbled around the hood, slipping past the crumpled wreckage. The fire roared hotter on this side, but there it was—an opening. A way in.

Smoke filled the air, burning my lungs. The fire was everywhere, but I covered my face and leaned into the wreckage. The flames licked at my clothes and skin.

The heat was overwhelming, suffocating, but I pushed forward.

Finally, I saw her.

It was hot as hell, the inferno creeping dangerously close, but it hadn't reached her yet. At least, not entirely. The car's interior was like a gas stove, the fire boiling from below, reaching higher. Leah was slumped in the driver's seat, motionless. Blood stained her face, and her body was limp against the seatbelt.

My stomach twisted in fear. Was she dead?

I pulled at her seatbelt, but it wouldn't budge. My fingers were numb, and my body was shaking as I fought against the buckle. That goddamn seatbelt again. "Leah!" I coughed, choking on the smoke.

Then, through the chaos, I heard Rose's voice cutting through the roar of the flames. "Richter!"

She appeared beside me, her face set with grim determination. Without hesitating, she pulled out a pocketknife. The fire burned her hands as she sliced through the seatbelt in seconds.

"Pull!" she screamed, her voice raw.

Together, we hauled Leah from the wreckage, my muscles burning with every pull. We dragged her across the ground, away from the inferno, collapsing onto a patch of grass by the tracks.

"Are you okay?" the train conductor shouted from a distance, running toward us.

I ignored him and kneeled beside Leah. My burnt hands trembled as I pressed my fingers against her neck, desperate for a pulse.

If she was dead...

The seconds stretched out painfully as I waited for a sign—any sign. My breath caught in my throat. Then I felt the faintest thump beneath my fingertips. A pulse. Weak but there.

Relief washed over me like a flood. I gasped, pulling her limp body into my arms.

Rose knelt beside me, her eyes wide with panic.

"Is she alive?" she asked.

I nodded, my throat tight with emotion.

Rose nodded and pulled out her phone. "We need an ambulance at the train crossing on Pine Street, near Wilkers Manufacturing. A train has collided with a vehicle." She hung up and turned to the conductor. "Are you hurt?"

"No," the man replied, his voice trembling.

"Good. Step back and wait by your train," Rose ordered, her tone sharp as she knelt beside me again.

We sat there in silence, staring at the wreckage. The flames danced in the distance, casting eerie shadows over the twisted metal that was now Novak's final resting place.

"In some fucked-up way, this might be the ending we all needed," Rose murmured, her eyes fixed on the burning wreckage.

I wanted to agree. I wanted to say yes, as if we were in a movie where a neat, happy ending resolved everything. Novak dead. Leah alive. We could twist the narrative—two lovers stranded on train tracks, their car giving out at the worst possible time.

But deep down, I knew it wasn't that simple.

Novak had texted me the location where Leah planned to kill him. He'd even told me how to save her. It left an unsettling taste in my mouth. Even in death, Novak was pulling the strings, the puppet master playing his final game from beyond the grave.

Had he planned all this?

But why?

"I hope this really is the end," I muttered, my eyes narrowing as I stared at Novak's crumpled, burning wreckage. "Jesus, Allah, Buddha, or even the goddamn devil ... I'll offer my soul in exchange for this being the fucking end of it all. The end and nothing else."

CHAPTER
FORTY-FIVE

Rose

A few months later

I was sitting in the sleek, modern meeting room of Obligato's underground compound. Polished black marble floors reflected the soft overhead lighting. Egyptian art lined the walls. It was the kind of place that felt cold, impersonal—designed to impress but reveal nothing. Novak's touch was everywhere, a strong reminder of him at every turn.

On either side of me sat cunning lawyers, their expressions unreadable as they reviewed the contract I was about to sign. They were the best money could buy—the kind who could get OJ off.

Across the table, FBI Director McCourt and Senator Wheezer sat with an older, tired-looking federal attorney. The lawyer looked every bit the government official: cheap suit, worn demeanor. Bottles of water were neatly placed in front of each chair, the labels perfectly aligned.

McCourt was arrogant and unreadable as always, while Wheezer grinned with that familiar mix of slime and forced charm.

Wheezer's eyes darted to the pen in my scarred hands—a lifelong reminder of the night I'd pulled Leah from the burning car.

My lawyers nodded, signaling that everything was in order.

I signed several copies of the contract, the one that would officially reinstate Obligato as the FBI's cloud storage provider.

As the lawyers handed over the signed copy, Wheezer beamed. His voice was irritatingly cheerful. "It feels like coming home," he said, his eyes gleaming. "Especially after Obligato's generous donation to our superfund for the next race." He leaned forward, lowering his voice as if to share a secret. "If I can ever help you with anything—"

"That will be all," I said, standing.

A glance passed between McCourt and Wheezer. For a moment, Wheezer's smile faltered, but he quickly recovered.

"Yes, yes, of course. I'm sure you're busy here. Thank you," he muttered, clearing his throat. He flicked his eyes toward McCourt, waiting for him to echo the sentiment.

With a forced smile, McCourt added, "Thank you."

Wheezer clumsily handed the signed contract to the federal lawyer, who shoved the papers into his briefcase. Making one last attempt at a dazzling grin, Wheezer stumbled out of the meeting room like a fool, his lawyer trailing behind him.

McCourt stayed behind.

I didn't move as I watched the others leave.

"You can go now," I said to my lawyers.

Almost in unison, they rose like robots and left.

McCourt scanned the room one more time before looking back at me. "I bet they pay a hell of a lot more here than at the FBI, don't they?" he said, not even pretending to make it a joke.

I didn't respond. I didn't need to. "When I said 'you can go,' I meant you too," I said, cold and detached as I gathered a copy of the contract for my records.

When he didn't move right away, I shot him a hard look. He held my stare, almost daring me to show who was in charge.

"I meant now," I repeated firmly.

A few more seconds passed, but then he rose, knowing full well I could ruin him with one phone call.

He walked toward the door but stopped when I spoke again. "One more thing," I said.

He turned around.

"If I need anything, I'll let you know."

His face tightened with anger—he couldn't hide it—but he forced a smile before leaving.

I stood and straightened my suit. A soft grin tugged at my lips.

McCourt was right. As much as I sometimes missed the badge, this job paid a hell of a lot more than the FBI ever had.

CHAPTER FORTY-SIX

Liam

I sat beside Theo in what used to be his childhood bedroom. Bonnie had turned it into a space full of medical equipment, sterile surfaces, and the constant hum of life-support machines. The walls still held memories of his younger years—a few posters from Led Zeppelin and Playboy. But now the room felt like a cold, clinical space. The air smelled faintly of antiseptic mixed with the aroma of scented candles—something his mother had insisted on. She'd read somewhere that smell was important for people in a coma. Bonnie was always searching for the next hidden miracle that could help bring Theo back to her.

None of this would have been possible without Leah's generosity. For months, I'd lied to Bonnie, asking for bills and telling her that the FBI was covering the cost of Theo's care. In reality, it was Leah who'd hired the team of private nurses and the world's top brain surgeons. She was determined to do whatever it took to keep Theo alive for as long as his mother believed in his recovery. Every day, physical therapists came by to work on his muscles, moving his limbs so they wouldn't atrophy.

And every day, Theo lay lifeless on the bed, his body thin and motionless except for the rhythmic rise and fall of his chest as the ventilator pumped air into his lungs. The breathing tube in his mouth moved with each inhale—a constant reminder of the fight we were still in. His face was pale, his features drawn in, and though he was technically alive, it felt like I was talking to a ghost.

"It's crazy, really," I said, continuing my story about the documentary I'd watched the previous night. "I mean, who the hell keeps chimps as pets? At first, it's all fun and games. They dress them up like kids, teach them tricks. But it always ends the same way." I shook my head, recalling the vivid 911 call from the documentary. "One day, the chimp snaps, and out of nowhere, it tears them apart. Sometimes they even eat parts of their owners—usually the face and genitals."

I paused, looking over at Theo, hoping for some flicker of response—anything. But his chest kept rising and falling, the machines continuing their steady rhythm.

"People never learn. They think they can control nature, but they forget that animals like that ... they're wild. No matter how much you think you know them, they can tear you to shreds." I laughed bitterly. "Almost sounds like me and—"

Marcia, the young physical therapist, entered quietly. She'd been working with Theo for weeks, moving his limbs and keeping his muscles from wasting away.

She gave me a small, understanding smile as she approached the bed. "It's time for his muscle strengthening," she said, her voice soft but professional. Marcia began moving his leg gently, speaking to him as if he could hear her. "I'm going to pull the blanket down now, Theo," she said, her hands moving with care. She went through her routine, working each muscle, flexing and stretching his limbs as though willing life back into him.

I watched her, feeling the familiar ache in my chest. "Thanks, Marcia," I muttered, barely above a whisper. Turning to Theo, I added softly, "You behave."

It was always the same—a routine that gave me the illusion of control in a situation in which I had none. The guilt sat heavily on me, a constant presence I couldn't shake.

Theo had been too good at his job. And now, here he was, reduced to a shadow of the man he'd been, all because he'd tried to do the right thing.

I couldn't stay any longer. If I did, the guilt would paralyze me like it always did.

Rising to my feet, I glanced one last time at Theo. Then, without a word, I left the room, carefully closing the door behind me. The house was silent. Bonnie was still at work, and Theo's little sister was at school. It felt so empty. Too empty.

I made my way outside and stepped onto the porch. For a moment, I stood there, letting the silence of the street wash over me.

Then I turned to look at the doorbell camera. The small black lens was mounted next to the door. I stared straight into it, locking eyes with the unseen watcher on the other side. I held my gaze for a long, quiet moment as if I was trying to send a message—something unspoken.

Without a word, I turned and left.

CHAPTER FORTY-SEVEN

Leah

The sterile, glass-walled room felt cold, almost clinical, as I sat at the sleek desk of Obligato's underground compound. The faint scent of disinfectant clung to the air, barely masking the metallic smell that lingered on my burned skin. The glossy surfaces revealed my reflection: partly burned face, bandages peeking out from under my shirt sleeves where my arms and hands still bore the marks of that night. The light overhead was harsh, bouncing off the touchscreen desk in front of me.

I stared at the monitor on the wall. Liam's face filled the screen. He stared back at me through the camera with unwavering intensity. Even at a distance, there was something about him—steady, unflinching.

Before I could get lost in the image, the sound of confident footsteps echoed through the quiet room. Rose strode in, her presence commanding. Quickly, I tapped the touchpad to make the video of Liam disappear.

"Here's a copy of the FBI contract," Rose said, placing the file on the glass desk, whose surface glowed faintly from the technology embedded beneath. The entire tabletop was a touchscreen, modern and futuristic, like everything else here. "Strange that we have to work with this man now," she added, her tone tight.

"McCourt or Wheezer?" I asked, picking up the contract.

"Both," Rose said, her lips pulling into a grim line.

"McCourt is a good puppet, and Wheezer won't last. He'll be replaced in the next election," I said, gazing at the contract. "The donation wasn't for him. It was for his younger assistant. He'll make a push next year. The old fool just doesn't know it yet."

Rose nodded knowingly. Her sharp eyes assessed the room, the situation—everything, as usual.

"Have you made any progress on the system yet?" I asked, setting the contract down. Jan had named the AI system Seshat, after the goddess of writing, knowledge, and wisdom.

"Not much," she admitted, her fingers gliding across the touchscreen. With a few swift movements, a large folder system materialized on the glass wall across from us. Its digital contents were reflected in a cascade of blue light. Jan Novak seemed to have coded her himself. The code is genius—really. None of our staff knows much about her. Jan was the only one who truly knew how to operate her."

I frowned as the weight of this revelation settled in my chest. It would take months just to understand the basics of this massive AI system—a program designed to operate Obligato's vast cloud storage. It was enormous. Navigating it felt like David fighting Goliath—only this time, without the slingshot.

Another one of the secrets Jan had taken to the grave.

He hadn't survived the crash, but what baffled me was how he'd known about it beforehand. He'd sent a text to Liam, warning him, giving him the precise location where it would happen. I remembered the moment when Jan had typed something into his phone just before we'd reached the tracks. That must have been the message.

But something else haunted me: the fact that Jan had left me everything. As if he'd always known that I'd take his place. As if grooming me for this role had been part of his plan all along. His words echoed in my mind: *I hope you'll forgive me.* He'd told me this when he'd confessed that death wasn't in the cards for me yet. Peace wasn't in the cards yet.

It almost felt as though he'd saved himself by turning me into him.

Under my leadership, the company had done well—profits steady, the public façade intact. And with Rose's help, I was slowly learning how to navigate the company's vast cloud.

But the real question wasn't if we could use Seshat, but how we controlled her and what we'd do with the information she provided.

That question burned inside me as much as the thought of Liam Richter did.

I'd stopped my concerts after the "accident" on the tracks. The burns on my hands weren't severe enough to end my career or affect my ability to play at my usual level, but Obligato consumed all my time, and stepping away from concerts gave me space to let things settle. It kept me out of the public eye for a while. Naturally, the world was heartbroken, but after the train track tragedy, no one dared to push me back to the piano.

The official story was that I'd been Jan Novak's girlfriend, and we were headed to a vacation home when the car stalled on the tracks. The FBI had been following us, acting on a tip that Carl Carr was planning to make an attempt on my life. Theo McCourt had previously identified Carr on footage near my residence, raising concerns about him stalking me. It all made enough sense to avoid further questions. Nobody had ever heard of Jan Novak or his powerful company to begin with.

To the public, it was just a tragic accident. I was just another virtuoso who was living a life touched by misery.

In his will, Jan had left both the company and his estates to me. Another sick twist.

Luckily, Rose had accepted my offer to help run Jan's company. I trusted her completely, and after everything that had happened, going back to the badge wasn't an option for her. But she wasn't ready to give up the work either. So here she was.

For Liam, things were more straightforward. He'd stayed with the FBI. The badge was his way of fighting for justice in this world, and it always would be.

Rose interrupted my thoughts, her voice sharp and controlled. "As crazy as it sounds, Seshat helped me with something for once—the missing girls from the border. She wasn't even playing games like last time. She led me straight to them. Navigated the cloud with me."

This made me uneasy.

Not the fact that we might have found the missing girls from the truck full of illegal immigrants. A man had taken the underaged girls from the truck for sex trafficking after they'd crossed into the US.

What shocked me was hearing Rose talk about Seshat as if she were sentient.

And to be honest, maybe she was. When ask a question, Seshat responded like a top-notch lawyer, always careful to avoid leaving a trail of evidence. Her answers were never straightforward. They always led to more questions, and you sometimes spent hours getting the information you sought only to discover new questions in the process. If you asked her to open a file on Liam Richter's camera footage, she'd first remind you that this wasn't ethical or legal without a warrant. That was when the chase began— a conversation through the keyboard or voice command, back and forth, until you either outsmarted her or presented your request in a way she deemed acceptable. Legal or not.

Rose handed me a manila folder. For a moment, my eyes lingered on the burn scars on her hands—remnants from the fire that had nearly taken both our lives. My brow furrowed as I looked down at the folder. I wondered why she hadn't just pulled it up digitally on the screen.

Rose caught my look and shrugged. "Old habit," she said.

I grabbed the folder and opened it, then flipped through the papers inside. For a long moment, I sat there, frozen. It wasn't the content that shocked me—it was the decision I wasn't ready to make.

Rose watched me, her eyes piercing. "What are you going to do?"

I lifted my gaze slowly to meet hers.

"Are you going to give this to Richter or take care of it yourself?"

"I ... honestly don't know yet."

CHAPTER FORTY-EIGHT

Leah

A warm spring breeze from the ocean carried the scent of salt and seaweed. Seagulls circled overhead, their cries sharp as they scanned the endless blue for fish. I sat on the weathered bench by the old rope factory. It was a place where Liam and I had met many times before, though the atmosphere felt different now. It was almost like the ghosts of past conversations lingered, hanging in the air. My stomach twisted with a strange mix of anticipation and anxiety.

I heard his footsteps before I saw him. His shoes scuffed softly against the wooden dock. His shadow stretched out beside mine, long and thin in the morning light.

As Liam settled next to me on the bench, a faint smile tugged at his lips. His brown eyes sparkled in the sun, and he wore his usual suit, though the jacket was absent and his sleeves were rolled up. It was as if he was trying to shake off the weight he'd been carrying. He looked more relaxed than I'd seen him in a while, though a shadow remained behind his gaze. A weight lingered—Theo's ghost, haunting him still.

"Sorry I'm late," he said, his voice soft. "Josie had a parent-teacher conference."

I returned his smile, though it felt faint on my lips. "How's her piano practice going?"

"She plays every day. Obsessed with it, honestly. And I'm pretty sure you have something to do with that," he said. "She's watching your performances on YouTube every day. I spent a few thousand dollars I don't have on a real piano last month because she insisted her keyboard wasn't helping her build finger strength."

"Sorry," I said, my grin widening despite myself. "But she's actually right about that."

He shook his head, a playful glint in his eyes. "Why do I have the feeling you're not sorry at all?"

We laughed. The sound was light, but there was an underlying tension—an unsaid truth hanging between us.

"She's begging me to ask if you'd listen to her play," he said hesitantly as if he already regretted the words.

"It would be my pleasure."

Liam smiled faintly.

I offered him an easy way out. "When you're less busy, of course."

"Yes," he said. "When I'm less busy."

The sound of the waves crashing against the rocks below filled the silence that followed. For a moment, everything felt peaceful, as if the world had stopped turning and it was just us. I savored that feeling. The anger was gone from his eyes, and the hate that had once threatened to swallow him whole had dissipated.

But peace was fleeting.

My hand rested on the manila folder beside me. I'd learned my lesson the hard way. Revenge wasn't worth losing what I had with Liam, and I couldn't let the monster inside me take control again. Not this time. Not after everything. After the crash, after the hospital visits, after what Jan Novak had set in motion from beyond the grave.

Without thinking, I handed him the folder. My heartbeat quickened, and I almost regretted it, but I knew it was the right choice.

Liam took the folder and flipped it open. He furrowed his brow as he scanned the contents. His eyes narrowed in concentration. "If this is accurate, we might be able to intercept a truck transporting human trafficking victims from Texas to New York tomorrow," he muttered.

I nodded. My voice was quiet but firm. "It could even lead to the missing girls. The ones taken from the border. Same cartel."

His eyes stayed glued to the pages. He was deep in thought, planning every move in his head. He stood abruptly, the folder clutched tightly in his hand. "I need to get on this immediately."

I rose too and nodded, though something in me stirred—a hesitation, a doubt.

Liam paused, lingering longer than he usually did. His gaze softened as he pulled a folded piece of paper from his pocket. As he handed it to me, our fingers brushed. A strange energy passed between us.

When I opened the paper, I frowned. "What's this?" I asked, staring at the name written across the page.

Liam's expression darkened. "What do you mean? It's Massimo Chandler. The name you texted me about. The inmate at South Bay House of Correction? You asked me to look into him."

A chill ran down my spine. "I didn't send you that text."

He stared at me, his face a mixture of disbelief and alarm. "What do you mean? It was texted to my flip phone."

"I didn't send you anything," I repeated, my voice steady but my mind racing. Who had sent him that name? And why?

Liam snapped out of the confusion first, shaking his head as if to clear it. "We'll deal with this later," he said, raising the folder slightly. "I have to move on this now."

He placed a hand on my arm. His touch was warm through the burn scars that marred his skin. They were scars that connected the three of us—him, Rose, and me—to that night.

"I'll call you as soon as I can. Wait for me before talking to Massimo Chandler," he said, his voice low and urgent.

I nodded and watched as his hand slipped away, leaving a strange emptiness where his touch had been. He turned and walked briskly down the weathered dock. His silhouette shrank as he neared his car, which was parked by the old factory.

I stared after him, my mind a whirlwind of confusion, worry, and something else—something darker. Was this another one of Jan Novak's twisted games? Had they already begun?

My eyes drifted to the name scrawled on the paper in my hand.

Massimo Chandler. South Bay House of Correction.

Liam had told me to wait, but my instincts told me otherwise. As I made my way down the pier, I was already dialing Rose's number.

"Hello?" she answered.

"It's me," I said, my voice sharp. "I need you to call in a favor with the district attorney."

"What do you need?"

"An informal visit at South Bay House of Correction. Off the record. No cameras. Have Wheezer arrange it with him, and remind him of our donations."

"Okay," Rose said slowly, intrigue coloring her tone. "Who do you want to talk to there?"

I glanced once more at the name on the paper. My fingers tightened around it.

"Massimo Chandler. And I need more than just a room to chat."

CHAPTER FORTY-NINE

Leah

South Bay House of Correction looked like any other institute—a concrete fortress, cold and unfeeling, bathed in harsh, sterile lights. The building loomed like a monument to hopelessness. Its narrow, barred windows seemed to be trying to block even the faintest sliver of light.

I sat in my limousine, the engine humming quietly beneath me. Through my tinted windows, I watched the prison's back door swing open. A tall man in an orange jumpsuit shuffled out. Heavy chains shackled his wrists and ankles. He was flanked by several armed guards, each keeping a close eye on him as they approached my car. The man's gait was sluggish, and his massive frame moved like that of a bear. Even from here, I could see the crude sneer plastered on his face.

Mark, my driver, opened the door to the back seat, allowing the prisoner to clamber in. The man's grin widened as he lowered himself onto the leather. Immediately, the stench of sweat and unwashed skin filled the confined space.

"You can leave us," I said, my tone cold as ice.

The guards exchanged uncertain glances. One of them opened his mouth to object, but I cut him off with a sharp look.

"Now."

With a reluctant nod, they backed away from the limousine, closing the door behind them.

The man's grin spread even wider. He reeked of filth, his breath sour, polluting the air. "You wanna fu—"

"If you insult me with your primitive vulgarities," I interrupted, my voice as sharp as a blade, "I'll tell the guards to shoot you the moment you step back into that prison. They'll say you attacked them. Trust me, the fact that I have the power to sit here with you like this should reveal to even your small brain that I'm telling the truth. So are you going to get shot today? Or are you going to make some cash?"

The grin vanished. Massimo's eyes widened, and his macho walls crumbled in an instant. He muttered something, his voice barely a whisper.

"I can't hear you when you swallow your words like a child," I said, my patience wearing thin. "Speak up."

His breath was rancid, his body a walking reminder of decay. Every inch of him made my skin crawl. "Cash," he grunted, louder this time, the word grating like nails on a chalkboard. "I choose the cash."

"Good." I nodded. "Now tell me everything you know about the man who was pushed in front of the train on the Green Line last year."

A knowing smirk tugged at the corners of his cracked lips. "Don't know his name, but I can tell you it wasn't no crazy homeless guy that did it."

Sarcasm dripped from my voice as I leaned back in my seat. "And how did you come to this brilliant conclusion?"

Massimo chuckled, shaking his chains as he wagged a filthy finger in the air. "First, the money."

I rolled my eyes and tapped sharply on the window. The guards, who'd been waiting nearby, were at the door in seconds, ready to haul his ass back to his filthy cell. "Get him out of my car," I demanded.

"Wait!" Massimo barked, panic lacing his voice. "I'll talk!"

The guards looked to me for confirmation.

I nodded, and they stepped back, closing the door once again.

"Jesus fucking Christ," he muttered, shifting uncomfortably in his seat.

"I'm not your Jesus," I said coldly. "Talk or get the hell out."

Massimo rubbed his hands together. The chains rattled softly. "I know it because I'm the one who pushed him onto the tracks."

For a second, time froze. Rage seared through me like wildfire, burning every inch of my restraint. My fingers itched toward the gun in my coat pocket. I could see it now—spraying his filthy brains across the leather seats, the warmth of justice splattering my face.

But not like this. Not yet.

I took a deep breath, forcing the fire back down. No, he could die later. Slowly. Painfully. An inmate could do it for almost nothing—just a favor, a whispered promise. But for now, I needed this piece of filth alive.

"Why?" I asked, my voice cold and detached.

Massimo shrugged like he was talking about the weather. "Nothing personal. My boss paid me to do it, so I did it. At first, he just told me to keep an eye on him. But when that fuck boy started talking to the FBI—"

"Shut up." I cut him off, his voice grating on my nerves like broken glass. "Get out."

He opened his mouth again, but I slammed my hand against the door. The guards didn't hesitate this time. They ripped the door open and grabbed Massimo, pulling him out of the car.

"Wait! You lying bitch! You promised me money! I need the money!"

The guards twisted his arms behind his back, forcing him to the ground as he struggled, kicking and cursing. A few punches from the guards and his resistance crumbled, but his voice didn't.

"I need the money! It's for my daughter! She's sick! She has cancer!" he screamed, blood dripping from his nose, his eyes wild with desperation.

The words hit me, slowing the world around me. My gaze narrowed as I looked down at him. His face was bloodied and bruised, barely recognizable.

"You need the money for your daughter?" I repeated, my voice soft but laced with venom.

Massimo nodded weakly, his body trembling from the pain. "Please. I'll never get out of here. I just want her to have the money. She needs treatment. She's sick."

I stared at him for a long, quiet moment, watching as his body sagged, beaten and vulnerable. The desperation in his eyes reminded me of all the killers I'd faced before—pathetic and broken in the end. I should have felt something, maybe pity, but I didn't.

"You're going to die in here, Massimo," I said, my words slow and deliberate. "Painfully and slowly. And I'll make sure your daughter never sees a cent. So she can meet you in hell soon."

His eyes widened in horror, but before he could speak, the guards yanked him to his feet and dragged him away. His screams echoed. The pain and despair remained visible on his face until he was gone. Tonight, I'd arrange for another inmate to shank him. Let him bleed out. All for pennies.

As the limousine pulled away, I exhaled, calming the fury that had bubbled beneath the surface. I'd send the money for his daughter's treatment. Of course I would. She didn't deserve to suffer because of him.

But he didn't deserve to know that.

As I stared out the window at the fading prison, I gathered myself. Massimo had been the one to push Emanuel, but he hadn't ordered it.

Someone else had.

And I'd pay that someone a visit.

Tonight.

CHAPTER FIFTY

Leah

It was a warm spring night, and the air was thick with the scent of blooming flowers and leaves. The sky above was clear, the stars scattered like diamonds against a black velvet canvas. The moon hung low, casting a silver glow over the mansion's expansive garden porch. I approached, my steps silent on the grass. The wind rustled the nearby trees, causing their leaves to whisper secrets in the dark.

Luca sat alone on the porch, where the flicker of candlelight danced across his sharp features. He was listening to one of my recordings: *Beethoven, Quasi una fantasia, like a fantasy.* The melancholy strains of the piano floated through the night air. A half-empty glass of wine rested in his hand, and he slumped in his chair, staring off into the distance. No one else was around, and I'd approached unseen. Seshut had pulled the footage from the cloud, so I knew every blind spot in his security system.

When my shadow fell across the porch, Luca didn't flinch.

"Do you think Beethoven would have cared?" he said. "That people renamed one of his greatest works *Moonlight Sonata* after his death?" Luca's voice was low, contemplative. "I've thought about it a lot since you brought it up." He swirled the wine in his glass, staring at it as if it held the answer. "Do you think it would have mattered to him, knowing his music is pulling these beautiful emotions from people in ways he never intended? Under a name he didn't choose?"

He shook his head, but the motion was uncertain, as if even he didn't believe his own question.

"Maybe Beethoven would be delighted," he continued. "Or maybe ... indifferent."

He didn't turn. He didn't need to. He knew it was me.

I stood there, looking at the man I'd once called a friend. Someone who had, in his twisted way, almost cared about me more than anyone else in this ruthless world.

Almost.

But that loyalty had come at a cost.

"Beethoven was known for his mood swings and rage," I said, my voice ice-cold. "If he knew that people who'd never played a single key of music had the audacity to rename his masterpiece after he was gone—if you really need to know—he'd be *really* fucking pissed."

"Yes," Luca mumbled. "Yes, I think you're right."

"Why?" I pressed. "Why did you have Emanuel killed?"

Luca finally turned to face me, his dark eyes heavy with exhaustion. He looked more human than usual. His suit was as immaculate as always, but his expression betrayed a weariness I'd never seen before.

"It wasn't personal, Leah. It had nothing to do with you." He set his wine glass on the table. "I placed Emanuel with that escort agency knowing they'd send him to you. He had everything you liked in a man. My only intention was to keep an eye on you."

"You mean to have him report back to you," I corrected coldly. "About my affairs."

"To protect you," he insisted, his voice soft but steady. "My intentions were good."

"Then why did you kill him?"

Luca sighed deeply and leaned back in his chair. "You already know the answer, but you want to hear it from my lips, don't you?"

I said nothing, waiting.

"He was talking to the FBI."

"He never told them anything," I shot back.

"No, he didn't," Luca agreed. "But he didn't tell me about his meeting with the FBI. Others did. And that, I can't tolerate. Not in my line of work."

I clenched my fists, my thoughts racing. Emanuel hadn't betrayed me. He'd kept secrets, yes, but they were out of loyalty to me. He'd abandoned Luca for me.

Luca and I locked eyes again in a long, tense gaze. His voice softened as he spoke. "It wasn't personal, Leah. I hope you can forgive me."

I tipped my head back, looking up at the stars, trying to find some meaning in their cold, distant glow. I thought of Jan and Emanuel. But as always, it was Liam's face that haunted me the most. What would he think if he found Luca dead? Would this be the end of everything I'd fought for?

And yet ... what if Liam never found out it was me? Luca had plenty of enemies. Any one of them could be blamed for this.

Then the text came to mind. The one sent to Richter by someone else, connecting Massimo and now Luca to Emanuel's death. Another mystery left unsolved—one of many since Jan Novak had entered my life.

Was Jan still pulling the strings? Was every move, every breath, part of a larger game he'd set in motion? Was he testing me, even now, from beyond the grave?

I turned abruptly, ready to walk away.

But Luca's voice stopped me cold. "I'm the only person who will ever accept you for who you truly are, Leah. Do you really want to be alone for the rest of your life? I did all this for you."

His words hit hard.

That last part.

That he did it all for me.

It was exactly what Jan had said about killing Theo McCourt. But was it really true? Was any of this really for me? If that were true, why had Richter never made such choices for me, always leaving my fate in my own hands, even when it could cost him?

As if pulled by invisible strings, my body moved on its own. My hand slipped into my pocket and wrapped around the cold metal of my gun. In one swift motion, I pulled it out, turned, and pressed the barrel against Luca's forehead.

"You didn't do it for me," I said, my voice steady. "You did it for yourself. If it were for me, you would've fucking asked and given me a choice."

Without another word, I pulled the trigger.

The shot echoed through the night, startling a flock of birds from a nearby tree. Luca's body slumped forward and slid lifelessly from the chair to the ground. His wine spilled onto the porch.

I stood there for a moment, feeling nothing. No relief. No satisfaction. Just the cold, empty silence that followed death.

Then I disappeared into the quiet of the night, my mind racing. Liam's face burned in my thoughts.

What if he found out that I killed Luca? Would he desert me once and for all? Or would he finally understand who I truly was, knowing that I'd never harm someone innocent? Not someone like him or Josie. Or Rose or Nathalie. Or even Theo McCourt. I'd always protected those who needed it and saved those who couldn't save themselves.

Maybe he wouldn't see me as a monster, but just as the villain who killed them.

Liam saw a difference between the two—monsters and villains.

Rose was starting to accept me for who I was. God knew why, but she was. Surely Liam could too, as long as I stuck to killing those who deserved it. Killing killers.

Maybe the little girl who'd grown up in psych wards could have it both ways.

Deliver justice to killers.

And have him.

I reached my dirt bike and flipped on the headlights. As I kicked down the lever to start the engine, a huge buck appeared in the beam. It stood just a few feet away. Its massive antlers glistened. Something about them caught my breath.

The tip of the antlers.

The tip of the left side curved into the shape of an ankh—a symbol I knew too well. It wasn't a perfect resemblance, but if one looked closely enough, it was there.

The buck stared at me with deep, black eyes before turning and disappearing into the forest.

I smiled at the beauty of it, then cranked the throttle.

If Jan was still playing his game, then let him come.

I knew who I was.

I was a killer of killers.

And on a killer's playground, there was only one rule.

Win and live, or lose and die.

COMING SOON!

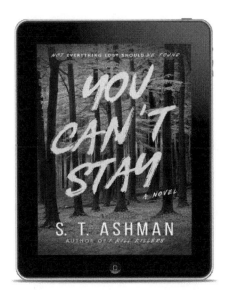

Not everything lost should be found. In the heart of the wilderness, some secrets are meant to die.

By preordering, not only are you supporting me as an author, but you're also saving money, as my preorders are always discounted! ☺ Thank you!

https://www.amazon.com/dp/B0DK8921KM

THANK YOU!

Dear Reader,

Thank you for reading "Final Kill." If you enjoyed the book, please consider leaving a review on your preferred retailer's website (like Amazon, Goodreads, Barnes & Noble, etc.).

https://www.amazon.com/dp/B0D5V4BG8W

I have a small, mom-run author/publishing business, so every review, share, and kind word makes a huge difference and means the world to me.

Newsletter: https://www.ashmanbooks.com

Instagram: https://www.instagram.com/booksbyashman/

TikTok: https://www.tiktok.com/@ashmanbooks

Join Ashman's Dark Thriller Facebook Group to Meet the Author:

https://www.facebook.com/profile.php?id=100094353614873

Contact: hello@ashmanbooks.com

Thank you for your support.

S. T. Ashman

ABOUT THE AUTHOR

S. T. Ashman is a writer who once delved into the criminal justice system as a psychotherapist. This role gifted her with a unique insight into the human psyche—both the beautiful and the deeply shadowed. She considers herself a crime-solving enthusiast, often daydreaming about being the female version of Columbo, solving mysteries while rocking a trench coat. Her writing audaciously defies norms and promises to keep readers engrossed in a nail-biting adventure.

When she's not busy crafting suspenseful tales, she's chasing after her nap-resistant kids, binge-watching TV with her husband, or ... actually, that pretty much covers it.

She aims to bend your brain, tickle your intrigue, and leave you pondering long after the last page. Come join her on her journeys.

Made in the USA
Middletown, DE
20 October 2024

62948511R00205